The Reluctant Heiress

ANNABEL LAINE is the pseudonym of a best-selling non-fiction writer whose work, published in Britain and the United States, has also been translated into French, German, Dutch and Japanese. One of her recent historical studies was a main choice of the American Book-of-the-Month Club. Annabel Laine is Scottish by birth and, most of the time, by inclination. She is married and lives in a Highland glen.

ANNABEL LAINE

The Reluctant Heiress

Collins
FONTANA BOOKS

First published in 1978 by William Collins Sons & Co Ltd
First issued in Fontana Books 1979

© Annabel Laine 1978

Made and printed in Great Britain by
William Collins Sons & Co Ltd, Glasgow

FOR MY AUNT
MARION W. WRIGHT
WITH LOVE AND AFFECTION

❈ *Chapter One* ❈

Charles Edward Graham Dornay, fifth Earl of Moriston – rich, fashionable, and respected by his wide acquaintance as a man of superior sense and impeccable self-possession – was on the verge of losing his admirable temper. Resting an inimical blue gaze on the contents of the wineglass balanced between his long fingers – 'Sir Augustus's best Madeira,' his hostess had assured him – he could barely repress a shudder at the thought of what Sir Augustus's second-best Madeira must be like. And as he shifted his position, achingly, on the gold satin chair that felt as if it had been hewn from the living rock, he reflected caustically that he had no one to blame but himself. If he had not allowed himself to be diverted from one minor matter to several major ones, he would not have found himself in his present infuriating predicament.

A few days earlier, his head groom had mentioned casually that Sir Augustus Home was thinking of selling that neat bay mare of his. The earl, inured by long acquaintance to Girvan's tactics, said nothing.

'Nice action, my lord,' Girvan persevered. 'And very good-mannered, by all accounts.'

'Oh, yes?' said his lordship politely, and allowed a few moments' silence to develop before he added: 'Touched in the wind?'

Girvan knew his employer as well as the earl knew his groom, and he was long past the stage of rising to that kind of provocation. But it did push him straight to the point. The mare, he freely admitted, might not be ideal for his lordship's own use, but it was late summer, and summer, in his experience, meant a steady stream of house guests expecting to be mounted from his lordship's stables. 'Which, as you know, my lord, could prove awkward. For what with Belshazzar having a strained hock and Miss Millicent throwing a temperament every time she feels a strange foot in the stirrup, I don't see how we are going to manage.' He stopped, pursed his lips, and concluded austerely: 'And that's a fact!'

The earl, amused at his groom's unusual loquacity but aware

that his stables had in some respects been neglected during his recent absences from England, directed his steps back towards the house with the laudable intention of sending over to Priory Court that very day to discover when it would be convenient for him to call and inspect the mare.

It was a glorious morning, and the air – fresh with overnight showers and scented with woodsmoke and new-cut grass – sparkled like a tonic in his lungs after the dank breezes of the Low Countries. Goldcrests were bustling about in the treetops and nuthatches darting inquisitively down the trunks. The gardens, generally held to be among Capability Brown's finest achievements, were at their best, the sheet of ornamental water mirror-calm, its capes and inlets thrown into sharp relief by the angle of the sun, its graceful stone bridges etched against a backcloth of shade. The smooth, vivid green of the banks was broken here and there by informal plantings of fan-vaulted gunnera, spiky irises, and mop-headed galingale, while the rising ground behind was swathed in shrubs and trees whose contrasts of shape and colour and leaf-form were both subtle and immensely satisfying to the eye.

But the final touch of genius had not been Capability Brown's. At the very summit of the hill that sealed the gardens off from the outside world was a delightful little temple carved in pure white marble, shimmering palely exquisite against the deep blue summer sky. Looking at it, this product of his grandfather's youthful passion for Classical Greece, the earl's eyes glinted and he felt the old familiar surge of affectionate amusement. An artificial ruin on an artificial hill, a folly by every definition of the word, but – he shrugged his shoulders in mock despair – irresistibly charming.

Smiling, he turned away, so much at peace with the world that he scarcely even winced at the sight of a rabbit breakfasting on the young growth of a magnolia he had brought back from North America two years ago, tending it on the voyage, he remembered, with as much care as a new nursery-maid left in charge of her employers' firstborn son.

'Bang!' he said cheerfully, and the rabbit stiffened, hesitated, and then scuttled for cover. A moment later, the earl had to suppress an ignoble impulse to do the same. Someone was approaching. Matthew, he thought with a groan. Who else? No one else he had ever met was capable of projecting a wave of atmospheric turbulence before him that announced his coming as clearly as a flourish of trumpets. The need to worry was as ingrained in him as the need to eat and sleep, and though he was the earl's cousin and the very competent manager of his estates, his lordship had long since given up hope of changing him.

Young Mr Somerville's fair, anxious face was pink and faintly reproachful when he finally hove into view. 'Charles!' he exploded breathlessly while he was still some yards away. 'I am so glad to have caught you. You have been abroad for so long that . . . But perhaps you are not in the mood for estate business? I did not wish to intrude on you when you arrived so late last evening, but if you will not give me some of your time . . . I have such a list of things that need your decision! There is the matter of the water meadow. And the tenancy of the farm at Norbury. And perhaps the time has come to purchase one of the improved seed-planting drills? And . . .'

The earl's hand, raised in surrender, brought this precipitate speech to an equally precipitate halt. Matthew's eyes dropped under the quizzical gaze as he became hideously aware that he had omitted even the courtesy of a 'Good morning', not to mention the more extended civilities that might be expected by an employer – even one who was a cousin – whom he had not seen for six months.

A swan hooted derisively from the lake, and the earl, impressed by its sense of timing, had difficulty in repressing a chuckle. Instead, with an affability that successfully completed Matthew's discomfiture, he said: 'Good morning, Matt. I am very well, thank you. And you? Let us by all means talk of water meadows and tenants and – seed-planting drills, was it? Tomorrow, I suppose, will not do?'

In the event, it was not until noon on the fourth day that his lordship was able to call a halt, pointing out that they had catered for every crisis that might conceivably arise in the forthcoming six months. 'You now have a full larder of decisions,' he said cordially, gathering his papers into orderly sheaves. 'You may pickle them, or dry them, or salt them, or smoke them. You may even preserve them in goose grease, if you so wish, for future use.' He laid the papers down on his desk-top and thoughtfully squared up the edges. 'But you could, you know, have made at least half these decisions without referring them to me. Do try to cultivate self-confidence!'

Half an hour later, subsiding into a chair and contemplating the luncheon table with disfavour, he lamented to his sister: 'Really, I am quite worn down!'

'Oh, yes?' she said.

'Matthew is the most exhausting company. I suspect it would add years to my life if we could break him of this habit of losing himself in a morass of half-sentences!'

Lady Susan opened her mouth and then, closing it again, devoted her attention to the bowl of fruit that had been set before her.

The earl waited patiently. At last, he remarked: 'You were saying?'

'Don't be sarcastic, Charles! You know perfectly well I was holding my tongue. Anyway, your brother has the matter in hand.'

'And what does *that* mean?' he enquired with foreboding.

'He found he was catching the habit, so now, when one of Matt's sentences stops short, John finishes it for him.'

His lordship groaned. 'I can imagine it. All it will do is drive poor Matthew into even further incoherence.'

'Yes, well,' his sister replied, assiduously dissecting a peach. 'I told him you would be displeased, but he paid no heed. You had best tell him yourself when you feel able to devote a few moments to family affairs.'

There was a brief, ominous silence.

'What this household lacks,' said his lordship forcefully, 'is occupation! John, now he is down from Oxford, appears to have no intention of *doing* anything – other than bait Matthew, of course. While you fritter away your time on managing servants and choosing gowns and paying morning visits!'

Lady Susan gazed with fixed intensity at the Stubbs painting over the fireplace – which depicted a much younger Girvan proudly grasping the halter of the fourth earl's favourite mare, Scheherezade – and when she was able to control her voice again exclaimed with the greatest innocence, and as if she had not been consumed with curiosity for the better part of twenty-four hours: '*A propos* of occupation! What was that official-looking missive that sent you into such profound melancholy yesterday? Or is a mere sister not permitted to know?'

Her brother's air was one of mild reproof, but he submitted to the change of subject without comment. 'If a mere sister is interested, it contained the news that Ross's force – you know, the one that has been harrying the eastern seaboard of the United States – has reached Washington and set a considerable part of it alight.'

There was a moment's silence. Then: 'Washington?' she said.

'Yes, Washington.' The silence persisted. 'In America,' he added kindly. 'You know – that place on the other side of the Atlantic? The place we've been at war with for the last two years?'

His sister took a deep breath. 'But you have just spent months at Ghent – and why Ghent I have never understood! – arranging a *peace* conference between ourselves and the Americans!'

'Quite. Enough to make anyone melancholic, isn't it? The reason for Ghent, though, is simple enough. It's neutral territory, but – more important – it gives the Americans an opportunity to compare the decadence of the Old World with the youthful dynamism of the New. And since moral superiority always engenders benevolence, they sit down at the conference table in a thoroughly good mood! Which suits us very well.

'Anyway, though I was, to begin with, annoyed by Ross's antics, I was very soon revived by the thought that I am safely here in Wiltshire rather than facing John Quincy Adams at Ghent.' He smiled faintly. 'Nothing makes John Quincy happier than to have something to complain about. If I were there, he would purse his curly lips at me, look down his long New England nose, and enquire in the most censorious way how our burning of the United States Capitol may be expected to further the cause of peace between our two countries. How, in fact,' and the earl's crisp, clear voice took on the flattened cadences of Boston, Massachusetts, 'it may be equated with "those principles of eternal justice to which you and I, my dear Moriston, are both so sincerely dedicated." Poor John Quincy, to be deprived of his most appreciative audience on such an occasion!'

His sister smiled dutifully. It was all quite beyond her. Why, she wondered, as she had so often wondered before, did her brother persist in involving himself in other people's tiresome affairs? Boredom, of course, was his besetting sin, but she felt he ought to be able to find some other way of alleviating it!

✠

All in all, it was hardly surprising that the minor matter of the neat bay mare should have escaped his lordship's mind. But when he walked down to the stables early that afternoon, looking forward to a brisk cross-country gallop that would shake four sedentary days out of his system, one glance at Girvan's wooden countenance was enough to set him searching his conscience. The mare, he remembered grimly. His eye fell on the laconic instruction carved into one of the harness room timbers by some disciplinarian long departed – 'Do it now!' – and recognizing with a sigh that it was advice as fitting for earls as for their stable lads, he swung himself up on the big chestnut and turned its head southward in the direction of Priory Court.

It was a ten mile ride along leafy country lanes and roads confined on either side by cultivated fields, so that by the time the earl turned in through a Gothic archway to arrive in the courtyard of the grey stone mansion that had sheltered the priors of Merton before the dissolution of the monasteries, he was more than half asleep. As a groom ran forward to take his horse, he reflected absently on what a gloomy, oppressive house it was, convenient enough as a religious residence in the sixteenth century, no doubt, but damned inconvenient as a gentleman's at the beginning of the nineteenth. Wondering why its owner did not dispose of the Court and commission Smirke or Wilkins to build something new, he tried to remember whether Sir Augustus, with whom his acquaintance was slight, had any antiquarian interests.

Though the earl's memory was believed by some to be a wayward instrument, it being his habit to attribute all sins of omission and commission to its deficiencies, it was perfectly capable of functioning – when he chose – as smoothly and effectively as one of Mr Trevithick's high-pressure engines. As he dismounted, he recalled that though the owner of the house had no interest whatsoever in the antique, he was said to be far too clutch-fisted to waste money on those whom he described as 'scaff and raff like architects and builders'. But what snapped the earl irritably awake was the remembrance that Sir Augustus Home was known to the irreverent as Sir Augustus Away-From-Home, through his habit of always being somewhere else when he was wanted. This elusiveness appeared to be his only talent, for he was humourless and of uncertain temper, and the one subject – other than economy – that had ever been known to engage his interest was protocol. Gossip had it that anyone who cared to follow Sir Augustus up St James's Street might learn, from the depth of bow he accorded his various acquaintances, just what position each held in the social register. It was generally believed that Home's preoccupation with the subject arose from the fact that he was nephew and heir to the Most Noble the Marquis of Wayne, an elderly recluse whose sole purpose in life appeared to be to outlive him.

It was too late to retreat. Swiftly reviewing the possibilities, the earl decided that if Sir Augustus should in fact be away from home he might as well take advantage of his own position in the social register and demand to be shown the mare's paces, regardless.

He had reckoned without Sir Augustus's butler. This lugubrious individual proved to be very unctuous, very French, and for all practical purposes very deaf. The reluctant earl found himself whisked indoors and through to her ladyship's noticeably shabby drawing-room as inexorably as air into a vacuum, there to be greeted, seated, presented with a glass of wine, and pinned to his chair with the assurance that Sir Augustus could not be long delayed. With a strong sense of ill-usage, the earl noted that the butler's hearing had been miraculously restored the moment he entered his mistress's presence.

Though the earl did not much care for being cast as a captive audience, which was clearly his immediate fate, he had met too many statesmen in his day to be unaccustomed to the role. The first exchange of civilities with his hostess would have given him a very fair idea of what to expect if he had not already known, through the agency of her irrepressible son Louis, that she was an inveterate talker who required no more from her hearers than an occasional murmur of 'Indeed?' or 'Just so!' Louis, a close friend of John's, had regaled them at dinner one evening with the report of an occasion when she had begun a story to a large circle of auditors who had melted away one by one, on a variety of pretexts, until she finished it to a footman who happened to come in with the coals.

Her ladyship, an imposing matron who was just, though only just, on the right side of fifty, gave the impression of having been built more for endurance than speed. Her figure was substantial, and the high-necked gown and light shawl she wore failed to conceal the buckram armour beneath, which spoke volumes for her stamina and for that of whoever was responsible for lacing her in. The rather bizarre turban set squarely on her sandy-grey head surmounted a long, expressionless face whose most notable features were a pair of slightly fishy grey eyes and a mouth that appeared to be unusually full of teeth. The earl suspected that her butler's accent owed more to Drury Lane than to Paris, but Lady Home's was undoubtedly genuine.

He had not met her since he was a boy, and then only rarely, but he remembered his mother saying that she had married straight from the schoolroom and adding the acid rider that the longer she was away from France the more painfully French she became. When the Revolution broke out, no one had been more minutely informed than she on its grislier aspects, and no one

11

more devotedly attached to the interests of the Bourbons. Though her elder son, Ludovic, had by an unfortunate oversight been born and christened some years before the fall of the Bastille, she had been able to name the son who arrived in 1793 Louis, after the late king, while the daughter who followed in 1794 was baptized Marie, after the almost equally late queen. Fortunately, said Louis, by the time he and his sister were old enough to be favoured with their mama's conversation, the days of the Terror were long past and all they were subjected to was a running commentary on the iniquities of that upstart Bonaparte – unlike poor Ludovic, who had been reared on tales of blood and horror almost from the cradle until he was old enough to go to Eton. 'And look what it did for him!' Louis had concluded gaily. 'Made him so dashed self-righteous that there's no bearing with him at times!'

Devoutly hoping that he would not have to suffer Lady Home's eloquence for too long, the earl resigned himself to the role of listener, and if the greater part of his hostess's discourse at first flowed unnoticed over his head, he was too well-bred to allow it to show.

Lady Home was both gratified and surprised to find her guest attending to her with every appearance of courtesy. She knew her delivery to be compelling, her English flawless, and her opinions both original and stimulating, but it could not be denied that after half an hour her audiences usually showed a tendency to fidget. The earl, however, sat tranquilly through an extended monologue in which her ladyship progressed from the subject of the neat bay mare to the shortcomings of grooms and stable lads, the inefficiency and indolence of servants in general, and the abysmal taste and criminal incompetence of carpenters, stonemasons, and other *soi-disant* craftsmen.

Her pale, protuberant eyes surveyed Lord Moriston approvingly, and she wondered for a fleeting moment whether she might interest him in Marie, who despite two very expensive London seasons had failed to attach an eligible suitor. From the viewpoint of an ambitious mother he was endowed with every desirable quality, including a considerable fortune. About thirty years of age, she supposed – neither too young nor too old to make a satisfactory husband – and distinguished in air and address. Handsome, too, she thought judicially, if one cared for that dark, aquiline style of looks. The only thing she could cavil at was the very odd coat he was wearing. However, what one would condemn as freakish in a commoner, in an earl must be regarded as an interesting eccentricity. For a dizzy moment she pictured his lordship side by side with Marie at the altar, but the image did not carry conviction. Although she chose to think of herself as a doting parent, there was a strong streak of realism in her nature, and she was regretfully aware that Marie had neither the wit, style, nor beauty to recommend her to one of the most eligible bachelors in the country. With a sigh her ladyship took a sip of ratafia, assured her guest once again that Sir Augustus could not be long delayed, and launched with renewed vigour into her monologue.

If Lady Home had been a woman of perception, she might have noticed that the earl's tranquillity had begun to cloud over. He had been at her mercy for well over an hour and the strain was beginning to tell. The first flow of her platitudes had been delivered in something of a monotone, but as she warmed to her theme her style had become increasingly melodramatic and her accent was beginning to grate on his nerves. Her voice, penetratingly high at one moment, would sink in the next to a level so confidential that his lordship was quite unable to discover what she was being confidential about.

His head was beginning to throb, and his suspicion that Sir Augustus had not been 'delayed' at all but had never been expected back before dinner had developed into a certainty. The late afternoon sun, striking through the embrasured windows, latticed the floor and pooled it with amber reflections from decanter and glasses. Ten minutes more, the earl decided, and not a minute longer. His hostess's voice scraped across his consciousness again, rather like a badly played fiddle.

'. . . in a salon *chinois*,' she was saying, 'full of jars and mandarins and pagodas . . .'

She was almost unbelievable.

'. . . Egyptian, all *hiéroglyphes* . . .'

It was surprising that the three younger Homes had turned out to be quite reasonable, normal people. Ludovic was a model citizen, though a little prone to moralize.

'. . . they sleep in Turkish tents . . .'

But Louis had a quick wit and a great deal of charm.

'. . . and dine in a chapel *gothique*!'

Marie, of course, was so negative that one had the greatest difficulty even in recognizing her when one met her. Yet, all in all . . .

With a sudden access of panic, the earl realized that his hostess had come to the end of her peroration and was waiting for some response from him. He could think of nothing whatever to say.

'*Formidable, n'est-ce pas?*' she prompted him.

The words sprang unbidden to his tongue. '*Oui, sans contredit!*' he said decisively, and had to make a conscious effort to smother the laughter that welled up inside him. Just like the Hindu, who never spoke English on a Monday! It was really too much. Consigning Lady Home, Sir Augustus Home, and Sir Augustus Home's neat bay mare to a joint perdition, he prepared to rise and take his leave.

At this precise moment the door opened to admit a whole concourse of people. His lordship, the words of firm but graceful farewell frozen on his lips, was afforded an excellent view of two male backs, which he identified as those of Louis, slender and topped with a thatch of curly brown hair, and Ludovic, taller, admirably tailored, and several shades fairer than his brother. The two ladies whom the young men were ushering into the room were obscured from his lordship's vision, but behind them, to his considerable relief, he could see the long-awaited Sir Augustus, his pallid features a little flushed, and the tonsure of fluffy brown hair standing out like some inappropriate halo.

As the earl rose and acknowledged Louis's boisterous welcome and his brother's more restrained one, Sir Augustus bustled forward with effusive enquiries after his well-being. In imminent danger of having his shoulder patted, the earl could not prevent himself from stiffening slightly, but he contrived to respond courteously enough.

Lady Home bore these exchanges in majestic silence before drawing his lordship's attention to the two young ladies. 'My daughter, with whom you are already acquainted, of course,' she announced with a perfect disregard for the conventional priorities. The earl bowed to the nondescript mouse of a girl who was Marie. 'And,' waving the other young woman forward, 'our charming guest, Mees Mallycollum.' His lordship, for the second time in a very few minutes, was afflicted by an almost overpowering desire to laugh. No one – really no one, and certainly not this astonishing beauty with hair like an autumn sunset – could possibly be called 'Mees Mallycollum'. He bowed again, his expression more than usually impassive.

'And this,' continued Lady Home, addressing the young lady, 'is our neighbour Lord Moriston, who lives at Atherton Hall. A *château*,' she added graciously, 'which is of a grandeur quite remarkable.'

With the deepest surprise, the earl saw the girl's colour

drain away until she was as white as the ribbons that trimmed her elegant grey gown. Since his coming of age, he had been the target of a great many match-making mamas and had seen numerous hopeful debutantes blush or turn pale under his regard, but this was something quite different. Miss – her name *could* not be Mallycollum – looked as if she had just received the shock of her life. From the corner of his eye he noted that Ludovic, too, was observing the girl curiously while his mama rambled on about how empty Priory Court would seem when its guest returned to London on the following day.

In other circumstances the earl would have been tempted to linger and enquire into the mystery. But having at last been permitted to rise from his bed of nails, he had not the most distant intention of sitting down again. He stayed, therefore, for no more than the five minutes civility seemed to require before taking leave of his hostess and the younger members of the company and propelling Sir Augustus, with more firmness than courtesy, out of the drawing-room and off to the stables and the neat bay mare.

✗ *Chapter Two* ✗

When the earl arrived back at Atherton Hall, followed by a groom from Priory Court leading the mare on a halter, it was well after the hour for dinner. Without further ado, he handed the mare over to Girvan's delighted keeping, remarking only, 'You will never know what she cost me!' and adding a brisk injunction to see that Sir Augustus's man had some refreshment before he set off again for the Court. Then he strode swiftly away in the direction of the house.

He was half-way up the splendid marble staircase when Lady Susan, a vision in water-green sarsnet, emerged from one of the saloons on the entrance floor. Her exclamation halted him, and he said, without turning: 'Yes, I know I am very late. But give me thirty minutes and I will join you for dinner.'

'That's all very fine,' responded the vision tartly. 'But I do wish you wouldn't disappear for hours without telling someone where you are going. Suppose you were needed urgently?'

The earl sighed and turned to face her. 'Don't try me too far,' he said mildly. 'I have just spent close on two hours at Priory Court listening to that interminable woman, Lady Home, and another thirty minutes suffering her husband's repellent brand of flummery, and I warn you that I am feeling exceedingly frail. Unless you wish me to take to my bed for the next few days, you will handle me with the care and delicacy you would accord to the rarest piece of Chinese lacquer.'

His sister fixed unerringly on the essential point of this discourse. 'You have been over to Priory Court,' she said in failing tones. 'In *that* coat?'

'In this coat,' the earl confirmed, his brows slightly raised. 'Though I would prefer you to call it by its proper name, which is *wamus*. It may not,' he conceded, 'be quite what Weston or Schultz would choose to make for me, but it is a most convenient garment, and all the crack among American frontiersmen. A commoner would have his *wamus* made of buckskin, but being an earl mine is made of white deerskin, as you observe.' He leant a negligent elbow on the balustrade and went on dreamily: 'I wonder whether I should have some deerskin breeches as well. There is something so aesthetically satisfying about the way their fringed seams set off the fringes on the *wamus* itself.'

'If,' retorted his sister wrathfully, 'you have been over to Priory Court dressed in that – that – thing, and if you have been talking in that extraordinary fashion, I cannot imagine what Lady Home must have thought of you!'

'I wish I could say she has taken me in dislike, but that would be too much to hope for. An earl, even an eccentric one, is not as other men. She has probably conceived a maternal regard for me,' he went on blandly, 'and will call once a week from now on to reassure herself that I have not caught a chill.'

His sister regarded him with a fulminating eye, but before she could find anything suitably crushing to say, he grinned, turned away, and disappeared up the rest of the stairs two at a time.

It was not until they had risen from table, fortified by some turbot with lobster sauce, a cut of spit-roasted ham *au Madère* – 'Madeira!' groaned his lordship – a few fillets of hazel grouse, cucumbers in white sauce, a dish of summer truffles roasted in the embers, a mouthful or two of lettuce *farcie à l'essence*, and some fresh fruit from the succession houses, that the earl felt able to describe his visit to Priory Court. Lady Susan had some difficulty in maintaining her composure. She had seen her brother's public face often enough to know that it was one of cool reserve; indeed, he appeared on occasion to be so controlled that he was almost inhuman. She had never thought, before, about the problems sustaining such an image might present to a man who, in private, was entirely human, and her brother had never before been articulate on the subject.

When he reached Lady Home's diatribe on contemporary interior decoration her precarious gravity collapsed. An answering gleam crept into her brother's eye. 'You may laugh,' he said. 'If I had anticipated an afternoon of high farce, I might even have laughed myself. But tell me! The unspeakable Sir Augustus can't be purse-pinched, can he? Yet it must be twenty years, by the look of it, since anything was spent on the furnishings or decoration of that house. I do not ask,' he added plaintively, 'for pagodas or *hiéroglyphes*, but a little polish and paint and the services of a good chair-upholsterer would work wonders.'

'I think he's just naturally miserly. The estate is said to be in good heart, but Louis is always complaining of his pockets being to let and most of Marie's dresses look to me as if they came from the Pantheon bazaar. Even during her London seasons, poor child. Ludovic seems to contrive better, though of course he is such a pattern-card that one wouldn't expect anything else! But go on. What happened next?'

They were interrupted by a tap on the door and the entry of a footman bearing the tea tray. John and Matthew, returning from a convivial evening with some friends at Norbury, followed closely in his wake.

Lady Susan waited only until the footman had departed before ruthlessly abandoning the subject of Priory Court and embarking on a fluent and comprehensive denunciation of the sartorial habits of both her brothers. The earl, as it happened, was now clad in a dark coat of superb cut, beautifully tailored knee breeches and a plain white waistcoat adorned with a single fob at the waist. But John, as always, had the rumpled look of one who had scrambled into his clothes before breakfast and never so much as glanced in a mirror since. At twenty-one, he resembled the earl much more than did either of the other Dornay brothers – Robert, at twenty-five a promising cavalry officer, and Gavin, twenty-three years old and the incumbent of a parish in one of the less salubrious quarters of London. John had the same dark good looks as the earl, the same gentian-blue eyes, the same long, shapely hands, but his figure still betrayed his youth and he had none of his brother's polish. Not all the exertions of his excellent valet could keep him tidy, and his barber was beginning to weary of pointing out that the windswept head now in fashion was meant to be achieved by the expert use of scissors, not by running the fingers through the hair.

'Ragamuffins!' said her ladyship witheringly. For all the world, thought John, as if she were a ninety-year-old grandmother instead of a twenty-eight-year-old sister. 'Charles goes to pay social calls in a *wampum* . . .'

'*Wamus!*' wailed the earl.

'*Wampum* or *wamus*, it makes no difference,' replied his sister. 'And John returns from . . .'

'But it does!' rejoined her brother, goaded. 'A *wampum* is a string of Red Indian beads, and I will not be accused of going calling in a string of beads!'

Her ladyship ignored this caveat. 'And John returns from what I understood was a respectable dinner engagement with his neckcloth askew and his coat as creased as if he had slept in it. I cannot conceive why the pair of you should insist on making such figures of yourselves.'

Unwisely, John opened his mouth to protest, but he was forestalled by the earl who could see familiar breakers ahead. 'Yes. Well, let's talk about that some other time. At the moment, I am much more interested to know whether any of you can enlighten me about the young lady who has been visiting the Homes at Priory Court. Have you any idea who she is? Her name,' he cleared his throat slightly, 'is Mallycollum.'

The others exchanged mystified glances. 'You did say Mallycollum?' John asked with a grin.

'I did,' his lordship confirmed. 'Or, at least, Lady Home did.'

There was a silence, broken at length by his sister, who shrugged her fashionable shoulders and said: 'What kind of girl is she? Lady Home is one of those women who is never comfortable in the country without a visiting Miss at her beck and call. You know, someone to play the harp, or sing not too much out of tune, or cut the leaves of new novels, or sort her embroidery silks.'

The earl scarcely even troubled to consider this. 'No, I don't think Miss – er – Mallycollum would fall into that category. About twenty, I suppose. Well-bred, and a raving beauty.' He turned to his sister again. 'I hadn't reached that part of my afternoon's saga. It was quite extraordinary. She turned as white as a sheet when she heard who I was, and her conversation afterwards was confined to the most basic civilities, most of them inaudible. But I shouldn't think she would be particularly biddable. People with flaming hair rarely are.'

'Flaming hair?' said Matthew. 'You mean red?'

'No, I don't mean red,' his lordship replied a little testily, 'though I should be hard put to it to describe it. The first thought that struck me was that it was like one of those Highland sunsets, a blend of flame and gold and apricot and amber, all changing from moment to moment as the light changes. And you may take that quizzical expression off your face, Susan. It does not become you!'

His sister was spared the need to reply. 'It must have been Miss Malcolm!' said Matthew unexpectedly, and blushed to the roots of his hair as three pairs of eyes swivelled accusingly towards him.

'Well, I mean, I have only just realized . . . But she certainly had red – er, flaming – hair . . . Though I was not aware that she was acquainted with Lady Home.'

The earl waited with commendable patience, and then said: 'Well, I am relieved to know that her name is just Malcolm with a French accent, but perhaps you might like to tell us who she is? Or am I supposed to know?'

'Yes, but Charles, you must remember! Though now I think of it, you were in Scotland at the time, and Susan and John were in town. But I'm sure I wrote to you about it.'

His lordship took a deep breath. 'I'm sure you did, Matt – but *about what?*'

'The accident. The poor lady who was found dead on the pike road by the South Lodge.'

'Ah. But you gave me only the barest outline of what happened. It must have been – when? September or October last year?'

'September, because it was just before Stoke retired, which was what made the whole thing so very trying . . .'

The earl closed his eyes, and his sister, taking pity on him, said decisively: 'Matthew, will you be good enough to begin at the beginning and continue to the end of the story. If you can tell us about the accident, what Stoke's retirement had to do with it, and how Miss Malcolm was involved, I am sure we will all be grateful.'

'Very well,' replied Matthew obligingly. 'It was September. Was it a Wednesday? Yes, I think it was. And the weather was unseasonably warm. Stoke was up early for he was expecting the carrier from Wincanton. He stepped out from the lodge to glance up the road and caught sight of what he thought was a bundle of cloth on the verge, about twenty yards up. His eyesight was failing badly, you know.

'In any case, he wandered up to investigate and found it was the body of a lady. He hesitated about what to do, and then went back to the lodge and sent young Jeremy up to fetch me. It was a bit of a pantomime. Brandon refused to allow Jeremy into the house with his great muddy boots, and Jeremy said it was urgent, and Brandon said nothing to do with Stoke could be urgent enough to warrant interrupting Mr Matthew at his breakfast. By the time I emerged from the breakfast parlour Jeremy was almost incoherent, so I thought I had best go down and see for myself before I sent for the magistrate.

'As soon as I looked at the lady, I could see she *was* dead and not just unconscious, as I had thought she might be. You know how Stoke dramatized things! There was no sign of what had caused her death until . . .'

Matthew's voice tailed off. His eyes were on Lady Susan, and he said: 'You look quite pale. Are you all right?'

The earl's gaze had been fixed on the tea-leaves at the bottom of his cup, but at this he looked up. His sister had, indeed, lost some of her colour. 'Are you sure you want Matt to go on?' he asked.

'Of course!' his sister replied with spirit. 'I'm not such a poor thing that I have to be shielded from every unpleasant fact of life!'

'Or death,' murmured John *sotto voce*, and was rewarded with an exasperated look from his brother.

'Very well, Matt. Please continue.'

Correctly interpreting the earl's expression, Matthew mentally reviewed the rest of his story with a view to expunging its more harrowing details. 'Yes, well. It must have been a kick from a rearing horse, for I remember a groom of my father's dying from just such a blow. It was tragic. She must have been very beautiful . . .

'I could see no purpose in staying on the pike road, so I told Stoke to remain there while I went up to the house and sent one of the footmen for the magistrate. Unfortunately, by the time he reached old Hopkinson's house the man had ridden off somewhere on business. Peter hung around, waiting, until well after midday, and then decided he had better just leave a message and get back to Atherton. I suppose it must have been about two o'clock when he returned. Hopkinson lives a good eight or nine miles away, you know.

'I was a little concerned to think of the poor lady still lying there by the roadside, but I felt perhaps I shouldn't move her before the magistrate arrived. However, I decided to walk down the road and have a word with Stoke, expecting him to be in a thoroughly crabbed mood by that time. When I got there, I found him comfortably seated on the verge, with the poor woman's body laid out for all the world as if she were on a bier! He couldn't bear to see the pretty lady lying there so cramped and stiff, he said, so - er - so he just eased her into a position that seemed more natural-like. There wasn't much I could say. In a way . . .'

'Yes?' said the earl encouragingly, after a moment.

'Yes. Well, the magistrate arrived late in the afternoon, about five, if I remember, bustling in that way he has, as if there's something automatically improper in anything he hasn't witnessed personally. I told him everything relevant, and he questioned Stoke closely about whether there had been any night traffic on the road. Stoke swore there had been nothing - but you know him! Deaf as a post, but nothing would make him admit it. He turned very surly when the magistrate didn't believe him. It was all rather tiresome.

'It seemed fairly clear what had happened. If the lady had been walking along the road at dusk - though goodness knows why she should have been; that was something that was never explained - she might have been overtaken by a carriage or a saddle horse. She was wearing a pale-coloured pelisse, a kind of creamy shade. If she had suddenly turned into the road, she might very easily have terrified the horse, which could have reared - striking her - and then bolted. The ri̇ḋer or driver may have taken some time to get the animal under control again. If so, by the time he returned to see whether the ghostly figure was real and had been injured, it would be too dark to discover anything, especially if he did not know the road.'

'Maybe he didn't return at all,' John said soberly, 'in case he *had* injured the "ghostly figure".'

'That thought crossed the magistrate's mind, too,' Matt said, 'for when he couldn't budge Stoke about the traffic on the road, he decided to have the tollkeepers questioned.

'Well, really! We all know what tollkeepers are. They go off with their cronies in the evening and leave their wives and children to take the tolls. The wives hear nothing because they're clanking away at pots and pans or out at the back feeding the hens, and the children fall asleep. Anyone who wants to can pass through the gates without being observed! I heard afterwards that it was just as you might have expected. One tollkeeper swore that nothing whatever had passed through the gates between sundown and sun-up. Another said that ten horses and vehicles had passed, *none* of which he could describe. There's a likely tale, if you please! A third – old Joseph at the Norbury pike, you know? – had passed through two men on horseback, a sporting curricle, young Walter Totton's farm cart, and old Lady Dorville's carriage.'

'There was an enquiry, presumably?' the earl's soft voice intervened.

'Yes. It produced nothing. The verdict was accidental death – a rearing horse and an irresponsible rider. The coroner made some extremely pointed remarks about civic duty and held forth at length on unfortunate ladies slain in the flower of their beauty by drunken reprobates. *He* at least seemed to have no doubts about who should bear the blame.'

'Poor Matthew!' said Lady Susan. 'What an unnerving experience for you! And I can quite see why you wished Stoke had retired earlier than he did.'

The earl had been sitting with his chin sunk in the folds of his exquisite cravat. Now, he turned and placed his empty teacup on the tray. 'One thing you haven't told us,' he said. 'Where does Miss Malcolm come into all this?'

His sister looked at him in astonishment. He must really have had a tiring day, for he was not usually so slow.

'Oh, dear! Didn't I say?' Matthew looked crestfallen. 'I met Miss Malcolm at the coroner's enquiry. The lady who died was her mother.'

The room seemed unnaturally quiet. A flower shivered in a vase in the corner and a petal dropped. A candle, unevenly trimmed, flickered slightly and guttered in some invisible eddy of night air.

'Hell and the devil confound it!' exclaimed his lordship, sitting up abruptly. 'No wonder the poor girl turned pale at the mention of Atherton. And she must have thought it very odd of me not to say a word about it, even at this late date!'

'On the contrary,' his sister said. 'She was probably grateful that you refrained from embarrassing her.'

'I wish I might think so, but I was behaving in such a high-handed fashion at the time . . .' He rose to his feet. 'It is late. You may burn the midnight oil if you wish, but I am going to bed. For if one thing is sure, it is that I have had quite enough of today!'

✠

Next afternoon, Peter the footman brought back from the receiving-office a number of letters for the earl. Among them was one from Field Marshal the Duke of Wellington. Dated four days earlier, it began with Wellington's characteristic 'My dear Lord,' and continued in equally characteristic fashion:

As you know, I have agreed to Lord Castlereagh's wish that I should become the ambassador at Paris, for I must serve the public in some manner and under existing circumstances I could not well do so at home. I am about to set out for that place.

I shall be much obliged to you if you will give me the benefit of your assistance in a matter concerning a young friend of mine, who has just told me of some circumstances to which I will not at present advert but which have somewhat shocked me. I am highly sensible of the demands on your time. It rarely happens that a man in your situation has leisure to attend to his own private affairs, much less to those of any other person. However, the matter is so extraordinary that I have told the young lady she must seek advice, and that you are the man for her. I suggest to your lordship, in case you should have no objections, that you might call upon her when you are next in town or whenever you may find it convenient. The name of the young lady is Miss Caroline Malcolm and she is residing at present in Hill Street, in the house adjoining Lady Orinford's.

Believe me, &c
Wellington

✠ *Chapter Three* ✠

Caroline Malcolm returned to London with her composure seriously ruffled. She had accepted Lady Home's invitation to spend a week in the country only because it would have been unsuitable for her, while still in mourning for her mother, to visit fashionable Brighton, and none of the less fashionable resorts seemed to have much to recommend them. But her acquaintance being with the younger Homes, she had not anticipated just what a trial their parents would turn out to be, nor had she quite realized how near to Priory Court was the scene of her mother's accident. Marie and her brothers had made valiant attempts to entertain her, riding out, walking with her, and arranging picnics and expeditions to all the more accessible beauty spots. These, Caro noticed, not sure whether to feel provoked or relieved, seemed without exception to lie in the opposite direction from Atherton Hall. Her mother's purpose in visiting Wiltshire had never been satisfactorily explained, and Caro had suffered ever since from recurring attacks of curiosity about the Hall and its unknown occupants.

As a result, she had spent much of the week on edge, torn between hope and fear lest there should be some neighbourly contact between the two households. By the end, her nerves were frayed as much by suspense as by Ludovic's unfailing consideration, Louis's relentless high spirits, and Marie's doe-eyed gratitude for her company. It was with a premature lightening of the heart, therefore, that she had entered Lady Home's drawing-room on that last afternoon, aware that only a few more hours at the Court remained.

The dark, striking man sitting with Lady Home had turned as she and the others entered the room, the expression on his face unreadable. There was only the faintest relaxation of the long firm mouth as he responded to the younger Homes' greetings, and his reaction to Sir Augustus verged on the glacial. Caro was just trying to decide whether he was insufferably proud, or merely found the Homes as intolerable *en masse* as she did, when Lady Home summoned her forward to be introduced. Suppressing the now familiar shudder at hearing herself referred to as 'Mees Mallycollum', she was diverted by noticing an odd gleam in the deep blue eyes before his heavy lids were lowered and he made her a polite bow. The introduction found her wholly unprepared.

It was the words 'Atherton Hall' that caught her attention first, even before his name, and her heart thumped against her ribs with a shock all the more telling for having been half expected and then dismissed. Several seconds passed before the rest of what Lady Home had said penetrated her mind and plunged her into a confusion as paralyzing as it was complete.

Her mind flew back to the morning a few weeks ago when she had had that long, private talk with Uncle Arthur, whom she had not seen for nine years. During that time, from being plain

24

Arthur Wellesley, a major-general in faraway India, he had become the iron-nerved, intolerant darling of England, a field marshal, and a duke. But she found that behind that terse, high-nosed competence he was still the honorary uncle of her childhood, who soothed nursery hurts with sugar-candies and bracing exhortations, took Caro up on his shoulder, and hoisted little brother Richard up to the dizzy eminence of his high military saddle. She had poured out her troubles to him as if she were ten years old again, and he had listened attentively, taken aback at first, but very firm that she should not let matters rest.

'What you need,' he had said, his profile beakily outlined against the window, 'is advice from someone who knows how to go about such things. I have been in England so little these last twenty years that I would scarcely know how to begin.' He sat silent for a few minutes, his forehead creased and his fingers drumming steadily on his knee. 'Hmmm!' he erupted at last with a suddenness that made her jump. 'Yes. I know who you want. He's abroad at the moment but he should be back soon. I'll write to him. Get him to call on you. That's it! That's the thing!' He took her hand and patted it sustainingly. 'No doubt about it. Moriston's your man!'

'Moriston?'

'Not know him? No, I suppose not. But he's a useful fellow. Does a bit of diplomatic work for us now and again, instead of sitting about on his estates driving his farm managers frantic.' Observing her raised eyebrows, he said: 'No need to look like that, child. You've no idea how handy it is to have an earl about the place – impresses the foreigners, you know.'

'An *earl*?' she said, considerably astonished. 'I'm sorry, Uncle Arthur, but you misunderstand me. I was surprised enough when you mentioned estates and farm managers. But an earl . . .'

'Oh, I see,' said His Grace, enlightened. 'Don't let that worry you. He's eccentric, I grant you, but perfectly conversable. No, I have nothing against him except that he can afford to pick and choose. Refuses to waste energy on rubbishing missions to China and suchlike. We'll probably have to send Amherst next time, though Moriston thinks he won't even be received and swears that this embassy to the Celestial Kingdom will be even more of a fiasco than the last.

'But that's all by the by. One thing most people don't know about Moriston – and this is what concerns *you*, m'dear – is that he has a genius for getting to the bottom of things. I know for sure of serious problems he has helped to clear up for three people, and I strongly suspect that a certain gentleman – no! I shan't say who! – would actually have been tried for murder if Moriston hadn't taken a hand in the game and found the true culprit. He only does it for intellectual exercise, mind you, so you will have to make sure you engage his interest!'

From Uncle Arthur's description, Caro had deduced a middle-aged or elderly gentleman, sharp, scholarly, of a meddlesome intelligence – an austere busybody, if such a combination were possible. Could this be the same man? And if it was, had he or had he not received a letter from the Duke? And if he had, had he been irritated by it? Was that what the gleam in his eye meant? Only too conscious that she was reacting to his practised civilities like a rabbit mesmerized by a stoat, she was quite unable to gather her wandering wits together. There was no possibility of speaking to him in private, and even if there had been she would scarcely have known how to begin.

She spent the rest of the evening with her brain in a whirl, contributing little to the conversation and even less to the game of whist with which it was Lady Home's habit to beguile the hours after dinner. An innocent question about the earl and his household opened the floodgates of Lady Home's eloquence readily enough, but all Caro learned was that he lived – when at home – with his youngest brother and a young, widowed sister; that there were two other brothers, and two elder sisters; that his father had died ten, or was it twelve, years earlier; and that his mother had not treated Lady Home with the distinguishing attention she felt to be her due. And all the while, Caro was aware of being covertly observed by Ludovic who was, she thought crossly, far too interested in her for comfort.

Back in the privacy of London in late summer, she was still not able to settle her mind. She could hardly discuss matters of a confidential nature with her hired chaperone, Sarah Nicholas, twenty-nine years old, well-bred, briefly married to a gentleman who had – providentially, said his widow – died before he quite ran through his fortune. But though she had not been reduced to penury, Sarah, a fair, talkative, wispy young woman with more style than beauty, did not hesitate to admit that her portion was by no means large enough to maintain her in the comfort she preferred. Living with Caroline suited her very well, and she anticipated that it would suit her even better when Caro's year of mourning was over – as it very soon would be – and they could attend balls and receptions and routs and all the other festivities of social London. Sarah had the kindest of hearts but her tongue ran on wheels, and Caro had made it a rule to tell her only what she did not mind having repeated to the entire circle of Sarah's acquaintance.

If Richard had been at home, it would not have been so bad. Admittedly, he could not understand why his sister was making such a piece of work about nothing – well, almost nothing – but since it was not his problem, there was no reason why she should heed his opinion. And that was Rich in a nutshell, she had thought at the time with affectionate exasperation: reasonableness carried beyond the bounds of reason. But at least, if he had been there, she might have talked some of the disquiet out of her system. However, he was on an extended visit to a friend in Lincolnshire and would go from there straight back to Oxford.

The outcome was that she spent several days fretting, and then received a brief and exceedingly uninformative note from the earl saying that he regretted he would not be in town before the second week in October but hoped to give himself the pleasure of calling on her one morning early in that month.

Having uttered what in anyone less exquisite would have sounded remarkably like a snort, Caroline – in intervals between visiting milliners and modistes, writing notes accepting engagements for the forthcoming season, and walking or riding in the Park – devoted the next few weeks to convincing herself that she would rather die than expose her private problems to that cool, detached blue gaze.

As a result, when her butler at last conducted his lordship to Miss Malcolm's elegant drawing-room, she was perfectly able to conceal her gratification at his visit. The butler withdrew, his countenance expressive of what the earl, mildly surprised, recognized as strong disapproval, and he was left stranded a few steps over the threshold with his hostess nowhere in sight. Then, turning his head, he saw her rise from a desk in the other part of the pleasantly proportioned double room and hesitate before coming towards him. A swift glance assured him that there was no one else concealed in the shadows, which at least explained the butler's disapproval. Unmarried young ladies did not commonly receive gentlemen without a third party being present.

Her beauty was quite as dazzling as he remembered, and her expression – if anything – even more discouraging.

'Miss Malcolm?' he said politely, and noticed how gracefully she moved as she came forward.

27

'How do you do?' she replied. 'Pray forgive me, but you have taken me a little by surprise.'

'But I understood you wished me to call on you?'

'Yes, I – or, rather, my uncle – thought that . . . But I have considered the matter further and . . .' She broke off with a sharp little sigh of vexation as her disclaimers disintegrated on her tongue. 'The thing is . . .' and she broke off again as she raised her eyes to his face and caught there a lingering trace of amusement, swiftly suppressed.

My God, the earl had been thinking, Matthew in the shape of Diana! Was it nervousness, or did she really intend to send him to the rightabout? Since he had no intention of relinquishing a promising mystery without at least discovering what it was, he chose his next words with care.

'Miss Malcolm,' he said. 'I beg you to believe that I have no desire to embarrass you or to intrude on your private affairs. I am here simply because the Duke of Wellington solicited my aid on your behalf. If you had rather I went away, you have only to say so.'

With a certain sympathy, he watched her work out the implications of this disingenuous speech, which had made it impossible for her to send him away without appearing, at the very least, either gauche or ill-bred. A spark flashed in the grey-green eyes, and he thought appreciatively how much she would have relished putting him in his place. Finally, accepting the inevitable, she inclined her head and said with a touch of constraint: 'Pray, won't you sit down?'

He bowed, and paused for her to seat herself before disposing his long limbs in a chair on the other side of the fireplace, where he waited placidly for her to collect her thoughts. It was a comfortable room, and the fire was welcoming on a crisp October day. At last she began, with a creditable attempt at self-possession. 'I am truly grateful to you for coming, and if I seemed ungracious I hope you will understand that it is because I have a reluctance to discuss private problems with someone who is a stranger to me.'

Very neat, he thought. Aloud, he murmured: 'Very natural.'

'The Duke is an old friend of my father – of my . . . Well, we have always been in the habit of treating him as an adopted uncle, and he has most strongly advised that I should consult you. I believe that you have some experience in solving problems of a delicate nature?'

Not so neat, he thought. 'A certain amount. Though since

such problems are usually confidential,' he went on apologetically, 'I fear I cannot provide you with references.'

The colour flared in her cheeks. 'Lord Moriston,' she said, her voice a little uneven, 'this is difficult for me, and I hope you will not choose to misinterpret what I say.'

His lordship was not in the least perturbed. In his experience, people who lost their tempers came to the point a great deal faster than those who clung to their self-control.

'The situation is,' Miss Malcolm continued in a rush, 'that I wish to find my father!'

It was not what the earl had expected. 'Forgive me, but how did you come to lose him?'

'I haven't lost him. I have never had him. I have no idea who he was, or is, nor do I even know his name!'

'But surely your mother . . .'

'No. It was only after she died – you must know about it! She met with a fatal accident almost on your doorstep, which is something I was not aware of when the Duke told me about you – it was only after she died that I discovered that Papa Malcolm was not, in fact, my father. Though he could not have been kinder if I had been ten times his daughter. I think that was what made the shock so very particular.'

'I take it Mr Malcolm is no longer alive?'

'Lieutenant-Colonel Malcolm. He died two years ago, which is why my mother brought us back to England. He was an army officer in India, and then transferred to civil and political duties when I was still very small.'

'You said "us"?'

'My brother Richard and I. He is two years younger, though he is always taken to be the elder – he is unusually tall for his age, you see, and rather serious-looking. But his birth is incontrovertible. Even without anything else to go on, he is the image of Papa Malcolm.'

The earl hesitated for a moment. 'You must have some other relatives. What about your mother's or your step-father's families?'

She smiled ruefully, and spread her hands wide in a gesture of negation. 'No one. My – step-father's parents died many years ago, and there was a brother who was killed in the Peninsular War. He wasn't married. I know nothing at all of my mother's family. She never mentioned them, and there was nothing among her papers when she died. I looked. In fact, I cannot even tell you her maiden name.'

The earl wondered how best to phrase his next question in such a way that it would not offend her sensibilities.

'Do I take it,' he said carefully, 'that you believe Colonel Malcolm to have been your mother's second husband?'

She looked up from the fire. 'There's no other answer, is there?'

If the earl had not had excellent control of his facial muscles, he might have blinked. Instead, expressionless, he changed the subject. 'Were you and your brother born in India?'

'Richard was, about two months after my parents – my mother and step-father, I mean – arrived there. I was born in this country, but I have no idea where.'

The earl frowned. 'One last question. You appear to me to have two problems rather than one. In other words, your mother's early life, and the identity of your real father. Which concerns you more?'

She looked at the slim, delicate hands clasped in her lap and allowed a pause to develop before she began, with difficulty: 'The answer is, I suppose, that I have known my mother all my life and she has given me – everything. So finding out more about her, about things she did not tell me because, perhaps, she did not want me to know, would be almost an intrusion. But my father, my true father, has given me . . .'

She stopped abruptly, a thoughtful look on her face, and the earl watched her, wondering if what came next was going to be the whole, unsullied truth. '. . . nothing of himself,' she resumed. 'I must know *some*thing about him. Who he is. What he is. Whether he is alive or dead – he must be dead, I suppose. I daresay it seems foolish to you, and you may be right. But you, presumably, know who you are. All my life I have thought I knew who *I* was – and now I don't. I feel that I can never be sure of myself again until I find out.'

'I understand. Are you sure you have told me everything you can?'

'Yes.' She was not looking at him.

'You realize how little it is?' She nodded. 'Miss Malcolm, you have asked me for advice, and I'm afraid you are not going to like the only advice I can give you. For it is to forget the matter.' He observed the faint movement as her clasped hands tightened. 'Think,' he went on, only too aware that he was sounding magisterial. 'All your life, you have regarded Colonel Malcolm as your true father, and he behaved as such. Doesn't it seem disloyal to begin searching, now, for someone to whom

30

you owe nothing but the accident of conception?' A faint blush rose to her cheeks, and he wondered whether it came from shocked gentility or was connected with whatever it was she had so carefully avoided telling him. 'Further, if your mother never made any mention of your true father, she must have had good reason. She may have been deeply hurt either by his death or by a marriage disastrous enough to end in divorce. It isn't a unique situation, but the people involved are often extremely sensitive on the subject. However,' and he paused for a moment, 'it is rare for the children of such marriages to become obsessed by the question of their paternity.'

Was he being a little too pointed? he wondered. The graceful figure opposite him did not stir, so he went on, his tone authoritative. 'Now. If you are determined on it, I must tell you that a search for your real father would prove not only difficult, but lengthy, expensive, and probably painful. You would have to employ people to ferret out a great many secrets from the past that you might find would have been better left to lie. And they would not, I fear, be people on whose discretion you could depend. If you want names, I will send you a list of the less unreliable ones. But I warn you, with the exception of one or two of the Runners – Townsend might do you, I suppose, if he's still practising – they will not be people of the type you are accustomed to dealing with, and you will have to think very seriously indeed before you place your mother's reputation, and yours, in their hands. If you can tell them no more than you have told me, you may find in the end that it has all been for nothing.'

And that, he thought, ought to do it. He could not see her expression, for the burnished head was bent, but he rose smoothly to his feet. 'Perhaps you will let me know when you have reached a decision?'

She looked up, at that, meeting the cool blue gaze abstractedly. 'Engage his interest,' Uncle Arthur had said. It seemed as if she had failed, but whereas half an hour earlier she would have been relieved that he had chosen not to involve himself, now, perversely, she was determined not to let him slide out so easily. She, too, rose. 'Would you wait a few moments?' she said, and left the room.

She was absent for what seemed a very long time. While he waited the earl, surveying his surroundings at leisure, decided that though the house was probably hired, the furnishings were not. The curtains were a pleasing shade of russet, and the chairs were upholstered either in the same russet or in a rough-textured, creamy Indian silk. The carpets were pale, too, and in one corner there was a magnificent urn full of autumn leaves and berries, green and gold and bronze and scarlet. Thank God there were no Benares brass trays or damascened sweetmeat boxes or all-too-familiar gouaches of 'Hindu festivals', mass-produced by Indian artists in vivid colour and picturesque detail for their British overlords. Only two fragile little watercolours of Indian temples, delicately executed – by Miss Malcolm, or her mama? – bore open witness to the greater part of a lifetime spent in the dominions of the Honourable East India Company.

The butler entered, soft-footed, with a tray of refreshments. 'Madeira, my lord?' The earl eyed it dubiously. But since he could hardly go through the rest of his life refusing to drink Madeira in other people's houses, he accepted and raised the glass to his lips.

Miss Malcolm, returning at that moment, interpreted his expression with unexpected accuracy. 'You needn't worry, my lord!' she assured him. 'Even the most unregenerate nabob can be depended on to be a tolerable judge of wine. My brother's palate has been rigorously educated. I will have sherry, please, Sime.'

Well, that was something in her favour, thought his lordship. Most young ladies drank ratafia, and he had never been able to understand how they managed to swallow it without retching.

Miss Malcolm waited until the butler had withdrawn and then went to her desk and took from one of its drawers a square of thick, resilient black cloth which she spread out on a marquetry table near the earl's chair. Next, unlacing the throat of a small black velvet pouch she had brought back into the room with her, she drew from it a cylinder which, unrolled, revealed itself as an envelope of black velvet and baize with a flap along one side protecting the mouths of a number of individually-stitched pockets.

Glancing at the earl to ensure that she had his undivided attention, Miss Malcolm folded back the flap and poured from the pockets on to the cloth a rivulet of brilliant, flaring, coruscating, perfectly matched diamonds.

The earl looked at her. Clearing her throat slightly, she said: 'There are twenty-one diamonds, and they came from my father.'

He stretched out a languid finger and gently flicked over a stone that had come to rest against another. 'May I?' He groped for his quizzing-glass, and with his left hand picked up one of the stones and raised it to the light so that it flashed out needles of radiance. Holding it perfectly still, he scanned it carefully through his glass. 'Has a jeweller seen these?' he murmured.

'Not to my knowledge.'

Nervously, she watched as he gazed into the blue-white heart of the stone, wondering whether its icy, unassailable purity aroused in him – as it had done in her – some faint understanding of the passion for diamonds that had seduced men through the ages. He gave no sign as, laying down the first stone, he picked up another and studied it with equal care. Slowly, attentively, he scrutinized every one of the twenty-one stones while Caro sat and waited.

He put the last diamond down, allowing his eyes to remain on the little pool of light for a few moments before he spoke. 'Yes. Quite remarkable. Genuine, without doubt. Twenty-one superlatively matched stones; fine blue-whites; double cut brilliant; and about twenty-five carats each, unless I miss my guess. I really have no idea what their combined value might be.' His lips curved sardonically. 'Your father had given you "nothing of himself", I think you said? Now tell me about it, please.'

She coloured a little. 'You see now why I can't have dealings with the kind of people you described as indiscreet ferrets? But I was speaking the perfect truth when I said I knew nothing whatever about my father.

'What happened was this. Mr Kidd, who was my step-father's and then my mother's man of business, came to see me soon after she died in September last year. It was the oddest thing. He is an unassuming little man who usually comes and goes without creating the least fuss, but this time he arrived surrounded by a whole phalanx of large young men. Though I wasn't finding much to laugh at, at the time, I had the greatest difficulty in containing myself when I looked out of the window and saw them all debouching from a single carriage. They must all have been piled up inside like a layer cake.

'He knew Rich was back at Oxford. In fact he had waited until term started, because his business was with me, and me alone. He was carrying a small, brass-bound teak box, this size.' She held her open hands about six inches apart. 'He gave it to me with a key he produced from his pocket, and told me he knew something about the contents but would like me to open the box before he said anything further. Inside was the wallet of diamonds and an unsealed note in my mother's hand saying merely, "For Caro, from her father". Nothing more.'

The earl's quizzing-glass swung idly in the long, lean fingers, and his gaze was abstracted. 'Your immediate reaction, of course, was that they were a legacy from Colonel Malcolm?'

'My immediate reaction,' she echoed, 'was to gape like a perfect ninny.' A twinkle came to her eye, but his face was in shadow and she did not see the answering gleam. Nor would she have believed it if she had, for she was finding his lordship rather formidable. 'Yes, I assumed the stones were from Papa Malcolm, but when I had finished exclaiming over them it occurred to me to wonder why Mr Kidd had been so cryptic about the whole thing. When I looked at him he was wearing an expression I can only describe as hunted, and it was then that I began to feel uneasy.

'Anyway, not to take too long about it, he told me with a great many hums and hahs and fidgets that my mama had intended to explain everything to me on my twenty-first birthday. The first diamond had been sent to her a few weeks after I was born, and another on each of my birthdays from then until my nineteenth, which was in February last year. I listened to all this, as you may imagine, with increasing mystification. The last diamond, he explained, had made the round trip out to India and back, for by the time it arrived there in February of 1813 we had sailed for England. I suppose I should by this time have seen what was coming, but I didn't, and poor Mr Kidd had to brace himself to tell me that Colonel Malcolm had been my step-father, not my father.'

There was, he noted, the briefest pause before she continued. 'The shock was considerable, of course. When I had slightly recovered, I asked him a great many questions, but he knew almost nothing more than I have told you. All he could tell me was that when we were settled in London my mother sent for him and put the box, which then contained nineteen diamonds, in his care, telling him only that Colonel Malcolm was my step-father and that these had come, year by year, from my own father. It was not until after she died that something I said made him realize that I believed Colonel Malcolm to be my real father. In July last year the twentieth diamond had arrived, readdressed from India to my mother in the care of Mr Kidd's office. We had not known when we left India where we should be living in London.

'And that is all. Except that this year the twenty-first diamond

34

arrived – three months ago – having made the round trip to India like the one before.' She hesitated. 'I should add that I don't want the diamonds. I don't need them. If they are my father's only heritage to me, I confess to being a most reluctant heiress. I had rather – infinitely rather – that both he and they had stayed out of my life forever.'

When he spoke, his tone was dry. 'Really the complete story this time, Miss Malcolm?'

She nodded, a little wearily.

'Who else knows it?'

'Mr Kidd, of course. My brother. And the Duke.'

'And who knows of the existence of the diamonds?'

'The same three people. No one else.'

'Except the person who sent them,' he reminded her. 'Was the package that arrived in July – was it? – addressed to your mother or to you?'

'To my mother.'

'So the sender,' he remarked thoughtfully, 'was probably unaware of your mother's death, or wished to appear so.'

The ghost of a shiver crawled down her spine. 'Wished to appear so?' she repeated.

He took so long that she thought he was not going to reply at all. Then he said decisively: 'I apologize. Merely a passing thought.'

Caroline rose restlessly to her feet and walked over to the window, looking out at the busy normality of a pleasant autumn day. She had been so sure during all these months that she wanted to know who her father was. It was true – she *had* been obsessed. But talking about it to the detached, elegant gentleman by the fireside, her determination had begun to waver. Was he right? Was she about to stir up secrets that would be better left to lie? To open long-locked cupboards, so that their skeletons tumbled out rattling? She could still call everything off, she supposed – and then found that she did not have the courage to turn to her disquieting visitor and say so.

The earl, had she known it, was by no means unaware of the way her mind was working. He had seen too many people expose their fat, well-nourished worries for the first time to an outsider's gaze. The initial feeling was one of relief, then came regret – even fright – and at last release. Not that Miss Malcolm looked particularly frightened, but she would certainly be a happier person when the burden was lifted. He studied the straight, slim back in its fashionable gown, the colour of poplars at leaf fall; the neat, poised crown of sunset hair; the small hands clenched revealingly on the sill.

'And now?' she said abruptly.

'And now the problem appears a little more susceptible to solution. Diamonds are notoriously easier to trace than people. Will you trust me with them for a few days?'

Silently assenting, she turned to the table and began to replace the gems, one by one, in their black baize pockets, and then wrapped the velvet pouch in two sheets of hot-pressed note-paper, sealing the folds neatly with dark blue wafers. He accepted the package from her, and said: 'I must go now, but you will hear from me in a day or two.'

She reached out to the bell-pull, and while they waited for Sime to escort him out he looked down at her and said: 'I would like you to become acquainted with my sister, Lady Susan Channock. Would you object if I asked her to call on you tomorrow?'

Miss Malcolm met his eyes, her own a little startled. Damn it, thought the earl, were they grey or were they green?

'It would give me great pleasure,' she replied politely.

He smiled. 'Don't worry. I will tell her nothing without your leave, I promise.'

When he had gone, Miss Malcolm sank into her chair feeling as if during the last two hours she had run through every emotion in her repertoire, and a few new ones as well. Silently, she apostrophized His absent Grace, the Duke of Wellington. Uncle Arthur, she thought, dear Uncle Arthur! I wonder whether I *should* have listened to you!

✖ Chapter Four ✖

There was no possibility of insinuating a small but bulky package into any corner of the earl's elegant dark blue coat, tailored by a master and moulding his figure to perfection, so he sauntered thoughtfully back from Hill Street to his house in St James's Square with the diamonds held negligently in his hand, meeting on the way several persons of his acquaintance. Mr Gilbert Smyth, encountered in Bond Street and dumbfounded to see a man of fashion burdened with anything so dowdy as a parcel, levelled his eyeglass accusingly. 'Toothbrush, dear boy,' responded the earl blandly, and said the same to the Honourable Thomas Gaydon, whom he met in Jermyn Street. As a result, the two young gentlemen later spent several hours in bewildered conclave, trying to penetrate the mystery of his lordship's latest start. 'Mark my words!' concluded the Honourable Thomas, a dedicated student of the *ton*. 'He's going to make toothbrushes all the go, though I don't know how. But we had best buy some tomorrow, old fellow, before they are quite sold out!' Unaware that when he next saw Mr Smyth and Mr Gaydon he would find them with small tufted objects inserted in their hatbands – 'Not in the buttonhole, Gil!' Mr Gaydon had remonstrated. 'Spoil the lapel!' – the earl proceeded serenely on his way.

Arriving at St James's Square, he relinquished his hat and gloves to a footman and then strolled into the office of his admirable secretary, Mr Francis Mervyn.

Mr Mervyn was the fifth son of a clergyman of moderate means and immoderate powers of genesis, and he believed that his father's life had been blighted by a succession of early tutors who, instead of directing his impressionable mind to the self-denying doctrines of St Paul, had caused him to commit to memory large portions of the scriptures, notably those sonorous Old Testament rollcalls of who begat whom. Francis, like most of his seventeen brothers and sisters – and, indeed, his mother – had lost his taste for biblical studies at an early stage. If the case had been otherwise, said his employer, he would have made an excellent Trappist monk, for there was no one less talkative in the whole of London.

The earl entered to find Mr Mervyn seated at a desk piled high with reports, accounts, and correspondence, the daily routine of substantial estates in Wiltshire and Scotland. With a delicate shudder, he averted his eyes. 'Good morning, Francis,' he said. 'You will be ecstatic to hear that I have set aside two hours this afternoon so that we may settle any outstanding problems. I anticipate that I may be somewhat preoccupied for a week or two, so take advantage of the offer.

'And by the by,' he added, holding out the small, wafer-sealed package, 'would you put this – er – toothbrush somewhere out of harm's way for a day or two? The safe, I think.'

The saturnine Mr Mervyn, who regarded the whole Dornay family as slightly but harmlessly mad, accepted the – er – toothbrush without a flicker, and the earl departed, chuckling inwardly, in search of his sister.

Susan was just the person to deal with Miss Malcolm, he thought. The youngest by seven years of the three Dornay sisters, she had discovered early in life what it was to be condescended to by her elders, and brisk though she might occasionally be with her brothers – 'Well, *some*one has to keep you in order!' – she never made the mistake of talking down to the younger ones. It was a source of the greatest relief to both the earl and John that it was Susan who lived at home, and not Verona or Charlotte. Verona, the eldest of the family, did not care for the country, and since she was perilously close to being a bluestocking their paths in London rarely converged. Charlotte, with her husband Rothbury and their numerous progeny, was firmly fixed in distant Yorkshire, a circumstance for which John in particular – who was unable to see eye to eye with her on anything – was accustomed to thank God on the infrequent occasions when Atherton suffered a visitation from her.

Susan had been married, too, at the age of nineteen, to a handsome young naval officer who was killed within a matter of months at the battle of Trafalgar. Since then, she had been dangled after by any number of eligible *partis*, for she was excellent company, refreshingly witty, and with her slender build, fine features, and glossy chestnut hair, a pleasure to look at. But she was now twenty-eight years old and showed no sign of wishing to remarry. When the earl, concerned, had pointed out how wasteful it was for her to dwindle into a mere sister, she had replied with a twinkle: 'But you cannot conceive how delightful it is to have the freedom of a married woman without the tedium of a husband. If Channock had lived, our marriage *might* have prospered, but I doubt it. Even when I was infatuated with his dashing good looks and distinguished bearing, I could already detect a hint of prosiness in his manner that did not augur at all well for the future. I am afraid I would find it a dead bore to share *all* my days, even with a paragon.' She reflected for a moment. '*Especially* with a paragon. No! I value my independence. I would only exchange you and John for a husband if I could be sure of staying in perfect charity with him by seeing him as rarely as I see you!'

He had pondered these words and reached the conclusion that they were by no means as capricious as they sounded. In fact, the answer was clearly another naval officer, who would be likely to be away from home for the greater part of the year! Susan had not, he thought, discerned his fine Italian hand behind the recent expansion of her naval acquaintance.

When he found her, she was drawing on her gloves preparatory to going out. Surveying her charming French green bonnet and the matching pelisse with its sable trim, he exclaimed: 'You look very becomingly! Where are you off to?' and was pleased to discover that she was being taken driving in the park by his latest and most promising import, Captain the Honourable Adam Gregory, a crisply humorous gentleman of about his own age. Responding to this satisfactory piece of information in the most disinterested fashion, he resumed: 'I shall be incommunicado for most of the afternoon and am engaged to dine out this evening, so spare me a moment before you go. I have just been to visit Miss Malcolm.' Lady Susan's eyes opened wide. 'Yes, it was all very interesting,' he agreed, 'but I can't tell you now. However, I asked her whether you might call on her tomorrow morning. I would like . . .'

'Unfortunately, I have another engagement!' she interrupted, perfectly ready to break it but not without the appearance of a struggle.

'I would like you,' he went on as if she had not spoken, 'to get to know her. I think she may turn out to be quite agreeable, as it happens, but the main point is that she needs help, and if I am to help I must know a great deal more about her. No! Don't jump to conclusions. I'm not asking you to pry into her affairs! It is simply that she will talk much more freely to you than she can be expected to do to me. When she gives me permission to tell you about her problem – which I think she will – you'll understand what I mean. For example, I will need to know every little thing she can remember about her mother, and you are as well aware as I am that no well-bred young lady would ever dream of boring on *to a gentleman* about her mama!'

His sister laughed and acknowledged the truth of this. 'But what do I say to her tomorrow?'

'What do you ever say to a new acquaintance? But try to form some impression of her and, if it doesn't offend your sensibilities, ot her background. Also, would you ask her from me the date of her birth, and her mother's age when she died?

'That's all, I think,' he concluded, with the affability his family had long ago learned to distrust. 'Then we can have a splendid family conference tomorrow evening.'

'I have another engagement,' his sister replied grittily. But he was profoundly unimpressed, and she departed for her drive in the park with a slightly steely look in her eye that both amused and intrigued her escort, who had until now believed her disposition to be unfailingly sunny.

✄

After dinner on the following evening, Brandon having been instructed to turn away any unexpected callers, the earl, Lady Susan, and John settled comfortably round the fire in the library, the two gentlemen armed with writing blocks and the lady with her embroidery, which she said helped her to concentrate.

The earl, remarked his sister trenchantly, looked as if he were about to rub his hands like some latter-day Midas. 'Why the air of self-satisfaction?' she enquired. 'You don't appear to have done anything yet to warrant it!'

He smiled. 'Just think back a few weeks – to the day when I said it was high time you and John had some exercise for your minds. My precise words, as I recall, were that this household lacked occupation. Well, now we have it. A delightful little mystery for the pair of you to sink your teeth in.' His smile broadened as he observed the expression of outrage on their faces, and he settled back more comfortably in his chair. 'It is not, as you will have realized, the kind of mystery in which I would normally permit myself to become involved. Even with such an enchanting client. Even, indeed, with a walletful of diamonds to be accounted for. No. Genealogical research is not a pursuit that recommends itself to me. However, as a discipline for idle brains it is excellent, and just the thing for *you*. Which is why I agreed to help Miss Malcolm find out the truth about her parentage and her diamonds.'

He laughed outright. 'Come now! Don't look so depressed. I assure you it's not a matter of fossicking around among piles of boring and, no doubt, dusty books. In fact, John is going to be bouncing back and forth like a rubber ball for some time to come.'

'But I'm engaged to go to Newmarket next week!'

His brother looked at him reproachfully. 'Really, John! A lady in distress, and you talk of Newmarket!'

'Yes, but . . .'

'Wait till you hear the story.' He turned to Susan. 'Now, correct me if I misheard what you murmured so confidentially to me just before dinner. You were favourably impressed by Miss Malcolm – yes? And she herself told you about the problem over which she needs help – yes?'

'And she said,' continued Lady Susan, catching his intonation perfectly, 'that – yes! You are at liberty to divulge the story to

40

others, in whole or in part, at your discretion, if you feel it necessary to the success of your investigation.'

The earl regarded her straitly. 'Thank you. Now, John, the essence is this,' and gave him a swift résumé of the situation.

When he had finished, John said: 'The diamonds are really good ones?'

'Superb, as a matter of fact. I'll show them to you tomorrow. I have rarely seen such a number of large, perfectly matched stones.' He surveyed his sister and brother with the greatest amiability. 'So! Set your minds to work, if you please. General ideas to start off with, and then we will consider what is to be done. You first, Susan, I think.'

Feeling very much as if she were back in the schoolroom, her ladyship made a hasty snatch at the nearest facts. 'You wanted to know Miss Malcolm's birth date. It was February 22nd, 1794. And her mother was just two weeks short of her thirty-ninth birthday when she died.'

'Which tells us?'

'Which tells us, I suppose, that Mrs Malcolm was . . .' Her brow reflected an arithmetical struggle. 'Oh, dear! Twenty? No, nineteen when Miss Malcolm was born.'

'And?'

'And what?' she replied with some asperity.

'And eighteen when the child was conceived, which must have been around May 1793. That's the date that matters, rather than the date of birth. What, by the way, did you think of Miss Malcolm?'

'Beautiful, of course, and she also has style. We found we hadn't met before because by the time they were settled in London and just preparing to go into society, Mrs Malcolm died and Caroline had to retire into a year of mourning. It's over now, and I imagine you will soon see her everywhere. In fact, I think she might turn out to be the success of the season.

'I was a little surprised,' she went on tentatively, 'at how strongly this mystery about her father has taken possession of her mind. In fact, I have been wondering about it all afternoon, for it seems so out of character. The only answer that occurred to me was that she may always have been a rather self-assured girl – too self-assured, perhaps – and people who have never had any doubts about themselves are the ones who are most likely to be thrown all aback when this kind of thing happens. If you understand what I mean?'

" 'Thrown all aback", Susan?' said John artlessly. 'Is that a nautical expression?'

The earl hurriedly intervened. 'I do understand what you mean, and I think it's a valid point. I wish she were not so obsessed, for there seems to me to be one possibility that would disturb her even more than her present ignorance. John?'

John gave an extravagant shrug, his shoulders rising almost to his ears, and his sister took her revenge by pointing out that if he *would* do such things it was no wonder that his neck-cloth always looked like a dish rag. 'If Caroline was born before her mother became Mrs Malcolm,' he said, loftily ignoring her, 'then her mother was either married before – and her first husband was either dead or divorced – or not married before, in which case Caroline is illegitimate.'

'Excellent!' said his brother approvingly. 'Well-reasoned, concise, and unarguable. You may stay.'

'Thank you.'

'Now, Susan. You must have received some impression of Mrs Malcolm, however tenuous, during your visit to Hill Street. Does illegitimacy seem probable to you?'

'Be reasonable,' his sister begged. 'No one could answer a question like that without full knowledge of the circumstances. My instinct would be to say that it was most improbable. Even the fact that Caroline herself doesn't even seem to have *thought* she might be illegitimate is suggestive. I suspected at first she was just being incredibly naïve, but now I'm not so sure. Mrs Malcolm – her given name was Jane, by the way – appears to have brought her children up with devotion, certainly, but with strictness and propriety, too, and I am of the impression that she herself was of good family and strictly reared. But on the other hand, a romantic girl of eighteen is perfectly capable of rebelling against the entire world if she fancies herself in love.

'Matthew was quite right about her. She was astonishingly beautiful. Miss Malcolm showed me a portrait Mr Chinnery painted of her nine or ten years ago, just a small one, but Miss Malcolm says very like. Apparently Mrs Malcolm was one of his first sitters when he went out to India.'

'Well, that's something, anyway,' remarked the earl, pleased. 'If it had been Cosway, we would have been none the wiser, for his miniatures are too much like each other to be like the originals. But Chinnery is first rate at catching a likeness.'

'I think you should see this one, for I found it interesting. The resemblance between mother and daughter is very pronounced, but if the portrait is really to the life, as Miss Malcolm says, then I believe her mother must have been a less decisive, weaker – I don't know how to put it! – more yielding personality than Caroline.'

The earl smiled. 'Miss Malcolm hardly strikes one as compliant, does she? Very well, let's leave illegitimacy out of the reckoning for the moment. For one thing, Miss Malcolm would not be pleased, and for another it would make the search even more difficult than it already promises to be.'

'Why?' said John.

'Because, my good idiot, marriage and divorce leave legal traces behind. Illicit passion – if you will forgive the expression! – does not.

'Divorce,' he went on reflectively, 'appears to me unlikely. A well-bred young lady married and divorced by the age of twenty would have to be a very precipitate young lady indeed. With aspirations towards martyrdom, too, I shouldn't wonder. Divorce takes time. It also takes a great deal of money and the influence necessary to procure the passing of a private Act of Parliament. No, I am not enamoured of divorce. However, I will ask Francis to procure me a list from one of the parliamentary clerks of all Divorce Bills presented between the middle of 1793 and 1795. In the meantime, let's see what we can do with death.'

'But surely,' his sister remarked, raising her eyes from her embroidery, 'if the diamonds are still arriving, Caroline's father must still be alive?'

'Not necessarily. "For Caro, from her father" could simply mean "on behalf of her father". They might be sent by someone who feels a kind of second-hand responsibility.'

'Couldn't we begin by checking records of deaths between 1793 and 1795?' John asked.

'And how,' said his brother, 'do you suggest we decide which of the thousands of young men who died in that period happens to be the one we are looking for?'

Unabashed, John said: 'Marriages, then?'

The earl regarded him without enthusiasm. 'If you wish to check the records for a marriage which took place in 1792 or 1793 between a young man whose name we do not know, and a lady of whom all we know is that her Christian name was Jane – very uncommon, you will agree – you are welcome to try! And I would remind you that the marriage, if there was one, did not necessarily take place in England. As a matter of fact, Mrs Malcolm's reticence about her family connections suggests estrangement, and that in turn suggests a marriage at Gretna

Green or some place of the sort. Do make an effort,' he implored, 'to think things through before you speak!'

'I scarcely dare open my mouth,' said her ladyship, who had been pursuing her own line of thought, 'but I find it odd that Caroline should have learned so little about her mother in twenty years. One would think Mrs Malcolm must have dropped some hint, even without meaning to, about her background or her childhood. But Caroline says not. Or, at least, nothing more informative than passing remarks about how unlike the flora and fauna of England were those of India. Which gave me,' she added, 'no very great opinion of Mrs Malcolm's originality of mind.'

'I don't know, Susan,' John objected. 'How much did our own mama ever tell you about her younger days?'

His sister, setting neat little stitches in her embroidery, gave this question serious consideration and finally admitted: 'Very little, I suppose, if the truth were told. But when she brought me out, I don't think she ever *stopped* talking about what her own come-out was like.'

'I can believe it! But wasn't it of the order of, "How well I remember young Lewiston's father, such an attractive man! You will find yourself forced to dance with the son, but you must stand up with him only for country dances!" Related to something quite specific, I mean?'

It was an excellent parody, and Susan smiled. 'True enough. I suppose maternal confidences do tend to be of that kind. I don't recall ever having any *general* heart-to-heart talks with mama. What you are saying, in effect, is that life must have been so different in India that Mrs Malcolm didn't have the occasion to draw parallels between Caroline's experiences and her own?'

The earl had been listening to this exchange with appreciation. 'Come now, this is much better! You have not absolved Mrs Malcolm of a degree of reticence, but you think much of it may have been coincidental rather than intentional. You are probably right.'

'But I cannot see how all this helps us,' Susan complained. 'It's Mrs Malcolm's first husband we need to know about, not Mrs Malcolm.'

'Yes, but think! There are only two routes to Miss Malcolm's father, and Mrs Malcolm is one of them. If we could find out where she was and what she was doing between 1793 and 1795 . . .'

'Apart from getting married, having a baby, and getting

divorced or widowed!' said John.

'If we could find out where she was,' the earl continued with dignity, 'we would be well on the way to discovering something useful. But since we don't even know her maiden name, it rather takes the wind out of our sails.'

John did not trouble to hide his grin. 'I hope you are going to tell us that if we take the other route we will be able to crowd on full canvas!'

But his sister was not attending. An idea had occurred to her which she decided not to impart to her brothers. They were in need of a set-down, she felt, and it would give her much satisfaction to be the one to administer it. Undoubtedly, she would have to pay a call on Verona at the earliest convenient moment.

'The other route to Miss Malcolm's father. Well, John, what *is* the other route?'

John was caught off guard, and his sister, restored to the present, was able to reply with great good humour: 'The diamonds, of course.'

'The diamonds,' the earl confirmed, with a long-suffering sigh. 'Really, this first lesson in the art and science of deduction is even more exhausting than I had anticipated. If the pair of you will just deign to listen, I will tell you where we go from here.

'As you may or may not know, the pedigree of first-quality diamonds is usually as well attested as that of royalty – better, sometimes! I propose taking Miss Malcolm's stones to Rundell, Bridge and Rundell tomorrow in the hope that they will advise me on tracing the original owner.

'The other thing that does not seem to have occurred to either of you is the very interesting question of their transmission to India. The voyage from England to India takes roughly six months, as you know, and it is hazardous even at the best of times. During the French wars, when England was fighting first the Revolutionaries and then Napoleon in Europe and on the high seas, it was even more hazardous – and this, of course, was the time when almost all the diamonds were despatched. All except one, in fact, for I assume one must have been sent in 1802 during the peace of Amiens.'

'Diamonds to India is a bit like coals to Newcastle, isn't it?' John interrupted.

'Quite,' replied the earl. 'But when the first two stones were sent, in England, the sender probably had no idea that he would finish up sending all the rest to the East. When that situation arose, he was faced with a problem, and it tells us quite a lot about him that he didn't simply abandon the whole idea. His sense of responsibility seems to have been fairly well developed.

'Anyway, under the conditions that prevailed, there could have been no question of sending something so valuable by ordinary merchant ship. For a start, it would have been virtually impossible to find such a ship unless it was sailing under the American, Dutch, or Danish flag. Then it would have been necessary to confide the package into the personal care of either the captain or a passenger. And, of course, because of the length of the double voyage, the sender would have to find a new ship, a new captain, a new passenger every year. And always there would be the risks facing a single ship, armed or unarmed, running the gauntlet to the East.

'There is, therefore, no doubt in my mind that the diamonds were sent by the only ships officially permitted to ply between Britain and India until last year's Charter Act – the East India Company fleet. The Company's ships, remember, are armed, sail with some regularity and not infrequently in convoy, for part of the way at least. During the French wars they were usually given a Navy escort until they were out of the main danger zone.

'Now, if I am right, there must be records in the Company's letter or consignment books. From what I know of the system, goods ordered by an army officer in India – wine, books, furniture – would be sent by the London suppliers to a commercial packing firm, who would wrap everything in canvas, oilskin, and so on, and then deliver to the Company for shipping. If I remember correctly, such goods appear in the books under the name of the consignee only. But letters and packages sent independently from this country, without the prior knowledge of the consignee, are a different matter. Ordinary mail is despatched in bulk to the various Presidencies, and sorted at the other end. *But* – and you will be pleased to know that I have almost finished – packages despatched under the frank of a director or proprietor of the Company may in certain circumstances appear in the books under the name of both the director or proprietor, *and* the consignee.

'My instinct tells me that our mysterious sender, being a man of sufficient substance to part with a small fortune in precious stones, may also be of sufficient substance to have them sent under a frank – either his own, or that of a friend. Which is, John, where you come in. Tomorrow . . .'

'I am engaged to ride out with Gil tomorrow.'

'No,' said his lordship, not mincing matters. 'You are not. Tomorrow, what you are engaged to do is visit the East India House in Leadenhall Street, where you will seek out the clerk in charge, and ask, in my name, to see a number of letter books or consignment books. He will advise you which. It would be simplest, I think, if you worked backwards, starting with last year. Most of the diamonds appear to have arrived in India during the first three months of the year, which suggests a despatch date of some time between July and September. What you are looking for is records of a small package sent off at approximately the same time every year, addressed either to Mrs Malcolm or, just possibly, Colonel Malcolm. The name of the sender is likely to be the same in every case, but to be certain you ought to go right back to 1796.'

Observing his brother's expression, he laughed. 'Never mind,' he said. 'The first few years are said to be the worst. In fact, once you've found two or three the rest ought to be easy.'

'Thank you. If I am not home for dinner, don't bother to save any for me. I will dine in some chop-house and sleep on a doorstep. To save travelling time, you understand, since the matter is so urgent.'

There was a knock on the door and the tea tray was brought in. 'Yes, put it there, William,' said her ladyship, removing her workbox from the Pembroke table and beginning to fold her embroidery, while John scribbled hasty notes on his writing block, and the earl rose, stretched, and leaned his broad shoulders against the mantelpiece.

Pouring tea for her brothers, her ladyship remarked brightly: 'Well, you two are going to be busy tomorrow, are you not! By the by, Charles, I am going shopping in the morning. Have you any commissions for me?'

The earl looked down at her and his voice was like honey. 'Come, Susan! Why should you think *you* are exempt from all this activity? You too are going to be busy tomorrow, and not with shopping – unless, of course, you need fresh supplies of drawing paper.'

His sister regarded him with misgiving. 'Oh, yes?' she said.

'Yes, indeed. We are going to need a likeness of Mrs Malcolm at some stage, and since we can hardly carry a framed oil painting around London – even if Miss Malcolm would permit it – I want you to put your watercolour talents to work. I should

47

think Miss Malcolm will allow you to make a copy of the portrait.

'Two copies would be even better,' he added thoughtfully. 'For I think it may be necessary to take one down to Wiltshire and show it to tollkeepers, innkeepers, and that kind of person. It's just a feeling I have – a kind of "by the pricking of my thumbs" something very-slightly-suspicious this way comes. It might help us to know more about the circumstances surrounding the death of Miss Caroline Malcolm's mama.'

Chapter Five

Just before noon on the following day, resplendent in a many-caped driving coat and topboots polished to dazzling perfection – 'Blacking and champagne!' thought the crossing sweeper, who had been listening to too much backstairs mythology – the earl emerged from his house in St James's Square and ascended into his waiting curricle. He gathered the reins into his capable hands, waited until his groom had swung up beside him, and then gave the office to the splendid pair of match greys. They swept round the square and turned east into Pall Mall, where the earl – though he saluted a number of acquaintances – drove on without checking, past the colonnade of Carlton House with its garland of provincial sightseers, and on by way of Cockspur Street into the Strand. Since the greys chose to take high-bred exception to a carrier's cart, his lordship was unable to spare more than a glance for the beginnings of Mr Rennie's new bridge before swirling on his way, by Temple Bar and Fleet Street, to the sign of the Golden Salmon on Ludgate Hill. There, handing the reins over to his groom with an instruction to walk the horses if he should be delayed, the earl descended and strolled in through the portals of Messrs Rundell, Bridge and Rundell, London's most famous goldsmiths and jewellers.

The head salesman, instantly recognizing the tall, caped figure, hurried forward, all attention. His lordship was an excellent customer, to whom Mr Harpur had in the past sold a number of elegant and expensive trinkets for one or other of the succession of ravishing beauties who engaged his inconstant favour. Hastily raking in his memory for gossip about the earl's latest flirt – for he was anxious not to commit the solecism of suggesting emeralds for a fair-haired lady or rubies for an auburn one – Mr Harpur came up with nothing. The fretful recollection that his lordship had been abroad for some months explained this lapse, even if it did nothing to resolve Mr Harpur's difficulties. But he was reprieved, for the earl announced that he did not desire to make any purchases. He merely wished to consult with Mr Bridge for a few moments. In private, he added.

Mr Bridge, whose third ear had caught the ingratiating note in his employee's voice that betokened a customer of rank, had already appeared on the scene. He greeted the earl politely, ushered him into his private sanctum, and closed the door firmly, leaving Mr Harpur prey to a seething curiosity that was destined to remain unsatisfied.

The earl, having responded suitably to Mr Bridge's enquiries after his health and well-being, came straight to the point. 'I wish to ask your advice in a matter of some delicacy, and I would prefer not to burden you with the details unless, without them, you feel you are unable to help me.

'I am trying to trace the history of a number of large, exceptionally fine, matched diamonds, and it seemed to me that they might at some stage have passed through your hands. I assume that if such were the case you would recognize them?'

'Of course, my lord,' replied Mr Bridge.

'And that you would be able to tell, for example, whether the lapidary work had been done here or in India?'

'Of course, my lord,' said Mr Bridge.

'From the circumstances, I think it possible that you, or some other reputable jeweller, may even have been asked to collect these stones in the first place. Would you accept that kind of commission?'

'Of course, my lord,' said Mr Bridge.

'Is it a kind of commission you often receive?'

Mr Bridge cogitated. '"Often" would be too strong a word, my lord.'

Damn it, thought the earl, if he was going to go on like this the conversation could last all day. He tried the effect of silence and a raised eyebrow.

After a few moments Mr Bridge decided to amplify. 'It's a matter of planning ahead, you see. A client might have to wait years for us to find the requisite number of really fine, large stones.'

'But suppose your client required you to supply him with

only one stone a year over a period of, say, twenty or twenty-one years?'

Mr Bridge produced a charming gold snuffbox decorated with panels in grisaille, flipped it open, and offered it to the earl, who refused gracefully. He had tried Mr Bridge's snuff once before and it had proved to be a vile mixture that reeked of attar of roses. Mr Bridge inhaled contentedly, snapped the box closed, stowed it away again, and dusted his waistcoat vigorously with a large handkerchief.

'One a year, eh?' he said. 'For twenty-one years? It would still need forethought. We'd have to start two or three years in advance, because we would have to keep several in hand. Not only in case there was a year when we couldn't find one of the right quality, but because we would always need two or three for matching purposes. Can't simply match one stone against one other in a case like that, you know!' He surveyed the earl percipiently. 'Just ruined one of your theories, have I, my lord?'

The earl smiled ruefully. 'You haven't helped it,' he admitted. 'There could have been no question of two or three years' warning in this case!'

'Might I suggest you give me a sight of the stones, if that's possible, my lord? The problem may not be as awkward as you think.'

The earl was annoyed. He disliked having his hand forced. What he had intended to do was proceed gradually, using careful questions to sift out the probable from the merely possible. A collection specially commissioned for the purpose had now been ruled out, but he could think of several other sources for the diamonds. There were connoisseurs who specialized in precious stones. There was the loot brought back by nabobs from India or travellers from Brazil. A family fallen on hard times might be expected to part readily enough with unmounted gems bequeathed by an earlier generation. And fashionable jewellers had their own reserves of stones destined for a royal coronet, a peeress's tiara, or a necklace for the wife of some newly rich manufacturer. The earl had intended to narrow down the possibilities before showing the diamonds to Mr Bridge, so that even if he proved unable or unwilling to identify them, his lordship would still have learned a great deal.

He had chosen to visit Rundell and Bridge first among London's leading jewellers because they were not primarily dealers in precious stones, though they had profited greatly from the trade in jewels and other valuables brought to England by French émigrés at the time of the Revolution. First and foremost they were goldsmiths and silversmiths, producing in vast quantity every kind of plate from table cutlery to christening fonts, and employing artists like Storr and Chantrey, Flaxman and Theed. The earl's reasoning had been that an enterprise of this kind, patronized at some time or other by almost every household in the land with pretensions to gentility, and dealing with a vastly wider range of customers than any specialist diamond merchant, was not only the kind of place to which a gentleman might go for out-of-the-ordinary as well as everyday purchases, but would also be a powerhouse of information about its customers' more valued possessions. Lady A– would send in her late mama's pearl eardrops for cleaning. Mr B– would discuss the possibility of having his grandmother's sapphires reset in a more modern style for his affianced bride. Lord C– would wonder whether the Paul Storr épergne was going to look quite at home against a background of Holbeins. And the Duchess of D– would order repairs to the William and Mary wine cistern that had been dropped on a flagged floor by two clumsy footmen no longer in her service.

His lordship was now almost sure he had come to the right place. At the mention of twenty-one years a flicker had come into Mr Bridge's eye. Not quite at once – which suggested that the association might be with twenty-one stones rather than twenty-one years – but the by-play with the snuffbox had been designed to cover his reaction and give him a moment to think.

If Mr Bridge did know something, decided the earl resignedly, then beating about the bush was unlikely to flush even a hedge-sparrow. He brought out the black velvet pouch, extracted the cylinder, unrolled it, and handed it over. Then he sat back and watched with detached amusement as Mr Bridge went through exactly the same routine as he had done in Miss Malcolm's drawing-room two days earlier. The jeweller's glass was more professional than his own, the manner more practised, and he checked the stones against one another more thoroughly, but the scrutiny was just as slow and methodical. At last, Mr Bridge replaced the twenty-first stone and sat back, pinching the tip of his nose between thumb and forefinger as if he were suppressing a sneeze. It was, the earl knew, his substitute for what in another man would be a self-satisfied smile.

'Well, my lord,' he said expressionlessly. 'Blue-whites of the first water, twenty-seven carats each, brilliant cut – what we used to call mazarines. But I'm sure you know all that already. Very nicely matched, all things considered, though there are one or two that could be better. Now, what is it your lordship wishes to know?'

His lordship gazed interestedly at the ornate plasterwork of the ceiling, and decided to risk a straight question.

'Have you seen these stones before?'

'Once, many years ago.'

'Do you remember who owned them?'

Mr Bridge sat back in his chair and steepled his fingers. 'Ah!' he said meditatively. 'May I take the liberty of asking your lordship a question before I answer that?' His lordship signified assent. 'Do you have any ideas yourself on the subject?'

The earl hesitated. 'Let me put it like this. I know a certain amount about the owner, but I don't know his name.'

Mr Bridge heaved his rotund figure out of the vast leather chair. 'May I borrow these for a moment? I would like our Mr Wylie in the workshop to see them, just to be sure my memory's not at fault, you understand.' An absent-minded 'my lord' floated back into the room as he left it.

While the jeweller was absent the earl did some rapid thinking. If Mr Bridge had only seen the stones once, then they could not have been in the shop for very long. If 'our Mr Wylie' was the lapidary, he would never have cut, faceted and polished all twenty-one stones without Mr Bridge seeing them and approving them several times. So the stones were already finished when they passed through the hands of Rundell and Bridge. But if that were so, why should 'our Mr Wylie in the workshop' have been involved in the business at all? Not just cleaning them – that was an apprentice's job. He must have done some work on them. What?

And then he had it. Just because the stones were now unmounted, it did not mean that they had always been so. A necklace or tiara, a matched set of brooch and earrings and hair ornament – something of the sort – must have been broken up and the stones taken out of their settings. Well, that was something, at least! He wondered morosely what the chances were of finding out who had stopped wearing the family diamonds twenty-odd years ago if Mr Bridge wouldn't tell him. There was one interesting implication. Whoever had indulged in the work of destruction had presumably had no lady in the family who customarily wore the ornaments. Otherwise, the logical thing would have been to ask Rundell and Bridge to make a paste copy, and if they had done so Mr Bridge, again, would have been bound to see the originals several times, instead of just once.

Time passed. 'Our Mr Wylie' must be working his way through the diamonds, one by laborious one. The earl thought of his unfortunate groom walking the horses up and down Ludgate Hill, round and round St Paul's Cathedral. He grinned suddenly, remembering the Reverend Sydney Smith's response to the proposal that St Paul's should be surrounded by a wooden sidewalk. All it needed, he had said, was for the dean and canons to lay down their heads together.

The door opened and Mr Bridge reappeared with the diamonds. He settled himself comfortably back in his chair again, folded his hands over his stomach, and said: 'Yes, my lord, we do know them.'

The earl allowed a small silence to develop. 'How long ago is it since you last saw them?'

Mr Bridge was a careful man and he had taken the opportunity to look up the books. 'March the first, 1794.'

'You must have an excellent memory for gemstones.'

'One or two, I might have doubted. But twenty-one of that quality – unforgettable. And you remember I called them mazarines? The style of cutting was named after the great Cardinal of Louis XIV's time, and these particular stones are reputed to have belonged to Mazarin himself.'

'Am I right in thinking that the stones were set when they came to you, and that you were responsible for removing them from their setting?'

Mr Bridge frowned slightly. 'You seem to know a great deal, my lord!'

The earl permitted himself a fleeting smile. It did no harm to appear omniscient. Well, almost omniscient.

'Just how much do you know, my lord? If you will permit me to ask.'

'That's a very broad question! If you reduce it to what do I know of the identity of the owner twenty-one years ago, the answer is nothing.'

'I see. But you knew enough to bring you here.'

The earl smiled again. 'Where else?'

'Let me put it plainly, my lord. If you yourself were to choose, for personal reasons, to break up or dispose of some valuable piece of family property, you would regard it as entirely your own business. If you found out that I was prepared to talk to any Tom, Dick, or Harry – no offence! – about it, you would be justifiably displeased.'

The earl grimaced. 'You're right, of course. Would it clarify matters if I told you that I am trying to help a young lady discover who her father was – or is – and that I know the ownership of the diamonds to be relevant? I cannot, of course, tell you the young lady's name . . .'

He stopped. Mr Bridge, unbelievably, was laughing. And laughing so immoderately that his shoulders and stomach were heaving and tears coming to his eyes. Even the chair quivered in sympathy. The earl waited, intrigued, until Mr Bridge had sobbed himself into silence. 'Well, well!' he said. 'Well, well, well!' The earl went on waiting.

Mr Bridge giggled again as he took out his handkerchief to mop his eyes. 'So he has been paying off in diamonds for twenty-one years! Well, well, well!'

The earl was becoming somewhat bored, so he said: 'I find all this a little unintelligible, but I gather you have drawn certain deductions. I hope you will tell me the name of the gentleman concerned. But I must say, in all fairness, that I would not be able to keep the name entirely confidential. I would have to use it in the interests of the young lady I mentioned.'

Mr Bridge gave a residual hiccough and became serious. 'I would expect that,' he said. 'Half an hour ago I did not think I would be justified in revealing his name to you, but after what you have said, I will. In any event, I owe you something for the advice you gave me when we had that series of thefts three years ago. I take it very kindly in you that you have not reminded me of it. But I still feel an obligation. If you will just assure me once again that your interest is in nothing more than the identity of the young lady's father . . .'

'You have my word.'

'How old *is* the young lady?'

'Twenty. The first diamond arrived a few weeks after she was born, and one diamond a year from then on.'

Mr Bridge showed signs of a relapse. 'Well, well, well!' he said. 'Let me see. Twenty, and he must be about seventy by now. So he would be around fifty at the time. A very virile gentleman until recent years, I believe. You must know him, my lord. The Marquis of Wayne.'

The earl felt slightly stunned. 'Wayne?' he repeated on an ascending note. Seventy years old, tough as nails, a recluse whose only amusement was to quarrel with everyone in sight. Agricultural improvement was his occupation and his hobby. He had fallen out irrevocably with the regrettable Sir Augustus

Home, his nephew and heir, so long ago that it was now ancient history. The earl closed his eyes for a moment, and then opened them again to demand of Mr Bridge, who was still chuckling happily to himself: 'What the devil's so funny about it, anyway?'

'Nothing, my lord. Nothing, really. It is merely that I find the thought of Lord Wayne a prey to the tender passion quite irresistible. And having to pay for it, too! I confess that it gives me great satisfaction when I think how often he has tried to chouse Rundell and Bridge out of their reckoning in his day. Dear me! Dear me! I am quite carried away. I should not have said that. I beg you will forget it!'

⚔

Wayne! Wayne! Wayne! The greys' hooves beat out the rhythm in the earl's head all the way back to St James's Square. Possible? Probable? Plausible? Credible? How many degrees of likelihood were there? He was so engrossed in calculating the odds that he offended several luminaries of the polite world by entirely failing to see them.

Pausing only to divest himself of his hat, gloves and driving coat, the earl walked along the corridor to Mr Mervyn's office, which was beyond the library and had a pleasant view over the long, narrow garden. Handing his secretary the pouch of diamonds, he said: 'Put it back in the safe, Francis, please, and we will return it to its owner tomorrow.' He turned to leave, adding: 'You haven't yet had the opportunity, I imagine, to procure the list of Divorce Acts I mentioned to you this morning?'

The excellent Mr Mervyn picked up a sheet of paper and handed it to his employer, who accepted it with raised brows. It was headed 'Bills of Divorce passed in 1793, 1794, and 1795' but was otherwise completely blank. A twinkle crept into his lordship's eye. 'None at all?' he said. 'Not even *one* little one?' Mr Mervyn shook his head. 'You are a secretary *sans peur et sans reproche*, Francis. A paragon, in fact. Thank you.' And he returned the sheet. 'Is my sister at home, do you know?' Mr Mervyn inclined his head towards the door that connected with the library, and his employer looked at him severely. 'You would have been in difficulties if she had been in the parlour, wouldn't you?' he said, and was pleased to see that Mr Mervyn had the grace to blush.

In the library, he found his sister seated at her easel, draped in an artist's overgown and with a smudge of cobalt blue on her patrician nose. She had sketched in the outlines of the Chinnery portrait and was now, he was amused to see, testing her technique on the least important part of the painting, the patch of sky in the upper left corner. He transferred his gaze to the original.

It was three-quarter length and quite charming. Outlined against deep blue drapery which fell away at the left to reveal a view of trees, river, and sky, Mrs Malcolm was seated with her head held high and slightly to the side, one slender hand resting on the open book in her lap. She wore a square-necked blue dress, cut low and trimmed with white, with no jewels, but a coquettish little wreath of white flowers twined in the high-dressed sunset hair. It was a face that would turn any man's head, with fine and delicate features, lustrous grey eyes, and a mouth that tilted upward at the corners. But Susan had been right. There was something muted about it, the hint of a personality blurred around the edges. Though it would have been inaccurate to describe it as a soft or indecisive face, it had none of the chiselled clarity that was so apparent in her daughter's. She must have been approaching thirty when the portrait was painted, but it had a freshness – innocence, even – that was quite striking. Not, the earl thought, the face of a girl who would have fallen to a middle-aged satyr like Wayne.

Glancing up at her brother and observing the creased brow and speculative eyes, Lady Susan forbore to comment, but as he had taken up a position at her left she was forced eventually to say: 'Charles. The light.' He did not stir, and she said again: 'Charles, the light!' Then, exasperated at his lack of response, she poked him in the ribs with her paintbrush and repeated: 'Charles. The light. You – are – blocking – my – light!'

He started, and returned to the present. 'My apologies,' he said, moving back. 'How long will it take, do you think? I am sure we're going to need it.'

She did not look up. 'You found out nothing at Rundell and Bridge, then?'

'On the contrary. But if *you* can see the Marquis of Wayne as Miss Malcolm's real father, I can't!'

His sister was betrayed into a squeak. '*Wayne?*'

'At the beginning of March 1794 Rundell and Bridge broke up into its component stones a diamond necklace of rare quality. It belonged to the Marquis of Wayne, who sold the smaller stones to Rundell's and kept the twenty-one large ones himself.'

'There's no question about their being the same stones?'

'None. The stones fit. The date fits. But the marquis doesn't. I find him a most unconvincing candidate for the role of papa.'

Lady Susan looked, as her brother had done, at the Chinnery

portrait, and came to the same conclusion. 'Yes. If she had ever been entangled with Wayne, one would expect the scars to show.'

The earl perched on the edge of a sofa table. 'We must see what John has discovered at the East India House, for it is just possible that Wayne parted with the diamonds immediately and had no hand in sending them to Mrs Malcolm.'

Susan noticed that his voice did not carry conviction. She wiped her brush on a rag and said briskly: 'Well, we should know fairly soon, for I charged John not to be late. If we are to attend the Seftons' ball I want to be sure of having an extra hour in hand, in case he has to be sent back upstairs after he has dressed so that he may dress all over again! By the way, Miss Malcolm tells me she will be there. What will you say to her?'

'I must say something, I suppose, but I'd better wait and hear John's report before I decide what.'

It was well after six when John put in an appearance. His sister, on her way upstairs, paused to remark that he looked positively demented and would be well advised to go and dress immediately. 'For if you look like that, I shall be quite unable to concentrate on what you are so clearly anxious to impart.' John's hands went automatically to his hair in an attempt to smooth it down, and he twitched hopefully at his cravat, but his sister shook her head. 'Useless, my child,' she said. 'Besides, Charles is already changing, so you might as well save your news until dinner.'

When she herself descended again, charmingly attired in a gown of her favourite pale green trimmed with silver, and with a silvery gauze scarf draped over her elbows, she found her brothers in the parlour awaiting her, suitably clad for a ball in black coats, white waistcoats, and black satin knee breeches. Eying the younger of the two critically, she decided that he would pass muster, even if his cravat fell far below the standard of his brother's. They made a remarkably handsome pair, she admitted to herself, thankful as always that neither of them had any tendency towards dandyism.

The earl had already told John the result of his visit to Rundell and Bridge, begging him to reserve the tale of his own day's labours until Susan should be there to hear. But dinner was announced immediately, and the earl and his sister were soon driven distracted by John's attempts to tell his story in the brief intervals when the servants were out of the room. He was a convinced exponent of the theory that the only way to deal with

57

a narrative was to begin at the beginning and go on until one reached the end, and when he had been arrested in mid-sentence for the twentieth time, so that he was beginning to sound quite like Matthew, the earl said gently: 'I think perhaps we had better continue this conversation at a later stage. If you don't mind, Susan, John and I will bring our brandy into the library directly after dinner instead of leaving you to sit there in suspense. Then we can sort things out before it is time for us to leave for the ball.'

Lady Susan having acceded thankfully to this suggestion, all three moved straight into the library at the conclusion of the meal. The brandy was brought in, the doors were closed, and the earl said: 'Now, John! Have you learned anything? And try not to take too long about it!'

'I think so,' said John, scowling at his brother's peremptory tone, 'but I don't guarantee it. I saw the senior clerk as you suggested, and there was no difficulty there. But the letter books! You can't conceive how many there are. Letter books, consignment books, shipping books – and at least a hundred of them for every year. You said last night there wouldn't be any fossicking around among boring dusty books. Hah! It took me half the day to find out where to start. And, of course, since we were interested in the Bengal Presidency, that made things no easier. If only Colonel Malcolm had been posted to Bombay or Madras!'

In response to his sister's look of enquiry, the earl explained: 'Calcutta, the seat of government, is in the Bengal Presidency, so it naturally attracts a much higher proportion of what is sent out from this country than the Bombay or Madras Presidencies.'

'Anyway,' John resumed, 'since I was obviously going to be consulting hundreds of books by the time I was finished, the clerk had someone carry the first lot into the Court Room, where they hold the stockholders' meetings. I must say it *is* rather handsome, with a great dais and a window in the dome and niches full of Classical statues all round the walls. But, of course, you know, Charles, don't you? You must have been there many times. I sat there in solitary state, surrounded by folio tomes, and I can tell you I wished I had never heard of Miss Malcolm!

'I had to begin with the shipping books to discover which of the Indiamen had sailed in the late summer. I made notes of likely-looking items of cargo . . .' He interrupted himself. 'Charles, I know you only had directors and proprietors in mind, but I thought I'd best note anything at all that looked promising, for I saw from a glance at the general books that though most of the entries were of the order of "eighty-four packets for the Bengal regiments" there were occasions where a little more detail had slipped in. In any case, I made notes from the shipping books and then checked the notes with the directors' and proprietors' books, and with the general books as well. And I may tell you that my shoulder muscles are aching like the very devil. Just you try juggling with a dozen heavy ledgers for every note you make!

'I am telling you all this,' he said with a grin, 'so that you will appreciate why I haven't yet worked back beyond 1809! However, as I said, I think I may have something. If you rule out the possibility of the diamonds having been sent by Hatchards, who appear to have been among Colonel Malcolm's most enthusiastic correspondents – what a lot of books he ordered from them! it must have made quite a hole in their profits when he died – then the only other candidate between 1809 and 1813 is a gentleman called Erasmus Grant, who sent off a small package weighing only a few ounces to Mrs Colonel Malcolm every year in August or thereabouts, depending on sailing dates. Every year except 1811, that is. But the books for 1811 are so confused – you wouldn't believe! – that I may easily have missed it.'

The earl sank his head in his hands and groaned. 'It's too much! God knows, Wayne was bad enough. But Grant!'

'It's the best I can do for you,' his brother responded, 'and you can think yourself lucky to have even that. One of the clerks writes such a cramped hand that I had the greatest difficulty deciphering half the entries I was interested in! Besides, what do you have against Grant?'

'For a start,' said the earl bitterly, 'he must be a hundred years old! If I remember, he ceased to be director in about 1802, but of course he still has a director's privileges. At least he isn't a crusty old care-for-nobody like Wayne, but he *is* deaf as a trunkmaker and as finical as a spintext – in fact, what Girvan would call a real doddering old sheep's head!'

'Charles! Such language!' said Lady Susan with a gurgle of mirth. Then she looked at the clock and rose to her feet. 'The carriage awaits, milord. Or if it doesn't, it ought to. We shall be disgracefully late if we delay any further, and we don't wish to upset Maria Sefton. So you'll have to make up your mind on the way what you're going to say to Miss Malcolm. And I do not,' she added, as she preceded her brothers out of the room, 'envy you *that* problem!'

✳ *Chapter Six* ✳

In the three weeks prior to the Seftons' ball, Miss Malcolm had been made forcibly aware that the Duke of Wellington had not been idle during his short stay in London. Besides receiving congratulatory addresses from the House of Commons, taking his seat in the Lords, whisking back and forth from one government department to another, and unmercifully snubbing young gentlemen desirous of obtaining sinecures at the Paris embassy, he had found time to solicit for his adopted niece the good offices of several of the female dragons who ruled over the *ton*.

As a result, Miss Malcolm had been subjected to a series of morning visits which were as distasteful as they were exhausting. She had been looked over, she exclaimed to Sarah Nicholas, as if she were a prize heifer. That none of the starched-up ladies who called upon her had found anything to take exception to did not mollify her in the least. Indeed, she had been unusually silent during her inspection by the supercilious Mrs Drummond-Burrell, not because she was afraid of saying something that might offend, but because she was fighting an overmastering impulse to do precisely that. The Countess Lieven came, and asked a great many penetrating and offensive questions, while Lady Jersey, known to the polite world as Silence, chattered unceasingly for the full thirty minutes of her visit and appeared to pay not the slightest heed to her hostess's replies. Lady Sefton, kindly but dull, had been the last and least insupportable of Caroline's inquisitors, and after her departure Sarah had subsided into a chair with a sigh of relief.

'Well, my dear,' she said. 'That makes four patronesses of Almack's who have approved you, which, let me tell you, is a very reasonable percentage. We need be in no worry about receiving vouchers.'

'I'm not at all sure I wish to receive vouchers,' Caroline retorted. 'I can conceive of nothing more insipid than an evening in the company of persons who are accustomed to truckle to that kind of arrogance!'

'Mere irritation of the nerves,' Sarah assured her. 'The entrée to Almack's is essential if you are to be accepted into society, so you must make the best of it. Besides, once you know a few more people you will find an evening there quite like a family party.'

The lady patronesses had been followed by a stream of other visitors curious to see the Duke's protégée, so that by the end Sarah was complaining that her voice was worn to a thread with giving Caroline so much worldly advice. She warned her whom she should be distant with and whom she must butter her tongue for, who was of a cheerful disposition and who as melancholy as a gib-cat, who had a well-informed mind and who an empty head, who was a gazetted fortune hunter and who an eligible match. Caro listened, marked, and occasionally obeyed, but although a few of her visitors proved delightful she came to the regretful conclusion that the Upper Ten Thousand probably contained just as high a proportion of frankly dull people as the Lower Ten Million.

She said as much to Sarah as they went upstairs to dress for the ball, and Sarah replied: 'But consider how *very* interesting the interesting people are. Moriston, for example. I cannot tell you how much *his* approval would add to your consequence! I know you thought him forbidding when he called the other day – and I should dearly like to know why he did call – but though I am little acquainted with him I believe he is not always so. He does have the reputation of being difficult to please, of course,' she went on consideringly, and would have enlarged on this theme had she not, by a fortunate chance, happened to look up and observe the sardonic gleam in Caroline's eye. Hastily, she abandoned the subject and, exclaiming at the lateness of the hour, briskly propelled Caro towards her chamber and then disappeared equally briskly in the direction of her own.

The strain of these last weeks, culminating in the tensions of the interview with Lord Moriston, had left Caroline in no mood for a ball. She should, she knew, be looking forward to it with pleasurable anticipation, but her only feeling was one of indifference. While she submitted to the ministrations of her excellent dresser, she took herself silently but severely to task, banishing the wistful desire for a quiet evening at home with the latest novel – an enthralling Gothic romance – from Colburn's Lending Library, and telling herself that a ball was just what she needed to lift her out of this fit of the dismals. Lights and music, cheerful people, animated talk, the sheer pleasure of dancing. Everything bright and superficial, all problems temporarily locked away. She need not even worry, she assured herself, about encountering the earl. Since he could not possibly have made any progress in his investigation in so short a time, he would probably do no more than exchange a few words with her before moving on to more congenial company.

Persevering along these lines, she had, by the time the last curl had been coaxed into place, talked herself out of despondency if not into cheerfulness. Then Miss Dutton stood back to consider the results of her labours and permitted herself a twitch of approval. 'Very becoming, miss,' she said, her hands folded primly before her. 'Very becoming indeed, if I may say so.'

Caroline stood up and studied her reflection in the long mirror. Not at all bad, she thought critically. Her gown had been made for her by Madame Delisle, a modiste of the first stare, from some lengths of soft, heavily textured raw silk she had brought back from India. The robe, clinging and warmly creamy in colour, was open down the front over a slip of the same shade, this time with a rich, shimmering vein of gold running through it. Her only jewellery was a heavy gold filigree necklace set with huge creamy pearls and a pearl ornament that glowed in her piled auburn hair, while an antique fan and a pair of long blond gloves completed a toilette that was both striking and, she thought, quietly elegant. A little sophisticated, perhaps, for someone in her first season, but then she was no longer a seventeen-year-old miss straight from the schoolroom. At any rate, she concluded with satisfaction, it ought to make all those rose pinks and celestial blues look decidedly commonplace.

Sufficiently restored to be able to laugh at herself, she turned to Dutton and accepted the amber velvet cloak from her hands. 'Wish me luck at my first society ball!' she said, with a flash of her accustomed vivacity.

Miss Dutton smiled grimly. 'Luck, miss?' she said. 'Looking like that, there's no need for luck to stir a finger in the matter!'

⚜

When her carriage turned into the street in which the Seftons' mansion was located, it found itself at the end of a long line of other conveyances waiting to set down their burdens, and it was twenty minutes before Caroline and Mrs Nicholas drew level with the gaily-coloured awning and red carpet that had been laid across the flagway to the front door.

The marble-lined hall was full of unknowns greeting one another with the indolence of long acquaintance, and Caroline felt a momentary nervousness; but the Seftons greeted the two ladies kindly and Caro's spirits lifted again as she entered the ballroom, which was a blaze of light and colour, iridescent with movement as the early arrivals wove and intertwined in the intricate figures of the first country dance. There were little knots of people round the edges of the floor, gentlemen chatting, unpartnered ladies looking as if they did not really wish to dance anyway, dowagers and chaperones in a solid mass of puce and purple, their nodding, gossiping heads topped by a frou-frou of plumes, while the musicians scraped away busily, almost hidden behind their stockade of greenery. The tented ceiling trapped the heat from the huge chandeliers and reflected it downwards, so that many of the ladies were already slightly flushed and the gentlemen's foreheads faintly sheened with perspiration.

Caroline, quite unaware that her cool and exquisite person had been the focus of numerous pairs of eyes from the moment she entered the room, was still standing inside the door when the dance came to an end and the floor began to clear. 'Over to the right, I think,' Sarah murmured in her ear, and she had just begun to move when she heard a cry of, 'Miss Malcolm, by all that's wonderful!' and turned to see the Honourable Darius Thornton bearing down upon her, a smile of pure pleasure on his face. 'My goodness, Miss Malcolm! You look absolutely radiant!' he exclaimed, his admiration so patently sincere that she could not but warm to him. Sarah had said that he was a younger son and had not a feather to fly with, and that he should not be encouraged, but Caro felt that his particular brand of light-hearted good humour was just what the occasion required.

She stopped to greet him, but they had scarcely exchanged two sentences before she found herself surrounded by a throng of fashionable young gentlemen all eager to claim her hand. In rapid succession, she stood up for a cotillion with Mr Thornton, a quadrille with either Sir Daniel Lord or Sir Paul Allott – who were quite indistinguishable from each other – and a country dance with young Lord Inverwick, one of the most attractive of her morning visitors. Then, breathless and laughing, she insisted on a respite, so that when the earl and his party arrived just after eleven o'clock, they saw her almost at once, demurely seated at the centre of an animated group in the far corner of the room.

'There's Miss Malcolm,' Lady Susan said unnecessarily, and the earl nodded. But John, following their gaze, stood transfixed.

'*That* is Miss Malcolm?' He turned to his brother indignantly. 'Well, I do think you might have introduced me before now. I've never seen such a ravishing creature. She makes every other lady in the room look positively shabby-genteel!'

'Thank you,' said his sister.

'And look!' he went on, unheeding. 'There are Louis and Thornton and that antidote Gaydon all behaving as if they had known her forever. Whereas I suppose she doesn't even know that I – who have been working myself to the bone for her – so much as exist!'

Catching his breath on a choke of laughter, the earl agreed that it was a situation that must be remedied at once, and the new arrivals began to make their way towards the far corner, pausing here and there to exchange salutations with friends. When they reached their goal, they discovered some good-natured wrangling going on as to who should be permitted to take Miss Malcolm in to supper.

'But there is no question about it whatever,' Lord Inverwick stated. 'In such cases, rank invariably takes precedence.'

'Pooh!' exclaimed Louis. 'Just because you happen to be a viscount! I tell you this, Inverwick – length of acquaintance is what counts. Is it not, Miss Malcolm?'

Miss Malcolm's reply was drowned by a piteous wail from Mr Thornton. 'But dash it all!' he expostulated. 'It was I who asked her first!'

Laughing, she turned towards him, and for the first time caught sight of the earl.

Devil take the girl! thought his lordship irritably. Now the whole town would know that it only needed his appearance to frighten the life out of her! But he bowed smoothly, and said with his most charming company smile: 'Good evening, Miss Malcolm. If an impartial observer may be permitted to express an opinion, I feel that Mr Thornton's claim is unarguable. Otherwise, I should be tempted to enter the lists myself.'

Mr Thornton, gratified, exclaimed: 'That's obliging of you, Moriston!' while Caro, furious with herself, looked at him steadily for a moment and then turned to greet Lady Susan. By the time John was made known to her – 'one of your most ardent – er – supporters' – she had sufficiently recovered herself to bestow on him a smile that was both dazzling and faintly conspiratorial. He was enchanted, and swiftly regained his power of speech to beg the favour of her hand for one of the dances after the supper interval. The earl did the same, if from motives that were rather less ingenuous.

In the meantime, a swift survey of Miss Malcolm's admirers had sufficed to inform him that, though they were a harmless enough set of young cubs, they were undesirably lightweight. All the fault of that Nicholas woman, he thought, who was still a silly chit even if she *was* approaching thirty. There was no one here, certainly, who would add much to Miss Malcolm's consequence. Casually, his eye swept round the ballroom, and in a moment he had succeeded in collecting the attention of Captain Gregory, another naval gentleman, an army officer of his acquaintance, and two of his own particular friends, Lord Inchmore and Sir Andrew Cowan. As they all accommodatingly converged on him, the earl turned back to Miss Malcolm's gallants.

Raising his quizzing glass, he surveyed Mr Gaydon's waistcoat intently. 'Mmmm,' he said at last, and then, as if struck by some fleeting memory: 'Tell me, Gaydon. I caught no more than a glimpse of you in Cockspur Street this morning, but enlighten me, pray. I thought I saw something odd – deuced odd, in fact – in your hatband. What could it have been, do you suppose?'

Mr Gaydon's youthful countenance assumed a rich, fiery tint. 'Nothing at all,' he stammered, trying to be airy but not quite succeeding. 'Nothing at all. Merely a bit of fun and gig. Hoaxing it, you understand! Hoaxing it!'

'Oh,' said his lordship, bored, and allowed the annihilating glass to drop as he turned to another of the young gentlemen. Mr Gaydon, still blushing furiously and murmuring something about being engaged for the country dance that was forming, backed out of the group – for all the world, thought Miss Malcolm, incensed, as if he were some petty princeling dismissed the presence of the Holy Roman Emperor. Within a very few minutes the earl had ruthlessly contrived to send all but one of Miss Malcolm's court about its business, and only the pertinacious Mr Thornton remained to leaven a company that had suddenly become mature, civilized, and faintly intimidating. Caroline, with adjectives such as 'autocratic', 'overbearing', and 'arrogant' revolving in her mind, was relieved when Sir Andrew Cowan, a tall, quiet gentleman with a delightful smile, said: 'Miss Malcolm, if we hurry we might join that last set I see forming over there. I think the numbers are not quite made up. Will you do me the honour?'

She did not see his lordship again until after supper when he came to claim her hand for the quadrille. But when the moment came for them to take the floor, he said: 'Should you object to sitting down with me instead? I have something to say to you and I find one can never converse rationally while paying attention to the figures – especially the *grande ronde* and the *pas d'été*!'

Though this request was clearly designed to put her at her ease, and was accompanied by a disarming smile, Caroline felt her heart sink to her gold satin slippers as he led her to a sofa in one of the alcoves that was set back from the main part of the ballroom. She gave no sign of it, however, as she seated herself, flipped open her fan, and calmly began to ply it.

He sat down himself, saying: 'That's better – much better. I'm not an ogre, you know!' But her answering smile carried no conviction at all. With an inward sigh, he went on: 'You will, I hope, be pleased to know that I have discovered the source of the diamonds. To . . .'

Her eyes flew to his face, and the pose of tranquillity evaporated as if it had never been. 'Already?' she exclaimed. 'Is it possible?'

'Entirely possible, I assure you! But please don't run on ahead of me. As I say, I have discovered the source of the diamonds, or, to be absolutely precise, I have discovered who was in possession of them when you were born. Whether he himself sent them to your mother, or whether he handed them over to someone else who sent them, I don't yet know. But I hope to find out within the next few days.'

Her eyes dropped to her fan, and she engaged in an all too visible struggle to control her voice. 'Who is he? Is he alive?' She looked up. 'Do I – know him?'

He cursed himself for his stupidity. He had intended merely to reassure her that something was being done, but had instead landed himself in an impossibly awkward position. As far as this subject was concerned, Miss Malcolm seemed to have no sense of decent self-restraint whatever.

Finally, he said: 'I would prefer not to tell you his name at present, but he is titled, wealthy, something of a recluse, and . . .' He paused, choosing his words, '. . . no longer young.'

She was bewildered. 'I wouldn't expect him to be! What do you mean "no longer young"? Forty-five? Fifty?'

Drat the girl, thought his lordship for the second time that evening. He hesitated, and then said, salving his conscience with the reflection that it was the literal truth: 'Over fifty.'

'Oh,' she said rather helplessly. 'So he was quite a few years older than my mother. Are you *sure* you have the right man?'

'There is no doubt about who owned the diamonds when you were born, but that is not to say that the man concerned is your father.'

'Surely that is implied?'

'Perhaps, but it is not the only possibility. However, I wish to consult you on the next step – or the next step but one, for I have something else I wish to check first. Which is to go and see him. No, no!' He held up his hand reassuringly. 'I am not suggesting *you* should go. That's for me to do. But once I have been to see him, and no matter what his reaction is, you must understand that we are irrevocably committed.'

She looked at him blankly. 'Committed?'

'Just think about it. Whether he is your father or not, he must know something. And once I have been to see him, he will know that *we* know something. Do you follow me?'

'You mean,' she said slowly, twisting the fragile ivory sticks of her fan between her fingers, 'that if I insist on going on with this, I won't be able to keep anything you learn to myself. That I may be inviting – responsibilities? Setting off a chain of events that we can't foresee?'

'All those things. With no retreat back into the dream world of ignorance.' His voice was more sympathetic than his words. 'It would help, you know,' he went on reasonably, 'if you would give me some idea of what you would choose to do if it were possible for us to identify your father without his knowing. If the choice were entirely yours, would you make the relationship public?'

'Oh, no!' she exclaimed involuntarily. 'The scandal! Everyone knows me as Caroline Malcolm!'

'Precisely,' he agreed, a smile bracketing the long, firm mouth. 'So, I repeat, once we have taken the next step you may find yourself robbed of the freedom to choose. With your mother and stepfather both dead, your true father might feel that there is no longer any reason to keep the relationship secret.'

'But if that were the case, why should he not have come forward before now?'

'My dear girl,' said his lordship with a touch of asperity. 'It is perfectly possible that he does not know they are dead. Who should tell him, if *you* haven't? Remember that the last diamond was sent off from England more than a year after your step-father died, and at just about the time of your mother's accident.'

Miss Malcolm fanned her heated cheeks, and there was a long silence. When she broke it, it was to revert to an earlier point. 'Still alive,' she said flatly. 'So my mother was not widowed.' Her eyes were enormous in the delicate face. 'Have you been able to find any record of a divorce?'

All of a sudden she looked very young and vulnerable. The earl's own gaze became slightly abstracted, and it was a moment or two before he identified the unfamiliar sensation in his chest as the stirring of a protective instinct, long dormant. He was wryly amused. Helpless maidens, however fair, were not at all in his usual style.

It was with more gentleness than he had previously displayed, though also with duplicity, that he said: 'That is something that takes time. But I should not concern yourself too much for the moment. One thing you can be sure of – the gentleman who owned the diamonds when you were born had both enough money and enough influence to procure a divorce if one was required.'

There was another silence in the alcove while, in the ballroom, the orchestra wound itself up to the final bars of the quadrille.

'Well?' he prompted her. 'Do I go and see the gentleman or do I not?'

She gave a sharp little sigh. 'I don't know. I can't – I really *can't* decide now. Indeed, I wish you had not chosen to confront me with this right in the middle of a ball. I was not even remotely prepared for it.'

The earl's goodwill suffered a severe setback. Well, he'd be damned, he thought. From the one piece of information he had vouchsafed her she had built a full three-act melodrama – and was now holding him at fault for it! At least it settled one thing, however. He would tell Miss Malcolm nothing more about the progress of the investigation until he was able to present her with the complete solution.

'May I,' she asked, aware of how ungracious she must have sounded, 'consider it for a little and send a message round to you tomorrow?'

The earl bowed. 'As you wish,' he replied coolly. But her smile was so forlorn that, as he stood up and held out his hand to assist her, he could not help but relent.

She rose gracefully, lightly shaking free the folds of her gown, and made a determined bid for self-possession – successfully enough to be able to look his lordship in the eye and say with an attempt at drollery: 'If I recall, it was Launcelot Gobbo in *The Merchant of Venice* who said, "It is a wise father that knows his own child." Am I wrong, or is there also a version which runs, "It is a wise child that knows its own father"?'

The intimidating blue gaze relaxed, and Miss Malcolm, very much startled, felt a reassuring pressure on her fingers and heard him murmur approvingly – and with the greatest impropriety – 'Good girl!' But Ludovic Home was standing smiling at his elbow, waiting to claim her for the next dance, and she allowed herself to be led unprotesting out on to the floor.

It was some moments before she realized that Ludovic was speaking, and in a tone that suggested he was repeating something he had said before, perhaps more than once. She gave a little shake of her head, as if to clear it, and looked up at him. 'I *am* sorry,' she apologized. 'What were you saying?'

He smiled down at her. 'Don't distress yourself. I asked whether you were enjoying yourself, that was all.'

With a strong feeling of indignation, Miss Malcolm recognized that her tribulations were not yet over for the evening. There was a great deal too much warmth in Ludovic's pleasant grey eyes, and his smile held a quality of concern that was disturbing. He had always been attentive but correct. Why, she wondered despairingly, should he choose now – just when Moriston's inexplicable behaviour had thrown her quite off balance – to make his feelings so obvious!

She replied with a vivacity that was deliberately artificial. 'Enjoying myself? Yes, indeed, though I know it is quite provincial to admit it!'

His brother Louis, or Darius Thornton, or, she suspected, John Dornay, would at once have accepted the implicit rebuke. Ludovic, however, was not so easily diverted. 'Truly?' he said. 'I am relieved to hear it. I had feared that Moriston, who is perhaps a little – ah – susceptible, might have offended you in some way.' She stiffened slightly. 'No, don't misunderstand me!' he begged. 'It is just that men who have earned distinction in a wider world sometimes appear arrogant – eccentric – oh, I don't know! self-indulgent – in the eyes of more conventional mortals. I should not like you to have been put out of countenance by him!'

This was so much what Caroline herself had been thinking that she began to feel almost in charity with him and to credit him with more perspicacity than she had, hitherto, believed him to possess. But she was still sufficiently ill at ease to wish to turn the subject, and a condescending bow from the Countess Lieven provided her with an opening. When she had responded to it, she asked Ludovic in a lowered tone: 'And who is that plump little lady staring at us with such interest? Over there by the second window, standing with the tall, cadaverous man?'

Ludovic glanced casually to his right. 'Princess Esterhazy?

The Austrian ambassador's wife. She is one of the patronesses of Almack's, you know.'

Caroline gave a little trill of mock alarm. 'Oh no! Not *another* patroness. If I am catechized just once more I shall say my father was a missionary and my mother a Hottentot! I wonder what that would make me?'

'Confused, I should think. A cross between a missionary and a Hottentot would be – what? – a Missentot?'

She gave a gurgle. Ludovic rarely succumbed to levity, and she felt he ought to be encouraged. Forgetting, for the moment, that the last thing she wished to do was give him any kind of encouragement, she glanced up into the sturdy good-looking face and said mischievously: 'Then if I am a Missentot, Richard must be a Masterintot?' It was a mistake. But he was quick to observe the look of withdrawal in her eyes, and this time he respected it.

With a smile that held no more than conventional politeness, he said: 'And how, by the way, is Richard? Do we expect to see him in town soon?'

'In theory, no. But I am almost sure he is reviewing ways of having himself rusticated so that he may come and see how I go on. His last letter was full of concern lest I should be feeling the want of his presence, and if he had not also mentioned that Oxford was – I quote! – "devilish flat" at the moment, I would have been deeply affected by his brotherly solicitude! Two or three weeks should do it, I imagine.'

Ludovic's smile widened. 'Well, when his arrival is imminent, do not fail to let me know. He cannot be acquainted with many people in London and I should be happy to take him about a little until he acquires some town-bronze.'

Caroline was touched. Ludovic was full of surprises tonight. Though his offer, she realized, sprang as much from a desire to win his way into her own good graces as from kindliness for Richard, it still argued a certain generosity of spirit. The volatile Louis, she knew, was fretted by his brother's assumption of the roles of guide, philosopher and friend. 'It simply isn't natural!' he had exploded to her on one occasion. 'Dash it all, if only he would let himself go, and have some fun sometimes! It's not as if he was prosy all the way through. He'd be quite a good fellow if he didn't insist on being so – so – *upright*!' Oh, well, reflected Caroline, if Ludovic hoped that her brother would prove more amenable than his own, he was destined to be disappointed. Contact with Richard, in fact, might be the making of him.

While Miss Malcolm and her partner revolved upon the floor,

the earl had remained standing by the alcove, his eyes on the dancers but his mind elsewhere. After some little time, Adam Gregory found him there.

'I am charged with a message for you,' he reported. 'Your sister says that, at her age, excitement and late hours are bad for her and she wishes to be taken home, if you please.'

The earl did not stir, and the captain followed the direction of his gaze, a hint of speculation in his own.

'Do I catch a whiff of mystery?' he asked politely.

The earl's expression was unreadable. After a moment, he said: 'You do. In fact, I have a feeling that I may need your help, if you are prepared to give it.'

'Of course,' replied the captain cheerfully. His eyes rested quizzically on his friend's abstracted profile for a few seconds, and then he added: 'That's what a family's for, isn't it?'

The earl's head snapped round. 'My God!' he exclaimed. 'Adam, you haven't?'

'My God!' laughed Captain the Honourable Adam Gregory in reply. 'Charles, I have!'

⚹ *Chapter Seven* ⚹

Within a minute of first being introduced to the Lady Susan Channock, Adam Gregory had recognized that he had met his fate at last. And though her ladyship did not blush, or turn pale, or lose the thread of her discourse, she, too, felt her heart miss its accustomed stroke, falter, and resume its beat with a measured intensity that seemed to vibrate through her entire being.

It would have been maudlin to describe it as love at first sight. The earl, who had been present, privately defined it as a case of spontaneous combustion, and wondered enviously if he himself was fated ever to meet the other perfect, interlocking part of his own self.

He and the captain had been friends for several years, ever since a much younger Adam Gregory, commanding an eighteen-gun sloop of war, had been 'requested and required' by his masters at the Admiralty to convey an equally youthful Lord Moriston, 'with the utmost secrecy and despatch', to the Caribbean on an early diplomatic mission. The two young men had found each other's company congenial and had kept up a desultory friendship during the intervening years when Adam's rare, brief shore leaves and the earl's frequent absences abroad had allowed. The abdication of Napoleon, however, and his departure for Elba earlier in the year had resulted in a naval reorganization that gave Adam the enchanting prospect of several months of a freedom he had not experienced for more years than he could remember. Travelling up to London from his family home in Cornwall, he had broken his journey at Atherton, there to meet for the first time the other members of Moriston's household.

That had been three weeks ago, and in the interval Lady Susan and the captain had met occasionally, ridden out once or twice, and contrived to behave like perfectly normal, rational human beings whose relations with each other, in public and in private, were just what might have been expected between a lady of breeding no longer in the first blush of her youth, and a long-standing acquaintance of her elder brother. When they met, they met on easy terms, talked comfortably, and laughed at the same things. Not by so much as the flicker of an eyelid did they acknowledge the almost tangible current of awareness that flowed between them.

The captain, whose will-power was exemplary, had elected to go about his wooing in the cool, civilized, passionless fashion dictated by the polite world's idea of good taste. A little unsure of the modes and manners with which he had been out of touch for so long, he was anxious not to provide food for gossip – not because he cared in the least what society thought of him, but because the last thing he wanted to do was embarrass her ladyship. Moonstruck he undoubtedly was, but he had no intention of permitting it to show.

He had not meant to declare himself for many weeks yet, nor would he have chosen an occasion as public as a ball to do so. But as he whirled her round in a waltz at the Seftons', Lady Susan looked up in response to some remark of his with such a heart-stopping smile in her eyes that all his will-power, all his resolution, went to the winds. Without another word, he steered her to the edge of the floor and led her off, in defiance of all propriety, to an anteroom which by the greatest good fortune proved to be unoccupied.

Once inside, he closed the door and leaned his back against it, still holding her by the hand and turning her to face him. The muscles of his jaw were tight as he looked down at her, brown eyes into hazel ones, and said baldly: 'Marry me. Soon.'

Her own eyes were misty, and she gave a breathless little gasp of laughter as all the inadequate conventional replies flitted through her mind. In the event, she said with the most perfect simplicity: 'Of course.'

Then she found herself crushed in an embrace that was neither cool, civilized, nor passionless, and would have suited the polite world's idea of good taste not at all. Her ladyship, who had survived the years of her widowhood in the comfortable conviction that love and desire were weaknesses to which she was immune, discovered in a few brief, cataclysmic moments that she had been quite wrong.

When he released her at last, it was as if the marrow had been drained out of her bones. Nor did the captain appear to be in much better case. They stood there weakly for a while, her head on his shoulder, his eyes gazing unseeing at the far wall of the room, until at last he put a gentle hand under her chin and raised her eyes to his again. 'My dearest love,' he said, with a slight catch in his voice and the faintest tremor of laughter at the corners of his mouth. The ghost of an answering smile lit her face and she sighed, freed herself, and bent to retrieve the silver gauze scarf that had fallen unheeded to the floor. 'You are perfectly right, of course,' she said. 'This *is* neither the time nor the place. Just suppose someone had tried to come in!' She gave a theatrical shudder. 'But my darling, even so, I don't think I could possibly go back to the ballroom. If I remain here, would you go and find Charles, wherever he may be, and tell him I would like to be taken home?'

So he had kissed her again, once, lightly, and then gone off in search of his lordship.

✠

On the evening after the Seftons' ball, the earl's incomparable French chef, Alexandre, produced a private celebratory dinner for Susan and Captain Gregory, Lord Moriston and John, that was a masterpiece both of planning and execution. So it was not until the following day that the earl proceeded to the next step in his investigation of Miss Malcolm's antecedents.

Afterwards, he returned to St James's Square with his temples throbbing and his throat as raw as a November fog. Mr Erasmus Grant had proved to be all that he had feared – and more, for beside being deaf and finical he spoke in a toothless mumble that was reminiscent of nothing so much as a pot of broth left at a simmer.

He lived in one of the houses in Adelphi Terrace, built almost forty years earlier by the Adam brothers as part of an imaginative scheme that had come close to ruining them. They had saved the situation by running a lottery, selling more than four thousand tickets with just over one hundred houses as prizes. The earl, as he followed Mr Grant's ancient butler upstairs to the second floor, wondered if this was how Grant had come into possession of his home. The lower part of the house, though adequately furnished, had a curiously dead and disused look about it, which was explained when he discovered that the owner, now approaching eighty, had his personal suite of rooms on the topmost main floor and roosted there all the year round, never stirring outdoors and rarely even venturing downstairs.

Looking out of the window at the panorama of the river, thick with masts and bustling with wherries, the earl congratulated Mr Grant on his choice of residence.

'Choice?' mumbled his host. 'Wouldn't say that precisely. Won it in the lottery, ye know? Fifty pounds the ticket cost me, but it was the best investment I ever made. Gives me a lot of pleasure, watching all that coming and going, ye know?'

The man was rake-thin, his chin sunk between hunched shoulders, his bony knees projecting through the thick rug that covered them, and his arms tightly folded, palm to elbow. He looked old and chilled, and his eyes had the vagueness of someone who lived almost entirely in the past. But the earl had a suspicion that these die-away airs were deceptive. He had heard too much – and recently – about the malicious brain behind the frail exterior.

Tactfully, his lordship embarked on a monologue that began with the busy river traffic and led to the new East India Dock at Blackwall and then to the East India Company itself. He was just congratulating himself on having got thus far reasonably painlessly when Mr Grant muttered: 'What did you say? What did you say, eh? Wasn't attending. When you get to be an old man like me your attention wanders. What d'ye want, anyway? No one ever comes to see me unless they want something!'

The earl looked at him and for an agonized moment contemplated repeating his delicate lead-in at the pitch of his lungs. Then he thought – oh no! You don't catch me that way.

So he braced himself and took a preparatory breath. 'I need your help,' he thundered.

'Go on,' mumbled Mr Grant. 'Surprise me!'

'I believe,' his lordship bellowed, 'that over the last twenty years you have despatched an annual package to a gentleman

74

in India, a Colonel Malcolm who was stationed in the Bengal Presidency?'

The response was inaudible.

'I beg your pardon?'

'I said, who told ye that?'

'We discovered it from the Company's consignment books. May I ask whether you knew what the packages contained?'

'What business is it of yours?'

The earl gritted his teeth and persevered. 'I believe that the packages were sent under your frank, but on behalf of someone else. Can you tell me if that is so?'

The veiled eyes looked up at him from under their sparse white brows. 'Why *should* I tell you, eh?'

His lordship paused to recruit his voice for a moment. Then: 'I ask,' he continued, 'on behalf of a young lady who is trying to find her father. We believe the origin of the packages would help us in our search.'

'Father, eh?' The sound that emerged from between the clamped, colourless lips sounded remarkably like a cackle. There was a long, long silence.

Never before had the earl found himself forced to discuss a delicate matter at the full stretch of his lungs, and he did not care for it. But there seemed to be no alternative, and he was just considering how to phrase his next question when Mr Grant mumbled something that he failed to catch.

'I beg your pardon?' he said.

The pale eyes focused on him. 'Shouldn't be so hard of hearing at your age,' said the old man disapprovingly. 'I said, you must have some ideas of your own. Wouldn't have phrased your questions that way if you hadn't.'

You crafty old chutney-chandler! thought his lordship, aggrieved. Swiftly, he reviewed his strategy and then, attempting unsuccessfully to fix Mr Grant's wandering eye, gathered his breath and admitted with extreme clarity: 'I know the contents of the packages originally belonged to the Marquis of Wayne.'

'Didn't hear that,' muttered his host.

The earl tried again. 'I know,' he began, doing his best to achieve a roar, 'that the Marquis of Wayne . . .' He broke off. '*Did you hear that?* I said, the Marquis of *Wayne* formerly owned what was in those packets.'

'No need to shout,' the old man grumbled, with all the complacency of the selectively deaf. 'Just speak clearly.'

The earl inhaled deeply and offered up a silent prayer for

patience. 'Was it on Wayne's behalf that you sent them?'

This time he was fairly sure that Grant had not, in fact, heard him, had not even been listening because he was pursuing some train of thought of his own. His next words confirmed it.

'Long time ago,' he said in the abbreviated style he seemed to favour. 'Some time in the 'nineties it must have been. Showed me the diamonds. Pretty things. Said he owed them to someone.' He paused, wheezing a little, and then gave a disapproving sniff. 'Didn't hear about the girl until years after. Just slipped out one night when the brandy had gone round too often. He didn't say she was his daughter,' he added resentfully.

The earl restrained himself from saying, 'Neither did I!' and waited hopefully, but at last he had to prompt him. 'Did he not have sons . . . *I said*, did he not have sons from his marriage?'

'Sons?' The old man's eyes were filmed over. 'Sons? Yes, there were two, I believe. But they were both gone by the time I knew him. He was all alone then. Even his wife had been dead for two or three years.'

His eyes cleared and he peered at the earl malignantly. 'That what ye wanted, eh? Going to make a scandal of it, are you? Well, I don't care any more. Never liked Wayne much. Took me a long time to get to know him, and even then I always had to keep my eye on him.' He relapsed into a quaver. 'But take my advice, my boy. Don't cross him if you can help it. He was a dangerous man to meddle with in his fifties and I shouldn't think he's changed one little bit since then.'

Though the earl remained for another hour, he learned nothing more to the point. It was clear that Mr Grant, though prepared for his own inscrutable reasons to reveal a certain amount about Wayne and his association with him, had no intention of revealing one word more. At last he took his leave, thanking him with perfect if somewhat hoarse sincerity, and even succeeding in pitying him a little as he left him alone before the windows, with darkness falling, watching the lights spring up on the river.

Back at St James's Square he found Susan, John and Adam comfortably gathered round the fire in the parlour. He opened his mouth to greet them and his voice emerged, his sister said with a chuckle, crackling like a Christmas goose on the spit. Turning an affronted eye on Captain Gregory, the earl requested him to keep his future wife in order or he, personally, would forbid the banns.

'You couldn't do that, could you?' John asked innocently. 'Surely she's of age now?'

'Ha!' replied his lordship feelingly, and sank into a chair. 'Adam,' he went on. 'Since you are now, as you said yourself, one of the family, you will have to accustom yourself to the shocking laxity of our habits. Not to mention the abusive nature of our conversation! I am about to consume a large glass of something potent – what is there on the tray over there? – after which I will go upstairs and lave my hands and face. But I am damned if I am going to exert myself to the extent of changing for dinner. Susan, I hope, will forgive me?'

Since it was less in the nature of a question than a statement, Lady Susan gracefully acceded to his request, and the company sat down in perfect harmony to a neat plain dinner. Afterwards, his lordship, claiming rights of recovery, remained silent while the others reported on how they had spent their day. John had made his third and final visit to the East India House, where he had confirmed what his previous days' labours had already made almost certain, that Erasmus Grant was the key to the transmission of the diamonds. Susan, despite numerous distractions, had succeeded in finishing the two copies of the Chinnery portrait. Captain Gregory had spent his morning and part of the afternoon at the Admiralty, and had then escorted Susan first to Hill Street to return the original of the portrait, and then to the house in Cavendish Square which Lady Verona Dornay, the eldest of the family, shared with two other well-born, intellectual, and unmarried ladies. It had been Susan's intention to acquaint Verona with her forthcoming marriage before it was announced in the *Gazette*, but Verona, she reported with what appeared to her brothers to be excessive disapproval, was gone out of town. And not *just* out of town, but to Paris, if you please! That prosy Miss Fitch-Rossiter, who shared the house, had said Verona had always wished to see Paris but had been prevented by the wars. So now that poor dear Bonaparte had abdicated, she had decided to take the opportunity.

'Poor dear Bonaparte?' echoed John, his eyes popping slightly.

'Oh, you know Verona! She has always been the dearest of friends with Lady Holland, and *she* has the most extraordinary ideas.'

'I don't know,' the earl objected. 'I've always felt there must be good in her somewhere, ever since I heard her tell Sam Rogers, when he opened his mouth on one occasion, "Your poetry is bad enough, so pray be sparing of your prose!" Anyone who can squash Sam as ruthlessly as that cannot be all bad!'

The captain, who did not have the pleasure of Mr Rogers's acquaintance and was unable to appreciate the anecdote in its full splendour, looked slightly at a loss, so the earl decided it was time for Susan to tell him all about the mystery of Miss Malcolm's father. When she had finished, he added what he had learned from Erasmus Grant that afternoon.

At the end, the captain, who had listened intently, let out a low, prolonged whistle. 'The girl must be mad to stir all this up. And she's decided she wants you to go and see Wayne?'

'She sent round yesterday to say so.'

'Well, I can see nothing but heartbreak in it, can you? It's like a frigate engaging the enemy in fog – no idea, until it's too late, whether it's a sloop armed with peashooters or a thundering great seventy-gun ship of the line.'

This picturesque simile drew a beatific smile from his affianced bride, and the earl, addressing himself to the ceiling, remarked: 'I *did* mention, I think, that you were going to have to keep her in order?' The captain merely grinned.

John, who had been unusually silent for the past half-hour, stirred. 'Charles, why did you ask your mulligatawny merchant about Wayne's sons?'

His brother looked at him with exaggerated sympathy. 'I asked about the sons because I cannot see Wayne as the errant father. Errant, yes. Father, no. It was interesting that both Bridge and my – er – mulligatawny merchant were so ready to assume that Wayne *was* the father. And they leapt to the same conclusion quite unaided, for all I said was that the diamonds might help in the search. But both of them disliked Wayne, and neither of them knew anything about the lady involved, whereas Susan and I are agreed that Wayne and Mrs Malcolm just do not match.'

'So if Wayne didn't send the diamonds on his own account . . .' John said thoughtfully.

'He sent them on behalf of someone for whom he felt – or feels – a deep and continuing sense of responsibility. Precisely. A son seemed the most likely candidate. Unfortunately, I haven't been able to find out very much about his sons.'

'I hesitate to suggest the obvious,' ventured her ladyship mendaciously, 'but why not look in Debrett?'

'Why not indeed?' His lordship was suspiciously cordial. 'You will be happy to know that I have done so. But when Mr Debrett took over the *Peerage* from Almon, he appears also to have taken over one or two entries that have not been brought up to date since. In Wayne's entry, one wife and two sons are recorded, and there is a date of death given for the marchioness. But as far as Debrett is concerned, both the sons might still be alive.'

'That's odd!' said the captain.

'Not if you know Wayne. In his concern for privacy, he is perfectly capable of threatening a publisher with all kinds of lawsuits. At the very least, he would refuse to supply information – in which case poor Mr Debrett would have to find it elsewhere. And he would have to be very sure of his sources, or run the risk of litigation. Much safer just to leave out anything he was unable to confirm.'

'Mmmm. Any relatives apart from the sons?'

'Several,' replied his lordship gloomily. 'But they don't help us much. He had a brother a year younger than himself – but dead now – who fathered Augustus Home and another boy, Edmund. I haven't been able to find out what happened to Edmund, which is ridiculous when you consider that Atherton and Priory Court are only ten miles apart. But our families were never on terms of more than the most basic civility, and during most of what seem to have been the crucial years I was either away at school or being dragged round the country by my tutor, who was a fervent believer,' he recalled with a shudder, 'in the theory that travel broadens the mind. Wayne also had a sister, Emily, who married beneath her into a Northumberland family not sufficiently distinguished to be mentioned in Debrett. Their name was Marr, and Wayne may have a dozen Marr nephews, for all I have yet been able to discover.'

'Well, you need not think you are sending me up to Northumberland to find out!' John announced firmly, and was rewarded with one of his brother's sweetest smiles.

'What *exactly* did Erasmus Grant say about the sons?' Susan asked.

'He said there were two.' The earl closed his eyes and repeated carefully: 'He said, "But they were both gone by the time I knew him . . ." '

'Gone?'

'Gone. He said, "He was all alone then. Even his wife had been dead for two or three years." I could get nothing more out of him than that.'

'How very inconclusive!'

'Yes, wasn't it? The atmosphere of what he said conveyed

quite strongly that the sons had both died – in which case they can be of no possible interest to us – but Mr Erasmus Grant is a devious old gentleman, octogenarian or not, and I cannot rid myself of the suspicion that he used the word "gone" deliberately.'

'But even if they *were* both dead,' said the captain slowly, 'it still doesn't help you, does it?'

The earl had been sitting relaxed in his chair by the fire. Now he swivelled his head towards the captain and surveyed him with an air of polite enquiry. 'If either of my nearest and dearest had said that . . . However, I assume you are not, in fact, suggesting that Miss Malcolm was sired by a ghost. Do go on!'

Captain Gregory, in his time, had withstood the scrutiny of more than one Admiral of the Blue and was not to be put out of countenance by a mere civilian earl, however distinguished.

'I was thinking about dates,' he said. 'Miss Malcolm was born in February 1794, was she not, but her father could have died at any time after she was conceived. Any time after the middle of 1793, in fact. Now, the first two diamonds were sent while Mrs Malcolm and the child still lived in this country, were they not? And the third may possibly have been sent here, too, and then forwarded to India by normal channels. It depends how soon Wayne was told – or discovered – that Mrs Malcolm had married and sailed for India. It was only at the end of 1796,' and he looked at John for confirmation, 'that Erasmus Grant became involved. So, even if he had known Wayne for as much as three years before that date, it would still be perfectly true to say that the son involved – if either of them *was* involved – was dead or "gone" by the time he knew Wayne. Correct me if I'm wrong?'

The earl's face was expressionless. 'You're right, of course.' He slammed one fist down on the arm of his chair and then sprang to his feet. 'Damnation!' he exclaimed, striding over to the window and back. 'I have been so taken up with how the later diamonds reached India that I hadn't even thought about the earlier ones!'

He stopped and gazed into the fire for several long moments while the others considerately held their peace.

'You don't think,' John volunteered at last, 'that instead of trying to work backwards, as we have been doing, we might devote more attention to what happened at the very beginning?'

'That would be an excellent scheme,' replied his brother

shortly, 'if you can suggest how we investigate the events of twenty years ago without interviewing everyone in the country over the age of forty, and without running the risk of questioning people who should, for Miss Malcolm's sake, be left in ignorance!'

'Now, that's unfair, Charles!' Susan exclaimed. 'You know perfectly well that if any son of Wayne's had an affair with a girl of breeding like Caroline's mama, there must have been talk. A little selective enquiry among those who moved in the first circles at the time would be almost sure to produce something.'

His lordship had the grace to look ashamed of himself. 'Yes, it may come to that. But not until after I have seen Wayne. Even the most sensitive questioning would be bound to result in speculation that could prove extremely disagreeable for Miss Malcolm.' He turned to John and said ruefully: 'I'm sorry. Put it down to mortification at having missed what Adam was so quick to see. And it's I who am supposed to be the expert on matters of deduction!'

'But it is I,' rejoined the captain with becoming modesty, 'who am the expert on arithmetic. Navigational mathematics, you know?'

The earl stared at him for a moment and then burst out laughing. '*Touché!*' he said. 'I can see you are going to be a great asset to the family.'

John had been sitting fidgeting, oblivious to his brother's display of temperament. Now he broke in impatiently: 'If only you would listen! Surely the obvious person to go to is Augustus Home. If anyone knows, he should.'

'Gruesome Gussie?' His brother surveyed him with renewed dislike. 'Heaven forfend. Quite apart from personal considerations, it would be a serious tactical error to approach someone who might have a direct involvement in the business.'

'You could work round to it diplomatically, without revealing your interest!'

'Could I indeed? Well, allow me to tell you that diplomacy is about as useful as hobnailed boots when you are treading on sensitive ground. I'd be prepared to wager that at the first mention of his deceased cousins Sir Augustus would become as invisible as a corncake, and all you would hear would be the rurrp-rurrp, *diminuendo*, of him changing the subject.'

John looked unconvinced, but he was given no opportunity to argue, for the earl turned to Captain Gregory and asked: 'Incidentally, Adam, what do you know about Wayne?'

'Me? Not much. Should I?'

'It was just that I had a feeling in the back of my mind that, sometime or other, he'd been connected with the Navy.'

'Not in my day. I thought he was one of those reform-our-agriculture maniacs.' The captain's friendly brown eyes narrowed, and his lean tanned features took on a bulldog scowl. 'We must wage war,' he intoned, 'not only against the French, but against the unconquered sterility of unused land. Let us not be satisfied with the liberation of Egypt, or the subjugation of Malta. Let us . . .' and he paused to regard his audience sternly, '. . . let us subdue *Finchley Common*! Let us conquer *Hounslow Heath*! Let us compel *Epping Forest* to submit to the yoke of improvement!'

There was a burst of applause. The captain rose, bowed with neatness and economy, and sat down again.

'Bravo!' said the earl. 'The Board of Agriculture would be proud of you. And you're quite right – that *is* very much Wayne's attitude. I doubt if his passion for reform is purely disinterested, of course. Profits under the new farming system are not to be scorned. I know it even from my own land, and I haven't been imposing changes with anything near the vigour of men like Coke and Wayne. Some landowners, I believe, have been able to increase their rents by as much as a hundred and fifty per cent in recent years.'

'Where does he farm? Norfolk?'

'Where else? Not far from Coke's place at Holkham, and very much in the same style. In fact, if you can drag yourself away for a few days, why not come and bear me company?'

'Traitor!' murmured his sister under her breath, but the earl heard her. Enfolding her in a seraphic blue gaze, he said: 'But you must learn to become accustomed to separations if you will persist in marrying into the Navy!'

There was a slight quiver in the captain's voice as he said: 'I should like to come, thank you, provided you don't expect me to join you in the lion's den.'

'That, I think, would be unwise. I'd better see him alone. I don't propose, by the way, sending to ask if he *will* see me until we are actually in the neighbourhood. Informality, I feel, should be the keynote. It helps to disarm suspicion.' A brilliant idea occurred to him. 'In fact, I might even wear my *wamus*!' Lady Susan made a slight choking sound, but her brother went on as if he had not heard. 'We'll stay at The George at Fakenham.'

'What line will you take with him?'

'His answer would probably be a flat negative if I said truthfully why I wanted to see him, and an equally flat negative if I gave no reason at all. So I think I had better be a new recruit to the cause of agricultural improvement. That should at least help to get me through the door. After that, I shall just have to see how things go.'

'And you'd like me, I assume,' said the captain matter-of-factly, 'to stand by and pick up the pieces?'

'Certainly not. Your task is to have a large bowl of punch ready when I return to The George.'

'Oh, very well,' Captain Gregory agreed obligingly. 'Which d'you prefer, light rum or dark?'

✵ *Chapter Eight* ✵

More than a week passed before the earl's cavalcade rolled up to the doors of the rambling, half-timbered hostelry known as The George at Fakenham.

'Yes, Adam,' his lordship had conceded politely. 'I am aware that this continuing downpour appears to a seaman as no more than a slight mizzle, but my postboys have no ambition to be mariners and we would be forever stopping on the road in order to dry them out. Let's just wait until the weather clears, and then we can travel not only in comfort but at speed.'

He had been right, Adam admitted to himself as they bowled swiftly north and east to the coast of Norfolk, through the low-lying sodden countryside with its turned fields, straggling hedges, and half-bare trees whose leaves drooped disconsolate and yellow-grey, like drifts of smoke from a damp coal fire. The captain was accustomed to finding the air ashore oppressive, but it had never seemed as flat and enervating as now, tasting as if it had been used and used again, so that all the freshness had been sucked out of it. He shivered slightly and slid a glance at his companion, whose profile was intent under the rakish beaver as his hands controlled the powerful pair of bays harnessed to the curricle.

Somewhere on the road ahead of them was the earl's chaise, laden with servants and baggage, while behind them was Girvan, his lordship's head groom, with one underling and two hunters. Adam had surveyed the cortège preparing to set out from St

James's Square with disbelief. 'Do you always travel like this when you go out of town for a few days?'

'Why not?' had been the response. 'If I leave my valet at home *he* will have nothing to do and *I* will have too much, and we also need at least one groom. We can't all – you must see! – travel in a curricle. And as far as the chaise is concerned, if you can face with equanimity the prospect of two days cooped up in it with baggage, grooms, and valets – for, of course, you must bring your man, too – I cannot.'

'And the hunters?'

'In case we decide to come back by way of Leicestershire, of course,' replied the earl, mildly surprised.

Adam had raised a despairing eyebrow at Lady Susan, who smiled slightly and murmured in his ear: '*Not* his usual style. But I have no idea what he's up to.'

The earl had so far vouchsafed no explanation. Adam wondered if he were being taught a lesson. Until the revealing little episode of a few evenings before, he had thought he knew his lordship fairly well, but now, with nothing better to do than watch the dank, dispiriting landscape roll by, he began for the first time to consider their relationship and to realize that each of them still regarded the other as the young man of eight years ago – lightly armoured, perhaps, in a new carapace of command, and festooned with a great deal more gold braid, real or metaphorical, but basically the same, unchanged and unchanging.

Yet Adam knew how his own personality and character had been altered by eight years of harrying the French Channel ports and the coastline of Spain, of beating up the Baltic, sweating across the Atlantic, daily risking the wind and the sea and the guns of the enemy. What had the diplomatic equivalent, with its intense intellectual strains, done to Moriston? He had always had a precise and polished mind, excellent self-control, and a great deal of charm when he chose to exercise it. Also the heaven-sent gifts of wit and humour. But now, Adam suspected, he used the charm and the wit not only to mask the cleverness that all too often frightened people, but as an armour against involvement. However well endowed in most ways, Charles Dornay, Earl of Moriston, seemed to have chosen to draw some invisible, intangible curtain between himself and ordinary human weakness. Yet that spurt of anger over the diamonds, even if it had sprung only from injured vanity, made Adam think. Perhaps the detachment was not complete. Perhaps, somewhere under the cool exterior, there were fires deliberately banked down. Adam wondered how strong those fires might be, and whether it would be wise to have business elsewhere when they erupted. He sighed faintly.

'Bored, Adam?'

Jerked back from the unrewarding realms of speculation, he replied succinctly: 'No, cold. And comatose. I don't much care for the scenery, do you? Now, if you had been a truly considerate host, you would have arranged for the valets to travel in the curricle so that we might have gone in the chaise and whiled away the journey with a few games of chess.'

The earl was in a brittle mood. 'What, and let Sanderson tool these bays? You must be mad. Console yourself with the thought that he is even now supervising arrangements at The George and driving the landlord to distraction by rejecting every item on the menu as too coarse for my aristocratic taste. At least he ought to have more success at The George than he had last night at the Blue Boar,' he went on reflectively. 'I suppose the neck of mutton he forced out of the cook *was* better than the pig's cheek that was first suggested?'

Adam responded to the look of enquiry. 'Yes,' he said drily. 'And I suppose even the pig's cheek would have been preferable to the salt beef and dried beans you swallowed with such enthusiasm on the *Rosalinda* eight years ago. You used not to be so faddy about your victuals!'

'Ah, but I was younger then,' his lordship replied soulfully. 'Besides, salt beef and dried beans were a novelty.'

'After eating them twice a day every day for seven weeks?'

The earl laughed. 'It certainly taught me to lay in cabin stores the next time I went to sea! Well, we can now, thank God, abandon that singularly arid topic, for we are about to enter Fakenham.' He flourished an arm to the left. 'Observe that exquisite dung-heap! Does it not inspire you to poetry? And the hen-house! A veritable Acropolis of the countryside!'

'Necropolis, more like,' observed the captain, as a weedy youth in a crumpled apron emerged with the corpses of several chickens tucked under one insalubrious arm. The two gentlemen looked at each other with foreboding.

'A kitchen boy,' said the earl flatly. 'Adam! Are you thinking what I am thinking?'

Supper at The George, however, proved to be quite tolerable. Admittedly, it did include a dish of *poulets gras bardés*, which his lordship regarded with suspicion and then passed over in favour of an excellent game pie. Otherwise, Sanderson had acquitted himself very well. The gentlemen's rooms were well furnished and comfortable, warmed by seasoned log fires, and a comfortable private parlour had been bespoken.

Here, after supper, his lordship sat down to compose a note to the Marquis of Wayne. It did not take long, though its writing was accompanied by numerous animadversions on the quality of The George's paper and ink, and punctuated by much sharpening of pens. At last, he sat back and considered the result of his labours.

'Yes, that will do, I think. Neat but not gaudy. I am visiting the estates of noted exponents of the more advanced systems of agriculture . . .' He broke off and looked at Adam with a faint smile. 'Not entirely untrue, for I ought to call in and see Coke before we leave Norfolk.' His eyes dropped to the paper again. 'Most grateful to you . . . benefit of your advice . . . glimpse of your methods . . . The George until Thursday . . . then on to Holkham. Yes. It will do. Girvan can take it up to the Grange first thing in the morning.'

Both men passed a comfortable night, though the captain always had difficulty in adjusting himself to the quiet of the countryside. In London, the cries of the watch and the inarticulate murmur of a city not wholly asleep provided some substitute for the sounds on deck, the patter of feet as the watch was changed, the creak of timbers, and the flap of canvas. But the silence of a country village, he remarked bitterly to the earl as the latter drifted in to breakfast at the early hour of ten on the following morning, was enough to ruin any sensitive man's sleep.

'Indeed?' replied the earl, interestedly removing the covers from a succession of chafing-dishes. 'Have you breakfasted?'

'Hours ago! I've already been for a stroll. I must admit that it *is* agreeable to be able to walk a mile or two in a straight line, instead of being restricted to a few yards back and forth across the quarterdeck. Girvan has delivered your note to the Grange, by the way. I met him returning.'

'Did he bring a reply?'

'No.'

'Hmmm.'

'It's quite a place, you know,' the captain volunteered. 'I walked as far as the gates. A lodge like a medieval keep and a drive stretching away to infinity. I *think* I even saw a triumphal arch in the distance!'

'You would,' said the earl, unimpressed. He swallowed a mouthful of cold sirloin. 'Wayne doesn't suffer from delusions of insignificance. There's an obelisk, too, if I remember rightly.'

At this moment, the landlord entered with the coffee pot. 'Just what I needed!' said the captain enthusiastically, and the landlord smiled benevolently upon the pleasant naval gentleman. 'Would there be anything else, my lord?'

'Nothing else, thank you, but you might ask my groom to step in for a moment.'

Girvan, when he appeared, reported that he had handed the note to Lord Wayne's butler – 'a proper old Norfolk dumpling, me lord!' – and had then waited thirty minutes for the information that the marquis would communicate with Lord Moriston in due course.

'And that was all? Oh well, I suppose we must make the best of it,' his lordship said philosophically.

But Girvan was still hovering. 'There was something else, me lord.'

'Yes?'

'Not so long ago – about half an hour, I suppose – there was a fellow turned up in the yard here. Dressed like a valet of sorts. Very interested in your carriages and horses, me lord. He conjectured you must be making a long tour.'

'And what did you say?'

Girvan looked slightly offended. 'I said, "That's his lordship's business, isn't it?" of course, sir. That soon sent him to the rightabout.'

'Well done, Girvan. Thank you.'

When the groom had gone, his lordship turned to Adam. 'I trust that explains why we travelled with such a retinue?' There was a derisive twinkle in his eye.

Adam's smile was a little lopsided. 'You mean, anything less would have given away the fact that we are making a very short tour indeed? You're careful, Charles. I'll give you that!'

'Make no mistake about it – Wayne isn't a fool. I merely thought it wise to provide backing for my story.'

The 'valet of sorts' must have carried a satisfactory report back to the Grange, for at noon there arrived a reply from the Most Noble the Marquis of Wayne announcing that he would be prepared – not 'delighted' or 'honoured', just 'prepared' – to receive the earl at the estate office that afternoon, at the hour of four precisely.

✄

The earl was prompt, and at five minutes past four found himself seated on a rickety wooden chair in the small, graceless building that housed the offices of the Wayne estates. Most landowners merely set aside one room of the house for an office, but this casual attitude did not suit the men whose watchword was improvement and who regarded agriculture very much as if it were one of the new manufacturing industries. Wayne's office building comprised two rooms only, but they were divided from each other by a solid brick wall and double doors made of sheet iron.

Wayne had launched into his lecture almost before the earl had sat down. 'Good administration is the essence of efficiency,' he stated, his thick voice brooking no disagreement. 'And it must be safeguarded. Here, if a fire should break out in one room it is prevented from spreading to the other. All papers relating to men, stock, and land – agents, tenants, labourers, sheep, pigs, cattle, drains, fences, arable, woods – are kept here, classified and catalogued. One hundred and thirty-eight drawers of them.'

The earl glanced round. He could believe it. The room seemed to be filled with drawers, great massive banks of oak, with heavy bevels and sturdy, unbeautiful handles. They left little space for anything else except Wayne's solidly-built desk and chair and the gimcrack construction on which he himself was perched, and which he suspected was brought in only on the rare occasions when there were visitors present. Employees, no doubt, would be left to stand. The unplastered walls of the room, what could be seen of them, had been limewashed a long time ago, and hanging in the centre of the ceiling, a ring of smoke stains above it, was an oil lamp, which seemed to be the only artificial illumination the room possessed. It was a heavy grey day and had turned dark early, but the lamp was not yet lit. Through the single dirty window the earl could just see, in the distance, the tower of the village church huddling dispiritedly in a cluster of trees, with the cold, white-flecked sea as a backcloth.

He turned back to Wayne, a big man still, and powerful despite his age, with a blunt-featured face and harsh lines cut deep around an uncompromising mouth. There was a sour smell in the room, of dampness and unwashed linen and rancid breath.

Wayne gave no sign that he had met the earl before, or even heard of him. It was not unreasonable, thought his lordship, trying to be charitable, for he had been only twenty at the time and probably, in Wayne's eyes, no more than an insignificant young puppy. He had disliked Wayne then for his single-minded ruthlessness; dealing with him had been like dealing with a human battering ram. But he did not remember the almost tangible aura of intractability that surrounded him now, as if a temperament that had always been headstrong had become very nearly ungovernable.

The marquis's shoulders were hunched forward, his head set between them in a way that reminded the earl unpleasantly of a bull making up its mind to charge. But there was no red glare in his eyes – yet! thought his lordship pessimistically – as he went on: 'I'll begin with rotation systems. That's where the records are filed.' He flung out his heavy walking stick in the direction of a bank of drawers in the corner.

The earl braced himself. To let Wayne go on talking about farming for any length of time would, he thought, be a mistake. The longer he went on talking, the angrier he was going to be when the earl revealed that what *he* wanted was to talk about something else entirely.

He took a deep breath and raised his hand to stop the marquis, who broke off impatiently. 'Please. A moment,' he said. 'I do wish to see you very particularly, but not – and I apologize – about farming. Though I am sure it would be instructive to hear your views. What I very much want to talk to you about . . .' He hesitated. With any other man, he thought wryly, he would have led up to the subject with politeness and consideration, beginning with the story of a young woman anxious to find her father and proceeding tactfully to the point at issue. But that would be the civilized way of doing things, and though Wayne might be many things, some of them admirable, he was not civilized. The more time he was given to think, the less likely he would be to answer with the truth. The earl decided he was going to have to use shock tactics.

As he opened his mouth to try them, Wayne's face, with astonishing and visible suddenness, turned purple – a phenomenon the earl had heard of, but never before witnessed. He slammed one fist down on his desk so that the drawers rattled, and let out an ear-splitting bellow of 'Hogben!' The earl, startled, turned to see one of the iron doors open, and framed in the gap a square, stocky man of early middle-age, his muscles bulging through a coarse tweed coat. Scarcely moderating his voice, Wayne yelled: 'Throw him out!' He raised his hand and pointed at the earl. 'Throw him out! He's here under false pretences. Throw him out!' Hogben began to move forward.

The earl, after a moment of sheer frozen stupefaction, turned back to Wayne and looked straight into the congested eyes, their muddy whites cobwebbed with blood vessels. His own voice was under icy control as he said, very softly indeed, so that only Wayne could hear: 'I have a message from your daughter.'

Wayne returned his gaze, his finger still pointing accusingly, his breathing heavy, and his eyes narrowing to slits. The earl did not stir even when he felt Hogben at his elbow. Then suddenly Wayne's hand splayed out in a gesture of dismissal. 'Go away, Hogben,' he rapped. 'Go away, damn you. And shut the door.'

Both men remained perfectly still as Hogben withdrew. The door closed with no hint of a slam, and Wayne, his eyes still fixed on the earl, said: 'You're a liar. And a fool. Only a fool would think I'd submit to blackmail, and I take it you must be a blackmailer. So tell me more.' He achieved a sneer that was very creditable indeed, and added malevolently: 'Commit yourself. Go on! And *then* I'll have you thrown out.'

The earl could scarcely believe his ears. For anyone to accuse him – *him!* – of being a blackmailer! But his swift sense of the ridiculous came to his aid and he saw a vision of himself gobbling with rage like a character in one of Gillray's cartoons. Momentarily diverted, he also had a memory of his old nurse and one of her favourite adages. 'Losing your temper butters no parsnips, Master Charles!' Lord, how *had* he got himself involved in a situation like this?

Firmly smothering this ill-timed hilarity, he said: 'The situation would certainly have its attractions for a blackmailer, but I can assure you I am not one. I am here because Miss Caroline Malcolm, now that her mother is dead, would like to know something about her father.'

The eyes, cold and grey as the sea outside the window, did not flicker. 'Go on,' the thick voice said.

'Please understand. There was no real need for me to come to you. I could have dug into the past for details and proof. But it seemed superfluous, since all Miss Malcolm wanted to find out was who her father was. I doubt whether she even wishes him to acknowledge her – indeed, I am very nearly sure she does not, for she has no desire to provide food for gossip. Nor does she want money. She is very adequately provided and also has the diamonds you sent her, all twenty-one of them. That is something we *can* easily prove, you know, that it was you who sent them. "For Caroline, from her father". Since we know so much, would you not be prepared after all these years to tell us the rest?'

If Wayne felt the slightest response to this appeal, he showed nothing of it. Instead, his lips curling to reveal discoloured teeth, he said waspishly: 'What's *your* interest in this? Where's *your* profit?'

The earl sighed, aware that his distaste was showing. 'My only interest is in helping an innocent young woman who is being rendered extremely unhappy through no fault of her own.'

Wayne snorted, the wide nostrils flaring. 'Very fine talking! Those diamonds went under a frank. Who told you about them? That skinny little louse, Grant, I'll be bound!'

Though Erasmus Grant no longer cared what the marquis thought of him, the earl had reached the stage where he would be damned if he told Wayne one word more than he had to. So he shook his head, and waited.

Wayne slid his stick to the floor, lurched to his feet, and padded unevenly towards the door that led outside. Then, turning, he leaned against the jamb and said: 'Get out.'

The earl sat and looked at him for a moment, calculating, and then he too rose. From his pocket he produced one of Susan's copies of the Chinnery painting, unrolled it, and held it out.

'Caroline's mother,' he said. 'You remember her?'

Wayne looked at it, slantwise, for several long seconds, and his face, when he turned back, was again suffused with an unhealthy purple colour. For a moment he stared at the earl without speaking, and then burst out, his voice hoarse: 'Imbecile!' The breath whistled through his nostrils. 'You seriously think the girl is my daughter by that woman?'

'I believe it to be possible,' his lordship replied evenly, if not altogether truthfully.

'When was she born?'

'Just over two weeks before you sent the first diamond to her mother. February the twenty-second, 1794.'

'Then she was begotten in the early summer of 1793, wasn't she? Unless the birth was very much premature or delayed. Somewhere in May, shall we say?'

The earl nodded warily.

'Then listen, my pretty popinjay, my not-so-clever knight-at-arms!' Hell, thought the earl in annoyance. He was about to be put in his place. 'In February 1793, the Admiralty sent me to the Low Countries. Parliament was proposing to suspend the article in the Navigation Act that provided for crews of English vessels to be composed entirely of Englishmen. Misbegotten idea!

91

I was to find out what were the chances of recruiting in Holland. I was caught up in the French invasion two months later. That's when I got this.' He looked down at his leg, and his face was drawn and embittered.

The earl stood unmoving, with a very shrewd idea of what was coming. The marquis had called him a fool, and he had been right. He should have checked his facts. If he had known, he would have taken a different line, for, as it was, he had laid himself open to whatever insults Wayne cared to throw at him. Damn, damn, and damn. And it was small consolation that he had been right about the naval connection.

'The *Barfleur* took me off,' Wayne resumed, 'and I spent ten diabolic weeks on her being hacked about by that sheep-biter they called a surgeon before they were able to ship me home.' He looked up. 'You can ask Collingwood. No, he's dead now, isn't he? Elphinstone, then. Afterwards, it took Knighton another six weeks to get me on my feet again. You can ask him, too. He'll remember. I wasn't the most amiable patient.'

Triumph was plain on the big-featured face, exultation in the eyes and on the lips. 'So from February 1793 until the middle of August, you impudent puppy, I was in no condition to be bouncing around in anyone's bed but my own. If you want to find Miss precious Malcolm's father, you'll have to look elsewhere, won't you?' He savoured his victory, breathing as if after some great physical exertion, and then, as the earl remained silent, smiled and with a hideous parody of politeness said: 'And now – get out!'

The earl, conscious of dismal failure, had only one card left to play. It was a high one, but he had no great hopes of it. Wayne in his present mood, he thought, would in all probability tell him to go to the devil.

He studied the marquis coolly, trying to look as if he were sure of his facts. 'Not you, then,' he said. 'So I owe you an apology. But your son was not on the *Barfleur*, was he?'

He was quite unprepared for Wayne's reaction. The man's temper gave way completely. The blood, which had receded, flooded up into his face again, and a pulse began to beat in his temple like an exposed heart valve. His eyes dilated, and the earl could see their glare even in the dim grey twilight of the room. With a tearing gasp he whirled the cane above his head and brought it down in a fast, slashing, murderous arc. In the cramped little room, the earl was at a hopeless disadvantage. As he stepped sharply back, his arm up to shield his head, the chair behind him rocked and then crashed to the floor in a spray of rails and rods. He stumbled, off balance, and as the stick rose again, twisted sideways in an attempt to wrest it from Wayne's demented grasp. But, as he moved, one foot became tangled in the wreckage of the chair and the other came to rest on a rolling dowel.

It was as if the ground had been swept from under him. Quite unable to save himself, he keeled over backwards, his arms upflung, and his shoulders slammed into the corner of the desk. The reflex threw him forward again and to the side, where his head, with uncompromising violence, connected with the massive oak bevel of one of Wayne's hundred and thirty-eight agricultural records drawers. From there – irrevocably, insensibly, and not without grace – he slid quietly down to the cold, unwelcoming floor.

✠ *Chapter Nine* ✠

There was a pleasant, familiar voice speaking with unfamiliar urgency just above his head, and a hand shook him painfully and persistently by the shoulder. He was perfectly comfortable. Well, not comfortable, precisely, but aware that any change in his present position would almost certainly be a change for the worse. He did not wish – quite definitely not – to return to the world just yet. Muttering, he turned over.

The voice said, on a choke of laughter: 'I can't think where you pick up such language! Come along, Charles! Wake up, damn you!'

With extreme reluctance he opened his eyes a fraction and closed them again hastily as a blinding light stabbed through to his very brain.

'Wake up, Charles!' said the voice again.

'For God's sake, stop savaging my shoulder, Adam!' he said crossly. 'And if you want me to wake up, take those damned flambeaux away!'

'Headache?' the captain asked sympathetically, moving the candle so that it was screened by the bed-hangings. 'All right, I've moved it.'

The earl groaned and gingerly opened his eyes once more. It

was better this time. He blinked and focused. He was back in his room at The George, stripped, in bed, and by the feel of things intricately bandaged.

'What time is it?'

'Eight o'clock.'

The earl levered himself up on one elbow. '*Eight*? Have I been out cold for three hours?'

'So it seems,' the captain replied, eyeing him with amusement. 'What happened?'

His lordship groaned again as he achieved a sitting position, but was pleased to find that his head did not fall off. 'No. You first,' he said, as Adam helpfully plumped up the pillows. 'Though you can leave off being a ministering angel and supply me with something hot and wet before we embark on the post-mortem.'

'Delighted!' The captain produced a tray bearing a steaming bowl, with a napkin and spoon at the side. 'This is why I was trying to wake you. The sawbones said what you needed was some good sustaining broth.'

'Did he indeed?' said his lordship ungratefully. 'I'd rather have some of that punch you were supposed to have ready for my return.'

'When you thought I wasn't going to be needed to pick up the pieces? Have some sense, Charles. Not after such an ungodly crack on the head! Broth or nothing. Can you manage it yourself?'

Offended, the earl said he could, and while he applied himself to it the captain reported on what had happened during his temporary absence from the sentient world. By six o'clock Adam had begun to wonder what was delaying his lordship, and was just contemplating sallying forth in the direction of the Grange when a small procession of the marquis's servants had appeared, bearing the earl's inanimate form on a shutter.

The earl choked on a mouthful of soup. 'On a shutter!' he said, and raised his eyes to heaven. A searing pain flashed behind his eyeballs, and he made a mental note not to do it again. 'The indignity of it! That I should have lived to see the day!'

'Well, it wasn't you who *did* see it,' Adam pointed out. 'It was I, and a very nasty shock it was. They said you'd tripped over something in the estate office and knocked yourself out.'

'True, perfectly true,' said his lordship in tones of the deepest gloom.

'Was it? Well, I didn't believe them. You must admit it sounds improbable. However, I didn't take time to question them, since I thought it more important to find a doctor for you. Girvan and I got you to bed, and when the sawbones arrived he said you had no bones broken, only a cracked rib or two and a few contusions – and the knock on the head, of course. He slapped some cold poultices on and strapped up the ribs.' The captain's eyes gleamed. 'I told him what was supposed to have happened, and he kept muttering, "Dangerous place, that estate office. Obstacles! Lots of obstacles!" Anyway, he's left a draught for you to take tonight. Smells appalling.'

'Indeed?' said his lordship with a marked lack of interest, returning the empty bowl to the tray and settling back as comfortably as his bandages would allow. 'Well, you want to know what happened . . .'

'Not if you don't feel able for it,' Adam interrupted nobly. 'My curiosity will keep till the morning.'

'No, let me tell you, but we'll leave discussion for tomorrow. My brain is not up to it at the moment.'

Adam listened silently while the earl recounted, in detail, what had happened. It tired him, Adam could see, and he stopped from time to time, a faint shadow in his eyes. When he reached the end, he said: 'Without pausing for reflection, does anything immediately strike you about all that?'

Adam's lips puffed out on a long, thoughtful breath. 'Two things, I suppose. He was probably speaking the truth when he told you about those six months in 1793. He must have known the story could be checked, and guessed that you might very well check it. Unless, of course, he could be convincing enough for you not to go to the trouble?' He paused for a moment, chewing his lower lip. 'But more interesting – he had the dates right at his fingertips, didn't he? I don't know about you, but *I* would be very hard pressed to remember, week by week, how I spent my time in any given year, even if I did have a set point to start from. No, all that little exchange suggests to me is that – am I wrong? – he was actually *expecting* to have to supply an alibi.'

'That was my impression, too. That's why I asked you. The point is that unless Bridge or Erasmus Grant has been in touch with him – which seems unlikely – why *should* he expect it? The thought that came into my mind at the time was that something during those weeks, additional to his injury, might have happened to fix the sequence of events in his memory.'

'You mean that while he was laid up, things were happening

95

that he might have prevented – or influenced – if he had been on his feet?'

The earl stared at him, his eyes heavy. 'I hadn't got that far, but yes. That's precisely what I mean.' He had a mind-splitting headache, and every limb and muscle ached in tune with the beat of his heart. He wished Adam would go away, good fellow that he was. Dimly aware that he was being ungrateful, he said aloud: 'You're a good fellow, Adam.'

The captain rose athletically to his feet. 'But you'd rather I went away?' He smiled. 'I perfectly understand. I'll send Sanderson in to you, shall I? And don't refuse to take the doctor's potion. You'll feel much better,' he added bracingly, 'for a good night's rest.'

Next morning, the captain breakfasted early and, deciding he could not decently intrude on his lordship for another two hours at least, took himself off for a brisk walk. Returning damp but invigorated, he found the inn yard a bustle of activity. The earl's chaise was piled with baggage, Sanderson was pummelling the squab cushions, the postillions stood gentling four lively dappled greys, and the landlord came scurrying out with – of all things – hot bricks in his arms.

'What the hell!' exclaimed the captain, and strode indoors. There, at the foot of the stairs, fully dressed for travelling and in the process of smoothing on a pair of handsome kidskin gloves, he discovered his lordship.

'Good morning, Adam!' said the latter in pleased surprise. 'How very well timed. Are you ready to go? Your man has packed your things and they are already loaded. I'm afraid he isn't coming with us, but Sanderson can look after you on the journey.'

Fulminating, the captain looked at him. 'Better?' he enquired.

'Much,' his lordship replied sweetly.

Within ten minutes they were on the road, Sanderson riding on the outside of the chaise, the earl and the captain solicitously tucked up inside, 'as if,' swore the captain, throwing off a swaddling of rugs, 'we were silkworms or something!' The earl smiled abstractedly. 'Oh, come on, Charles! Don't be so damned irritating!' Adam complained. 'Where are we bound, and what's the hurry?'

'We're going back to London,' the earl said briefly, his eyes on the countryside.

Adam waited for a few moments and then, as the earl showed no signs of contributing further to the conversation, remarked with what he hoped was withering sarcasm: 'Thank you very much.'

The earl's set expression disintegrated into a smile of genuine amusement, and he said: 'Very well, have it your way! I suppose I can't make much more of a fool of myself than I've done already. We're in a hurry because I am concerned about Miss Malcolm's safety. No, don't look at me like that. I can't offer you any reasons. Put it down to instinct.'

The captain was taken aback. 'You think she's in danger? From whom – Wayne?'

'I know what's in your mind. The diamonds, and all that. It's not very convincing, is it? No, my uneasiness is entirely nebulous, and Wayne enters into it only because the fracas yesterday started me thinking. I invited trouble, you know. I could see that his temper was balanced on a knife-edge and tried to use it to force the truth out of him. I shall be more careful in future. But the man was in a blind rage, and perfectly capable of murder. Add to that Mrs Malcolm's presumed "accident", and the case takes on a smell of violence that I don't care for. I've been treating the whole search for Miss Malcolm's father much too lightly, and yesterday made me realize it. What we have on our hands could be something much more serious than just a pleasant little problem in deduction.'

Adam looked at him soberly. 'Susan said she thought you had allowed yourself to become involved because you believed her brain and John's were in need of exercise.'

'True enough.' The earl shook his head in disgust. 'And now I would much prefer them not to be involved.'

'You'll find yourself in difficulties,' Adam warned him, 'for they're both very much committed.'

The earl's shrug was a mistake, and he remained silent for several minutes while his muscles quietened down again.

Adam relapsed into thought. 'You seem to have been suspicious about Mrs Malcolm's death all along, of course.' The silence continued, broken only by the faint regular murmur of the chaise's excellent springs and the beat of the greys' hooves on the mud-caked surface of the road. Adam had been talking to himself, but the earl at last sighed and said: 'Not suspicious enough. When Matthew told us about it, he edited the story so as not to upset Susan and I didn't take the trouble to ask him for a fuller version afterwards. However, I've sent for him and he should be in London by the time we get back.'

'What do you expect him to come up with?'

'Hell, Adam! How should I know?' Restlessly, the earl turned to the window again. 'But there might be something, or some lead we could use. Otherwise, we'll be at a standstill!'

The captain, observing the slight, feverish flush on the earl's cheekbones and the blurring of indigo below his eyes, charitably decided to hold his peace, but before very long the earl turned to him and said: 'By the way, your man is travelling with Girvan in the curricle. They shouldn't be too many hours behind us.'

'And the hunters?'

'Following in the care of the second groom. And damn your impudence!'

'I can quite see,' said Adam, pained, 'why *we* are not travelling in the curricle, though if you felt your shoulders were not up to it, I would have been perfectly capable of handling the bays.' This optimistic remark having fallen on stony ground, he went on resignedly: 'But what I *am* curious about is why Girvan has been left behind at Fakenham?'

'He's wasting his time, probably. I have left him to fish in the carp pond of information – in a word, to gossip in the stables.'

The captain gave a crack of laughter. 'Poor Girvan! I shouldn't have thought that was his line at all!'

'It isn't. Sometimes I think he was created as Nature's answer to the Sphinx. But I have persuaded him that only he can find out something we need to know.'

'Which is?'

'Where Wayne was when Mrs Malcolm died. Not having bothered to check his whereabouts when Miss Malcolm was conceived, I don't propose to theorize about his part – if any – in her mother's death without first sorting out possibilities from probabilities.'

'You'll forgive me,' said the captain, suppressing a smile, 'if I point out that, had he been the father, his physical presence would have been essential at Miss Malcolm's conception. You can't be a father at second hand. But you *can* be a murderer.' He spread out his hands. 'He could have employed someone.'

'He could. But when I said he was capable of murder, I meant capable of it personally, in hot blood. Not necessarily in cold. However, we're not talking in terms of murder – yet – so let's forget about it for the time being.'

They tried. They talked of politics and politicians, of Europe's future now that Boney had abdicated, and of whether he would, so to speak, stay abdicated. They discussed Adam's ambitions and the earl's own plans. They compared the scenery through which they were passing unfavourably with that of Wiltshire, of Cornwall – Adam's home county – and the West Highlands of Scotland, where the earl owned several thousand acres. They argued over whether Adam should purchase his own estate now, or whether Susan and he should make their home with the earl until Adam retired from the sea. They discussed ships, and horses, and mutual acquaintances. The earl even produced a travelling chessboard and they played several games. But all diversions failed.

'Queen's bishop to knight's fifth,' said Adam. 'But what I don't understand is, why the diamonds? Why not money?'

'Knight to bishop's third. Money would have been too bulky. Or tactless? Too easy to send back?'

'Queen to bishop's third. No, it won't do. Surely diamonds would be just as insulting?'

'Prettier, though. Pawn to bishop's third.'

'Depends on your point of view. I like my prize money in cash. All right, then. Diamonds or money, why pay out at all?' His hand hovered over the board. 'Bishop to king's bishop's fourth.'

'Sense of responsibility on someone else's behalf, we decided. Someone close to him, like a son. Queen to king's second,' said his lordship. 'And check.'

'Damn. Bishop to king's second. Problem, find the "someone else" then!'

'And that,' remarked the earl mildly, considering his next move, 'is one of the most classic statements of the obvious I have heard for some time. We *know* that's the problem. How would you suggest we go about solving it?'

It was a question Adam was quite unable to answer. His defence, in the best tradition of the Service, was attack. 'It doesn't have to be a matter of family responsibility,' he responded briskly. 'Despite what Wayne himself said yesterday, I would still have thought blackmail was worth considering.'

'I don't suppose,' said his lordship, his dark brows lifting, 'that I have ever come across a less promising candidate for blackmail than Wayne. Not because he hasn't enough villainies in his past – and present – to keep a dozen blackmailers in clover for the rest of their lives, but because he is utterly impervious to what the world thinks of him. It wouldn't concern him in the least if his iniquities were the talk of every breakfast table in the country, and it certainly wouldn't occur to him to dip into his purse to prevent it. In fact, any aspiring blackmailer would find himself booted out of the door with a gargantuan flea in his ear and a few broken bones for good measure. Just take my own case . . .' concluded his lordship equably, moving his bishop to king's third.

Adam grinned. 'All right, so it wouldn't be worth blackmailing Wayne on his own account. But it was the element of secrecy about the whole thing that made me think of blackmail. What if we combine my blackmail theory with your responsibility theory? Would he pay out blackmail on our mysterious "someone else's" account?'

His lordship's eyes were on the board, and Adam hastily moved his queen's knight to queen's second. But the gentian gaze was unseeing. 'A weakling of a son, who couldn't stand a disgrace that would have left Wayne himself unmoved? But what kind of disgrace?' The earl was talking to himself. 'The child, presumably. But it's the unfortunate mother who reaps the whirlwind when a child is born out of wedlock, not the father. I shouldn't have thought Wayne would have given a brass farthing towards the upkeep of a child born on the wrong side of the blanket, far less a small fortune in diamonds. And neither of the sons seems to have been married, so there was no need for secrecy from that point of view.'

Amused, Adam said: 'You're determined to have poor Miss Malcolm born out of wedlock, aren't you? Why couldn't one of the sons have married her mama? Then she could have been the offspring of a legal union.'

'And what happened to the father?'

'Killed in an accident?'

'It's possible. But then we're back to the beginning again. If everything was legal and above board, why the secrecy?' The earl brought his attention back to the game. 'To hell with it. Let's forget Miss Malcolm. Castle,' he said decisively, and moved his queen's rook. Then he reached for the beautiful little pegged ivory king, lifted it, and stopped short with it still in his fingers. 'But if you substitute a weakling of a nephew for a weakling of a son, what do you have?'

'Sir Augustus?'

The earl leaned back, the unfortunate monarch swinging neglected between his thumb and forefinger. 'Let's see what we can do with it. Heading the cast is Wayne, the Most Noble the Marquis of. In his fifties, recently widowed – or do I mean widowered? – and father of two legitimate sons, both recently deceased. The closest surviving member of his family is Augustus Home, who is also his heir. Augustus is married to a tartar of a Frenchwoman, and they have a family of – where are we? 1793 – only one son, so far. Ludovic. You've met him, haven't you?' Adam nodded. 'But there's another child on the way. Louis.

'Augustus, out of sympathy with his wife, falls heavily for the gentle charms of young Jane Malcolm, who is just out of the schoolroom. Jane becomes pregnant. Augustus is paralysed at the thought of his wife finding out, and goes to his uncle and confesses all. Wayne is in a virulent mood, still recovering from his leg wound. But his sense of family responsibility, though stretched almost to breaking point, doesn't quite give way. He pours out the vials of his wrath on Augustus's bowed and balding head, says that he will relieve him of all responsibility for the child's future, but tells him never to darken his door again.'

'Balding?' enquired Adam, recognizing a flaw in this disquisition.

The earl looked at him. 'Oh, yes! I can see that you and Susan are going to get on very well! She, too, has a genius for fastening on the minor imperfections of an argument. He *looks* like the kind of man who would be bald by the age of thirty. As a matter of clinical fact,' he resumed, 'Augustus and his uncle have not been on speaking terms for twenty years.' Pausing, he considered for a moment and then decided there was nothing further to add. 'So there you are! No need for your mysterious blackmailer, and a perfectly logical sequence of events. How do you like it?'

'Not much,' said the captain, and was rewarded by an icy stare.

'Judas!' said his lordship amicably. 'No, neither do I. Odd, isn't it? There's nothing wrong with it except that the people don't fit. Augustus as Romeo, Mrs Malcolm as an immoral little hussy, and Wayne as a philanthropist who goes on dispensing diamonds even when, by anyone's standards, his responsibility for the child could be said to have ended with Mrs Malcolm's marriage to the colonel.'

'I don't think I ever realized before,' Adam said, 'what was meant by "a maze of speculation". What do we do now – think again?'

'No, I couldn't stand it. Let's get back to the game. Where were we?'

But it was impossible to leave the subject alone, and for most of the day Adam and the earl continued a desultory and wholly unproductive discussion of the mystery of Miss Malcolm's paternity.

They continued it for much of the evening, too, at The Duke of Cumberland, a hostelry in which the earl initially refused to set foot. 'What? Put up at an inn dedicated to Billy the Butcher? With *my* Highland ancestry? I wouldn't dare. Tearlath's ghost would come back and haunt me!'

'*Whose* ghost?'

'I am ashamed of you. Tearlath – Gaelic for Charles – and pronounced, roughly, Charlie. That's why my namesake, Prince Charles Edward, was known as Bonny Prince Charlie. You didn't think it was misplaced egalitarianism, did you?'

'I didn't know that,' said Adam, interested. 'Never mind, it was a long time ago. I'm sure his ghost has other things to think about by now. Let's go inside.'

But the earl hung back. 'The food will probably be terrible, too. Surely there's another inn?'

Sanderson assured him there was no other respectable house for several miles, and the captain, half amused and half mystified, was anxious for his supper. So the earl submitted and was bowed over the threshold by a beaming landlord who, whatever his other deficiencies, was perfectly able to recognize the Quality when he saw it.

It gave his lordship the greatest satisfaction to be able to pronounce the poached brill tasteless, the *timbale de macaroni* glutinous, and the ribs of beef tough and stringy. Adam, laughing, was just begging him for the tenth time to desist when a *salmis* of wild duck appeared which even the earl, with the best will in the world, found himself quite unable to criticize.

His lordship retired early, limbs and head aching after the long day of travel, and Adam, who had found the enforced physical idleness more wearying than a full day on the bridge, soon followed. But he slept badly, his dreams peopled with faceless figures dressed in the fashions of twenty years since, and woke in the morning unrefreshed and convinced that the 'someone else' in the Malcolm mystery could not be either of Wayne's sons, or his nephew, but had to be a person as yet unknown. He found it a depressing thought, and said as much to his lordship as soon as they were on the road again.

'None of them fits,' he complained. 'All we are doing is speculating – and on a basis of almost complete ignorance!'

The earl, his eyes clearer this morning and his movements easier, threw him a derisive smile. 'What, discouraged already?

You needn't be. We've come a long way considering what we started out with. And, you know, although we can't yet fit our discoveries into a satisfactory pattern related either to Wayne's sons or to his nephew, or, indeed, to any sons his sister Emily may have produced – for we haven't even considered *them* yet – it doesn't mean that there *is* no satisfactory pattern. Merely that we can't see one. Have you thought, for example, that the secrecy may have been for Mrs Malcolm's sake rather than for that of the man involved?'

Adam took a moment to react, and when he did, it was dismissively. 'Pooh!' he said. 'Do you think Wayne would make concessions to a mere slip of a girl? Especially one who was related to him only by mistake, so to speak.'

'He might. It would depend on the circumstances. He may very well have his own standards of justice.'

The captain thought about this and then said: 'One thing that occurred to me during the watches of the night. What if Wayne, as a young man, fathered an illegitimate son and it was he who was involved? If you simply substituted him for Sir Augustus in yesterday's tale, it would level out some of the inconsistencies. The secrecy could be connected with Wayne's relationship to the young man rather than the young man's relationship with Mrs Malcolm.'

'What an admirable pupil you are, Adam,' remarked his lordship in a tone that made Adam long to hit him. Then he grinned disarmingly and went on: 'The same thought struck me. It was talking about Wayne yesterday as "father of two legitimate sons, both recently deceased" that put it into my head.'

'Mine, too.'

'It's a notion that has its attractions. Would you favour introducing a blackmailer into that equation? And if so, who?'

'Well, you can't rule out the possibility. How about Mrs Malcolm?'

A trace of answering amusement touched his lordship's face. 'She certainly knew who the diamonds came from, and why. But does she really strike you as the kind of person who would not only bear a child to a married man but have the tenacity to go on hating and blackmailing someone like Wayne for twenty whole years?'

'No. But the mildest of people *are* sometimes capable of the most astonishing obduracy. They may hate rarely, but when they do, my God they do it thoroughly!'

'True, but I think the odds are against it in this case. However,

103

we'd better keep the hypothetical illegitimate son on our list of possibilities. If he were still alive, it would help to explain the secrecy that has been bothering us.'

When the chaise arrived back at St James's Square the evening was somewhat advanced. The earl was welcomed home with well-modulated surprise by his butler, and with Gallic imprecations below stairs by his chef, feverishly throwing together a supper that would not wholly disgrace him. The other members of the household had dined long since and departed to their various evening engagements, all except the admirable Francis Mervyn, who was discovered in his office relaxing with a glass of brandy and the latest volume of Mr Hansard's parliamentary reports. Lady Susan had gone to the Curson ball, he said, escorted by Matthew Somerville who had arrived at St James's Square on the previous day. John had gone out of town for a few days, but was expected back tomorrow.

'Out of town?' said the earl. 'Where?'

'Wiltshire.'

'Drat the boy!' said his loving brother. 'What is he up to?'

The Reverend Isaac Mervyn's fifth son became almost talkative. 'He told *me*,' he said sceptically, 'that he was going fishing.'

✕ *Chapter Ten* ✕

John was already on the way home from his fishing expedition, glumly conscious that, if he had caught anything, it was very small fry indeed, and quite unaware of the ripples he had left spreading behind him.

He had given long and serious thought to the problem of finding out what had happened in the Wayne family in the year 1793, and had begun to see why Charles was so strongly opposed to asking Augustus Home about it. It would, he realized, be almost impossible for the earl, however diplomatically, to extract the information he needed from Sir Augustus without starting bells ringing. But where his high-powered brother did not dare to tread, John thought that he himself, youthful and unconsidered, might rush in with at least some hope of success. Sensitive to the possibility that his lordship might not entirely agree with this viewpoint, he decided to act first and confess afterwards.

Louis had told him, with a wringing of hands that Mr Kean's Shylock would have envied, that he and Ludovic had both been summoned home for a week to celebrate their mama's birthday. It was an annual purgatory, he moaned, with the house full of old phiz-gigs exchanging reminiscences, his father in the devil's own temper, and he and Ludovic being talked to – and of! – as if they were still in short coats instead of adults who had much rather be in town playing pharaoh or boxing the charley or indulging in some other equally rational amusement.

'I may see you, then,' John had said promptly. 'I have to visit Atherton for a day or two soon.'

Scarcely had his brother left for Norfolk than John, too, was on his way as fast as his horse would carry him, undeterred by the prospect of so many hours in the saddle and hampered only by a cloakbag bearing a few overnight necessities. He made excellent time on the journey, and was greeted at its end with affectionate resignation by Mrs McColl, who had been house-keeper at Atherton since before he was born.

'Now, couldn't you have let me know you were coming, Master John? Here's me just finished putting the library under holland covers and taking the curtains in the small dining-room down for cleaning! Mr Matthew only left this morning and I thought I'd get a few things done while he was away.'

'Don't worry, Mrs Mac!' John replied buoyantly. 'I'll camp in the Red Saloon and eat in the breakfast parlour. As long as I've a bed to sleep in, I'm not worried. Matthew's gone, has he? He'll be in town before my brother, then.'

'He had a few calls to make on the way, so he expected to take three days on the journey. Now, you go upstairs and take off those wet clothes, and I'll see about getting you a nice hot supper.'

What was it Louis had said about being back in short coats again? John thought as he trod obediently up the stairs. But two hours later, warm, dry, and well fed, he came to the conclusion that perhaps there was something to be said for being coddled, and it was in a state of mild euphoria that he settled down in the Red Saloon to decide on his strategy for the morrow.

Mrs McColl, approached next morning, listened to his request with mild exasperation and said she would have to consult with Gaston, Monsieur Alexandre's young but promising apprentice who was left to practise on the staff while the family was in town. Gaston, it transpired, would be *enchanté* to produce a satisfying, sustaining, but nonetheless poetic repast for the young master and two other gentlemen on the following evening, and that hurdle having been surmounted, John sent a footman over to Priory Court with an invitation for Ludovic and Louis, carefully worded to imply that his only purpose was to help them to escape for at least one evening from playing whist with the old phiz-gigs. To his relief, the invitation was accepted.

Gaston surpassed himself, and the Russian fish soup, the *rond de veau à la royale*, the grouse pudding, the *gâteaux de feuilletage pralinés*, and the *brioche au fromage* had the effect of mellowing even Ludovic, who behaved quite like a sinful, civilized human being for once. It was in the most cheerful of spirits, therefore, that the three young men settled round the fire after dinner for what John, slightly overwrought, described as a comfortable cose – whereupon Ludovic cast him a quizzical glance, and John hurriedly gathered his wits together and embarked for the next hour on a conversation so much in character that it would have been suspicious in itself to anyone really well acquainted with him. Ludovic, fortunately, or unfortunately, was not, and his indulgent mood began slowly but surely to give way to a bored formality. Sensing this, John decided it was now or never.

Wielding the decanter with abandon, he dived into a long and complicated story of a wager with dear old Gil, who had been complaining of an elderly aunt of his. The old lady, Gil said, had a fund of scurrilous stories about her acquaintance which she told with the greatest gusto but without naming names. Time after time, Gil said, he was caught in the same trap. He would sit there with his eyes gleaming, drinking in details and trying to identify the parties involved, and just as he had come to the delighted conclusion that Mr A– and Lady B– were the ones, it would turn out that dear old auntie was talking about something that had happened a full fifty years ago. The thing was, Gil said, that she remembered so much detail you would think the whole affair was happening now. He and Gil, John said, had had a splendid evening trying to discover how fully they themselves could reconstruct the past, and they had done surprisingly well to begin with. It was when they got back to the age of ten that things began to fade, and by the age of eight they were in real difficulties. Gil had claimed that no one could remember details when they were that age, while John had said of course they could. The upshot was that Gil had bet John that he couldn't find anyone among their acquaintance with a month-by-month recollection of what had happened in his eighth year.

God! thought John suddenly. He must remember to have a word with Gil the moment he got back to town!

Louis let out a shout of laughter. 'Well, you're going to lose if you depend on me! I can't remember a thing, can you, Ludo?' Ludovic shook his head, smiling faintly.

'But you must, Louis!' John protested. 'We're the same age. If I started you off with what I remember about 1801, you ought to be able to go on from there!'

'Yes, but playing truant and climbing trees isn't quite what you mean, is it?'

'Of course not. In our house, though, it's memorable because it was the year Charlotte was married and went to live in Yorkshire. Praise be to God,' added the youngest of the Dornays, raising saintly eyes to heaven. 'It's events like that that start your memory working.'

'Oh! Yes, I see what you mean.'

Twenty minutes later they had exhausted Louis's recollections which were an unremarkable catalogue of measles, falls from horses, shooting lessons, departing governesses and arriving tutors. Even Louis soon recognized that his eighth year had gone unremembered because it was largely unmemorable.

Irrepressibly, he turned his attention to encouraging Ludovic, who did not trouble to hide the fact that he regarded the whole game as being rather childish.

'But you *must* remember,' Louis insisted. 'Dash it all. It was 1793, wasn't it? The year I was born. The year a charming little bundle of fun entered your lonely life!'

Ludovic eyed the charming little bundle of fun without enthusiasm. 'Yes, I do remember that. The entire household was in a state of immortal chaos for weeks.'

Louis chuckled. 'Admit that it wasn't all my fault, though!' He turned to John. 'It must have been like one of those primitive tribes, where they practise *couvade*.'

'Practise what?'

'*Couvade*. You know, when it's not the mother but the father who retires to bed when the baby's born.'

'I didn't know,' said John in a forbidding tone that made him sound remarkably like his brother.

Louis was apologetic. 'Heard about it from a fellow who'd been on one of those exploring voyages in the Pacific or some such place. Anyway, the thing was that mama was confined to her room for the better part of three months before, during, and after my advent, and papa was confined to *his* room for almost the same time. He'd caught a cold and it went to his chest, or something. Poor Ludo was left feeling like the orphan of the storm.'

Ludovic sniffed. 'Yes. I fear that parental loving care has never been a feature of our family, and that summer was a classic of its kind. For the whole of April, May and June, I don't think I saw our parents more than half a dozen times, and when they were both recovered they were in such an un-Christian temper that Nanny Sparks kept me as far away from them as possible.'

'That was the time Great-uncle Wayne got his wooden leg, too!'

'Didn't get his wooden leg, you mean. I have always held,' he went on in measured tones, 'that his famous evil temper might have been improved if he hadn't spent the last twenty years dragging a bit of painful, shrunken, useless flesh and bone around with him.'

'Is he as unpleasant as they say?' John asked.

Ludovic shrugged. 'I imagine so. I haven't seen him since I was a child, but he was crusty enough then, goodness knows!'

'Not seen him since you were a child?' John repeated ingenuously. 'I wish I could say the same for some of *my* uncles! How do you manage it?'

Ludovic's eyes were on the brandy glass twirling gently between his fingers, but his lips twitched expressively. 'Oh, he and my father quarrelled, I believe.'

'*That* was in 1793, too!' Louis exclaimed, much struck. 'We're doing quite well – we'll win your wager for you yet, John! And wasn't there some other great family upheaval about then, Ludo? Something to do with Uncle Edmund?'

'Uncle Edmund?' John asked encouragingly. 'Who's he?'

'Father's younger brother. He went to America years ago and hasn't been heard of since. *Was* the fuss about him, Ludo? I never did discover.'

'Nor I,' said his brother a little dampingly. He put his glass down. John groaned to himself. Ludovic was obviously back to normal again. 'And I doubt if John is interested in all this rattling of family skeletons.' A smile crept into the clear grey eyes. 'I fear Louis is wrong. You won't win any wagers if you depend on me, John. Come along, Louis, stir yourself. The moon is high and I think we should be off. Splendid dinner, John. You may tell Gaston, with my compliments, that if ever he should be looking for a situation I will be happy to employ him.'

As John turned back indoors after watching his guests ride off down the drive, he had the irritating sensation of having come close to something interesting but not quite close enough. He already knew of the long-standing quarrel between Sir Augustus and his uncle, so all the last half-hour had done was put a date to it – though it was an interesting date. He had not known about Wayne's leg, or Sir Augustus's illness. Or, indeed, of the exploits of Uncle Edmund. Did they fit into the mystery somewhere? If they did, he couldn't for the life of him see how.

He went to bed thinking about it, and worried away at the problem all next day and much of the day after as he rode back to town. It was only when he reached the village of Kensington, midway through the afternoon, that his mind began to concern itself less with that problem and more with the problem of how the earl was going to react to his youngest brother's solo enterprise.

✶

At much the same time, the earl and Captain Gregory were closeted with Matthew Somerville in the library at St James's Square. It was a comfortable room, whose two short walls were curved like shallow segments of a circle, one of them wholly lined with bookshelves and the other, on the garden side, pierced by three tall, slender windows. Set in the middle of the straight book-lined wall towards the front of the house were the great double doors that led to the dining-room, while the other accommodated a graceful Adam fireplace, a number of family portraits, and the small door that connected with Mr Francis Mervyn's office. It was the room where most family conferences took place, and where the earl, Lady Susan, and John naturally gravitated when they were at home, preferring its softly gleaming wood and supple, faded leather to the more elegant splendour of the parlour or the salons upstairs.

Today, three chairs were drawn up round the crackling log fire, and the candles, lit early to counteract the greyness of the skies, illumined three faces deep in concentration on the events of September 1813. Matthew had begun at the beginning, since Captain Gregory had not been present when he first told the story of the discovery of Mrs Malcolm's body. Dutifully, he repeated how Stoke, looking for the carrier from Wincanton, had found the bundle of cloth at the roadside that proved to be a body. He told how he himself had gone down to see it before sending for the magistrate.

109

'It only needed one look to see that she was really dead. I didn't touch the body, just walked round it, you understand. She had had a dreadful blow to the base of the skull, and it was pretty clear that was what had killed her. I think I mentioned before . . .' His voice drifted off into a characteristic silence.

'Matthew!' said his lordship firmly. 'You have been doing very well. Please don't start losing yourself in half-sentences unless you wish the captain to set you to the bilge pumps or lash you to the yardarm or something of the sort!'

The captain chuckled, but Matthew was sufficiently taken aback to sit up straight and collect his wandering wits. 'Yes. The blow to the head. A groom of my father's was killed by a very similar blow when a half-broken young horse reared and struck out at him. Anyway, poor Mrs Malcolm was lying there with her head at a horrible angle, her pelisse torn and muddied, her bonnet and reticule a few feet away, and her body all cramped together, sort of scrunched up, and quite, quite stiff.'

'Now, this is something new,' the earl interjected. 'You didn't mention last time that the body was stiff. And what precisely do you mean by "scrunched up"?'

'Well, I can't think of any other way of describing it. Though . . . do you remember, as a child . . .? Did you ever try to fold yourself up like a parcel so that you could fit yourself into the smallest possible space? Knees up to your chest, elbows tucked in, fists under your chin? Rather like that.'

'I can't say I ever recall having ambitions to be a parcel, but I see what you mean. How very interesting.' The earl looked at Adam, who looked back at him with a slight frown in his eyes. Matthew had a feeling that both had been struck by the same thought but that neither of them proposed to enlighten him on the subject. A touch petulantly, he said: 'Shall I go on?'

'Pray do.'

'I knew that I shouldn't touch the body, and I didn't in any important sense. But she must have been so beautiful, and she looked so tragic lying there. All broken, and stripped of – well, of dignity. Her mouth had fallen open a little. I don't know why it upset me so much, as if it were a final desecration, but I couldn't prevent myself from gently taking her by the chin and closing it again . . .'

'Did you have to force it?'

Matthew was shocked. 'Oh, no! The rest of her was stiff, but her face muscles were quite relaxed.'

'What time was this?' the captain asked.

'Time? I don't know. About nine o'clock, I suppose, or a little earlier.' Matthew looked enquiringly at the captain and then at the earl, but since there seemed to be no other questions forthcoming from either quarter he cleared his throat and went on.

'I went back to the house and sent Peter off for the magistrate, but he didn't return, and he didn't return, and by one o'clock I was wondering what on earth to do. It transpired the magistrate had ridden out early, so Peter waited a while and then left a message and came back home. It must have been about two when he arrived. I thought I'd better go down to the lodge, for Stoke would be sure to have his hackles up, and stopped on the way to arrange for Jeremy to relieve him in another half-hour. When I got to the pike road, there was Stoke, seated comfortably on the verge, guarding the body. When I say that my jaw dropped . . .' Matthew paused, his face a picture of remembered stupefaction. 'He had laid the body out as if it were one of those medieval tomb figures. Straight as a statue, with the hands crossed high on her chest. And draped, from the hands down, with a clean white sheet! He'd sent Jeremy up to the house to ask Mrs McColl for it!' He stopped again. 'I was annoyed, but touched, too, in an odd sort of way. I hadn't thought he could be so sensitive. He said he couldn't bear to see the poor lady lying there so cramped, so when the stiffness wore off he just eased her into a more natural position. Natural for a coffin on a catafalque!' he added hollowly.

'What in God's name did the magistrate say?' asked the captain, awed.

'Oh, him! He was so busy tut-tutting about everything else that his disapproval of that particular point got lost in the crowd! It was clear someone had moved the body, of course, but he didn't seem to be much concerned – except on principle, of course.'

'Stop there, I think, Matt,' said the earl, 'unless there was anything else about the body you haven't mentioned yet?'

Matthew considered carefully. 'No, I think that was all.'

'Medical evidence at the inquest?'

'Only the cause of death – a rearing horse – and a reference to the fact that it had probably occurred around dusk the night before.'

'But that was a product of deduction rather than a strictly medical opinion?'

'I think so, though I remember someone using the words "the

state of the body".'

The earl turned to Adam. 'It's a phenomenon you must have witnessed during the war?'

'Mmmm. Though I'm not an expert. To be frank, we tip our corpses over the side as soon as we can, so I don't have much opportunity for studying it.'

The earl smiled. 'Understandable. Very well, then, like Matthew you require instruction.' He turned to his cousin, who was looking singularly blank. 'What happens is this, Matt. Some hours after death – how long after depends on the mode of death, body temperature, the state of the weather, and a number of other factors – the human body becomes subject to a condition known as the *rigor*, or stiffening, of death. Beginning with the face and jaw, the corpse gradually stiffens up and remains stiff for a number of hours. How long this lasts depends, again, on external factors. Then the *rigor* begins to wear off in the same sequence as it came on. You follow me? Good. Now, one other thing. If a limb is bent before *rigor* sets in, it freezes in that position and cannot be moved, without breaking, until the rigidity has worn off.' He paused. 'Do you see what that means in connection with Mrs Malcolm's death?'

Matthew did not. 'You mean that this – er – *rigor* was wearing off between the time Stoke found the body and the time he laid it out?'

'That, of course, but a lot more.'

The captain said helpfully: 'The scrunched-up position?'

'Precisely. Think about it, Matthew. Mrs Malcolm couldn't have fallen back from a killing blow into the position you described, could she?'

'Oh, no!'

'So that position must have been shaped by something else.'

'Er – yes, I suppose so.'

The earl shook his head reprovingly. 'You're not concentrating, Matthew. But I'll tell you what your description of the body suggests to me. I think that Mrs Malcolm was killed by a blow to the head, whether from a horse's hoof or some other instrument. Not on the pike road, however. For after she was dead and before *rigor* set in, some person or persons unknown "folded her up like a parcel", hid her on the floor of a curricle or coach, and transported her under cover of darkness from where she was killed to the pike road near the south lodge. During the journey, her body stiffened up and she was tipped out on the verge, quite unavoidably, in that giveaway scrunched-up position.' He turned to the captain. 'Is that how you see it, Adam?'

The captain nodded sombrely. 'Would the magistrate have reached the same conclusion, do you think, if he'd seen the body before it was moved? Have Matthew and Stoke, between them, been guilty of perverting justice?'

'I don't know. But I have a strong feeling we ought to do something to rectify matters!' He turned to his cousin and smiled reassuringly. 'It's all right, Matthew. Don't look so pale – we'll protect you.'

Matthew's gaze was owlish, and he had just begun to stutter distractedly when the double doors from the dining-room opened and John marched in.

He was tidy, more or less. He had changed his boots, his neckcloth, and his coat. 'Hello, Adam!' he exclaimed airily. 'And Matthew! We must have passed on the road. May I join you?' He drew another chair forward, and Adam and Matthew obligingly moved over. 'Deuced damp and cold out,' he said, rubbing his hands busily and warming his coat-tails before the fire preparatory to sitting down. 'So! What's been happening while I've been away?'

During this somewhat selfconscious by-play, the earl had been surveying the cadet member of the family with ironic resignation, and when John's inconsequent burbling faded into silence, he allowed a few moments to elapse and then drawled: 'You sound a little feverish, dear boy. The fledgling investigator returning to the nest? Do enlighten us. What world-shaking discoveries have you made? We can scarcely wait. And for God's sake sit down or we'll all have a crick in the neck!'

John, glancing at Adam Gregory, surprised him smothering a grin, and sheer annoyance stiffened his spine. 'Very well,' he said, a trifle pink, and launched into an extremely full account of his doings over the previous few days, starting with his thought processes and leaving out nothing at all, not even the dining-room curtains.

'So there you are,' he concluded. 'I may not have found out anything to the purpose, but at least we have a hint of *some*thing that happened in the year in question.'

His brother, he found, was still gazing at him, an unreadable expression in the shadowed eyes. But John had exchanged a few words with his sister before he entered the library. As the silence lengthened, he added defiantly: 'And at least I contrived it without getting thumped on the head in the process!'

For a moment, he wondered whether the roof was about to

fall. He heard Matthew gasp nervously. Adam choked and closed his eyes. Inwardly quaking, John held his brother's gaze.

The earl was able to sustain his gravity for no more than thirty seconds, then he dissolved uncontrollably into laughter, in which he was joined by Adam and then, after an unbelieving pause, by Matthew and finally John himself. They laughed, all four, for what seemed a very long time, and just when the earl was beginning to recover he caught Adam's eye and was set off all over again. Eventually, his breathing still noticeably uneven, he said to John: 'Well, for pity's sake, if you are so determined to be helpful and enterprising, ring the bell for Brandon. I don't know about you others, but I am urgently in need of a reviver!'

When they were restored to sanity, the earl brought John up to date on what had happened in Norfolk and told him that it was now almost certain that Mrs Malcolm had been murdered – or, at the very least, that someone else had been involved in her death.

Adam turned to the earl and said: 'Well, at least John's discoveries have finally put paid to that charming little story we invented about Sir Augustus.'

'Yes. But how does the mysterious Uncle Edmund appeal to you – for it looks as if we are back to our old friend Someone Else again.'

'Which "someone else"?' John asked, confused. 'The one who was involved in Mrs Malcolm's death?'

The earl caught Adam's eye again and then removed his gaze, unfocussed. His hands were clasped under his chin and his forefingers steepled against his lips.

Adam took it upon himself to reply. 'We were speculating on the way home. Wayne was paying out, we knew, on behalf of someone for whom he felt responsible, but we couldn't decide why he was being so secretive. There was no need for secrecy, as far as we could see, if either of his two legitimate sons was involved. Blackmail seemed a possibility, and we thought he might be paying it on behalf of Sir Augustus, but if what the Home boys told you was true, then Augustus couldn't have fathered a child during the crucial period. The only other idea we had was that Wayne himself might have an illegitimate son, and that it was *this* son who had – or hadn't – married Miss Malcolm's mother, and on whose behalf Wayne was paying out. We fell into the habit of referring to him as Someone Else when we were talking round the subject.' He glanced at the earl.

114

'Is that a fair summary?'

The earl disregarded the question. 'What about this?' he said slowly. 'Put yourself in Wayne's shoes. You have an illegitimate son who had an association with Mrs Malcolm twenty-one years ago and became Caroline's father. The son is still alive, and for his sake, not your own, you maintain secrecy. Mrs Malcolm, who has been out of everyone's life for more than nineteen years, unexpectedly reappears, and her reappearance presents a threat to somebody or something. She dies suddenly, and violently. Question one – could she have been killed by this hypothetical son, the father of her child? And question two – if she was, would it be easier to find him in his role of murderer than in his role of father?'

❈ *Chapter Eleven* ❈

That same morning Miss Malcolm had received, by the hand of Mr Francis Mervyn, a communication from the earl which was as enigmatic as it was brief. She raised her eyes from it and surveyed Mr Mervyn in pained enquiry. 'Is this all?' she asked. 'No word-of-mouth postscript? No second sheet left off by mistake? No enclosure fallen by the wayside?'

Mr Mervyn shook his dark head politely.

'Then perhaps you are here in the role of interpreter?' Miss Malcolm pursued.

Mr Mervyn succeeded in looking blank.

Miss Malcolm, seated at her desk, her chin propped lightly between forefinger and thumb, continued to gaze at him. She longed to be five years old again and able to ask whether the cat had got his tongue. Instead, she remarked: 'As far as I am able to discover, his lordship wishes me to remain at home until he calls to see me – whenever that may be. From your acquaintance with your employer, would you take that to be merely a pious hope, or does it have the force of a command?'

Mr Mervyn found himself in a quandary. The earl's parting injunction had been: 'And do curb your tendency towards garrulity, Francis! No details. I simply want Miss Malcolm to stay safely indoors for as long as possible.'

He cleared his throat. 'A hope, I believe, ma'am, but – er –

possibly a forceful one.'

Miss Malcolm's eyes crinkled in amusement. 'Very diplomatic!' she said. 'You may tell him I shall obey insofar as I am able.'

His lordship was not entirely satisfied with this assurance when Francis relayed it to him, but circumstances were in his favour. Miss Malcolm was giving a small party that evening for several of the younger friends she had made in recent weeks, and for the rest of the day was wholly occupied with preparations for it. It was intended to be an entirely carefree occasion so, of the Dornays, only John had been honoured with an invitation. He found it when, after the session in the library, he took time to glance at the correspondence that had accumulated during his absence. With a whoop of glee he tore upstairs to change, and infuriated his brother and sister throughout dinner by addressing them with all the submissive respect he normally reserved for elderly valetudinarians.

But the evening was not to be one of unalloyed pleasure for him. As he walked through the door and glanced round to see who else was present, the first person who caught his eye was dear old Gil, deep in conversation with a back that was all too hideously familiar. Gil beamed at him and his companion turned, an expression on his face that was half smile, half frown. Taking a deep breath, John strolled over. 'Hello, Gil. You, too, Ludovic! I thought you were fixed in Wiltshire for another few days? Is Louis here as well?'

'Yes. He's over there, talking to Mrs Nicholas. We arrived back in town this afternoon.'

John was just casting vainly around in his mind for something to say when Gil broke in with: 'What's all this about a wager? Have you been taking my name in vain, dear boy?'

Damn! thought John, but succeeded in maintaining an air of unconcern. '*Your* name?' he said, his brows raised over candid blue eyes, and turned enquiringly to Ludovic. Then he allowed enlightenment to dawn. 'Oh!' he said, stretching the syllable out to several times its usual length. 'Did you think I meant *this* Gil? No, no. It was dear old Gil Sumner I was talking about.'

'Gil Sumner?' It was Louis, who had escaped Mrs Nicholas's clutches and moved over to join them.

'Yes, you know! Gloucestershire family, very old friends of ours. Our fathers made the Grand Tour together.'

'Oh,' said Louis, disappointed, and turned to his brother, his mouth turning down at the corners. 'And we had convinced ourselves that you were up to something sinister, hadn't we, Ludo?'

John gulped, and was just beginning to wonder whether he could salvage anything at all from what looked like a fully fledged disaster when he caught the gleam in Ludovic's eye and saw that Louis was trying very hard indeed not to laugh.

With a grimace at Louis he turned back to Gil and, nothing if not persevering, said: 'But I'm glad you mentioned it, for maybe *this* Gil can help me. It's like this, Gil. I have a wager . . .' Ludovic's eyes closed resignedly and he sighed, then, smiling politely and murmuring 'If you'll forgive me?' he drifted away in the direction of his hostess, closely pursued by his brother, who had no intention of letting Ludo have things all his own way where Miss Malcolm was concerned.

John looked after them. 'Whew!' he said quietly but forcefully to his bewildered friend. 'That was tricky. No, don't look at me like that, Gil, I haven't run mad. I'll tell you about it some day, but not now. Look, there's Mademoiselle de Rionne over there. Let's go and practise our French on the poor girl, she looks as if she could do with a good laugh.'

Later in the evening, in obedience to his brother's behest that he should keep his eyes and ears open for anything of interest, John wandered over to join the cheerful little group that surrounded Miss Malcolm. The Misses Mannering were there – unimpeachable, even if they did make a fellow nervous with their breathy little voices and clinging eyes. Miss Godmanly, plain as a nursery pudding and twice as wholesome. Inverwick, tall, sandy, impossibly thin, as pleasant with an income of sixty thousand pounds a year as if it were only ten thousand. Curly-haired Dan Lord; John looked around for the inseparable Paul Allott. And there he was, plump, dark, and nervous. That pair would have been splendid candidates for blackmail, thought John wistfully, if only their secret wasn't obvious to anyone with eyes in his head. Who else? Darius Thornton, of course – volatile, good-natured, as full of guile as a day-old puppy. And the Home brothers, who had known Miss Malcolm longer than anyone else there.

'How was Wiltshire?' she was asking Louis. 'Your mama enjoys her customary good health, I trust?'

He was shocked. 'Miss Malcolm,' he said earnestly, 'I beg you will never ask such a question in my mama's hearing! For you must know that only the sternest resolution keeps her on her feet. She suffers from at least three terminal illnesses, however nobly she contrives to disguise the fact!'

Since most of the assembled company was only too well

acquainted with Lady Home, this raised a general laugh, though Miss Malcolm's smile was a little uncertain. Ludovic frowned at his brother, but there was a betraying crease at one corner of his lips. 'Shockingly unfilial, isn't he, Miss Malcolm?' he said. 'But you must make allowances for him. He is trying to establish his credentials as the most outspoken member of our very outspoken family!'

'And talking of families,' said Inverwick, who liked Louis and thought his brother occasionally bore too hard on him, 'what news of Richard?'

'Yes!' Mr Thornton joined in. 'I thought he was supposed to be coming to town soon?'

'Tomorrow, and tomorrow, and tomorrow,' said Caroline with a smile. 'Or more probably the day after. In fact, I had hoped he would be here for my party tonight, but he was not going to be able to leave Oxford in time.' She felt, suddenly, that she was being watched, and turned rather sharply. There was no one in direct line behind her except the Honourable John Dornay, who was gazing innocently into his wineglass.

'Yes, I expect him on Monday,' she said, but her mind was not on her words. Inside, she was subduing a slightly hysterical giggle. John Dornay had been watching her all evening, off and on, and when he was not watching *her*, she had been watching him. It was ludicrous. She had made up her mind that sordid mysteries were not to intrude on her party, but it had taken considerable self-restraint not to corner him with a demand to know how the earl's investigation was progressing. She had heard nothing from his lordship – for that ridiculous note this morning could hardly have been said to count! – for almost two weeks, and the suspense was becoming insupportable. She might even have succumbed to temptation if John had shown the same anxiety as every other male guest to have a *tête-à-tête* with her. But the earl, knowing his brother's susceptibilities, had been quite explicit on that subject. 'No private conversation. However, you may tell her that I propose calling on her on Monday afternoon.'

'Thank you,' John had said, piqued. But he had obeyed, as he did not know how much his brother proposed telling Miss Malcolm and had no desire to be accused of blurting out something of which she was meant to be kept in ignorance. When he took his leave of her, therefore, thanking her for a most enjoyable evening, he added in a lower tone: 'My brother asks me to say that he will give himself the pleasure of calling on you on Monday afternoon, if that will be convenient?'

118

She replied with the utmost cordiality: 'How delightful! It would be useless, I imagine, to say that it will *not* be convenient?'

John's engaging grin spread over his face. 'Quite useless,' he assured her cheerfully, 'unless you wish to be left in suspense for another two weeks!'

Miss Malcolm was perfectly able to contend with his lordship – as long as he was at a safe distance. She smiled with untrustworthy sweetness. 'Then you may tell him that I await his coming as devoutly as a Believer before the gates of Paradise.'

It gave John some satisfaction to convey this message to the earl. 'Oh, yes?' said his lordship. 'Is she getting above herself, do you think?' But John refused to comment. In his opinion, Miss Malcolm had found her balance and might very well turn out to be what his old nanny had called 'a rare handful'.

When the earl, who had not seen Miss Malcolm since their provocative encounter at the ball, presented himself at Hill Street on Monday and found her perfectly in command of herself, he wondered with amiable cynicism how long it would last. But as their conversation progressed, touching, at first with butterfly lightness, on subjects that two weeks previously would have reduced her to a state of nervous distraction, he was amused to see that she was maintaining her poise. He was not to know what an effort it was costing her, and would in fact have been quite astonished to discover that it was his cool reserve, more than the mystery of her father, which was responsible for the state of paralysed apprehension which overcame her at the very sight of him. She was only too aware that, at their previous meetings, it had driven her to behave like a pettish schoolgirl. This time, she was determined to prove herself sensible, adult, and as much at ease as he.

He began by telling her that the elderly gentleman of whom they had talked at Lady Sefton's ball, although responsible for sending the diamonds, had proved not to be her father.

'Well, that's a blessing,' she said airily. 'I didn't like the sound of him at all. So who *is* my father?'

The earl's mouth opened slightly, and closed again. He took a breath. 'Not the old gentleman,' he said, with an internal quiver of laughter at the thought of Wayne as an 'old gentleman'.

'But it is just possible . . .' he hesitated elaborately '. . . that it may have been one of his sons.'

'Just possible?' Miss Malcolm echoed disparagingly. '*May* have been? No more than that?'

The earl looked at her. She *was* getting out of hand. 'You

119

will appreciate,' he said repressively, 'that it would be indiscreet to go around asking too many direct questions. I would like, therefore, to try a new line of enquiry. Your mother's visit to Wiltshire . . .' He saw her jaw muscles tighten but she gave no other sign of emotion as he went on, '. . . was never really explained, was it? Yet it seems more than likely that it could be relevant. Will you tell me all you know – just as it comes into your head?'

Miss Malcolm sat back in her chair and surveyed him pensively for several moments, her fingers twining and untwining in her lap. At last she said: 'As you wish. If I tell you strictly from my own point of view, there will be less likelihood of my missing anything out.'

'Please,' said his lordship. 'And I hope you won't object if I interrupt you occasionally with a question.'

'Very well.' She fixed her unseeing gaze on the fire and began. 'It was September of last year, as you know. Richard was soon to go up to Oxford and I had gone with him on a visit, partly to see the place – how is it described? a city of dreaming spires and screaming choirs? – and partly to be sure that he would have everything he needed when he was there. We had been in the city for a week when we heard of my mother's accident. The magistrate at Bishops Deverill had sent a message here to Hill Street, and one of the grooms brought it on to us. By then, of course, it was more than three days since it had happened, so we went direct from Oxford to Bishops Deverill.'

'Your mother is believed to have died on the Tuesday evening, and it was late on Wednesday before she was identified,' the earl interjected. 'So the message reached you – when?'

'Saturday midday. It had been sent off early on the Thursday and reached Hill Street on Friday afternoon.'

'Thank you. Please go on.'

She hesitated, collecting her thoughts again and remembering that drive through the unfamiliar English countryside, lush, mellow, beginning to turn faintly golden with the approach of autumn. The little market town of Swindon. Avebury, with its strange rings of standing stones. Peering back out of the window of the coach for a view of the White Horse cut out of the hillside turf at Cherhill in 1780 by the energetic Dr Alsop. The pretty little village of Erlestoke, every cottage decorated with a fragment of sculpture, Venus and Cupid peering coyly out from bowers of thatch and late roses. And then the Kingston valley and the chalk lands, the quivering willows, the clouds rolling white and gracious to the far, flat horizon. And Bishops Deverill with its grey, sleepy streets and the intricate ironwork of the old Ship Inn, with its embarrassed landlord, and the fussy magistrate, and her mother's maid greeting her in floods of tears. 'Oh, Miss! Oh, Miss! I blame myself. I should have stopped her.'

Reliving it, she knew that none of it was important in the present context, and was quite unaware of how much the earl, with heightened perception, had read in the delicate profile outlined against the fire, the almost imperceptible tightening of the lips, the shadow over the arched brows, the dropping of the long, unexpectedly dark lashes over the lustrous grey-green eyes.

At last, she drew a long, quiet breath. 'When we arrived at Bishops Deverill, we heard that my mother had arrived there at about noon on the day of her death, travelling post from London and accompanied by Abby, her maid. Much to Abby's concern, she then hired the landlord's gig, told Abby she did not require her, and drove off alone, saying that she would be back later in the afternoon.'

'Unconventional,' the earl remarked.

The grey-green eyes were raised quickly to his. 'Yes. And quite unlike mama. There was nothing unusual in her making a journey at short notice – one becomes accustomed to that in India – but to take only her maid! Not even a groom! She told Abby nothing about where they were going, or why, and apparently she was very quiet on the journey from London – not depressed, or out of temper, you understand. Simply not talkative.'

'Was that unusual?'

'I – yes, I would say so. I would have expected her to make casual conversation, at least.'

'When she drove off in the gig, which direction did she take?'

'Back along the road they had come – eastward. Abby first occupied herself with unpacking and hanging up clothes, and then spent the rest of the afternoon fretting. By early evening she was seriously worried but not quite sure what to do. If my mother had merely gone to visit friends and stayed longer than she had intended, she would not thank Abby for raising a stir. But if some accident had happened, the sooner Abby raised a stir the better.' She stopped, and then said abruptly: 'It was quite unlike my mother to be so inconsiderate.

'Anyway, when it was almost dusk, Abby insisted that the postboys should set out along the road to look for her. They found nothing before darkness fell. At first light, not only the postboys but the landlord and every available man began a serious, organized search which went on for several hours with no success. In the end, the landlord said there was nothing for it but to call in the magistrate. The local man was away, so a message had to be sent to Mr – yes, Hopkinson. When the message reached his house he had just gone out, in response, it later turned out, to the message from Atherton about the discovery of my mother's body.'

She took a few minutes to resume, her eyes once more fixed on the fire. 'Abby didn't know our direction in Oxford, so the magistrate sent to Hill Street, as I said, and our groom brought the message on. He, of course, didn't know what was in it, so while Rich was opening the note he took the opportunity to tell me what had happened in Hill Street. The house had been broken into the night before he left . . .'

The earl's head came up, and his eyes narrowed.

'. . . and although he thought not much had been stolen, everything was in a shocking mess, with drawers turned out and papers all over the place. The servants were not quite sure what they ought to do about tidying up. Should they wait, he asked, until either Madam or I returned? I must have looked at him quite blankly, for we had left my mother at home with – as far as I knew – no intention of leaving it. It was just then that Richard, having read the note, said rather brusquely that we would hear about that later, and dismissed him. Then he told me what was in the note.'

When the earl's calm, pleasant voice broke the silence, Miss Malcolm looked up with a start.

'This break-in. It occurred the night before the groom left Hill Street for Oxford. That would make it the Thursday, presumably?' She nodded. 'When you returned to London, did you find out anything more about what had happened? Was the intruder caught? What did he steal?'

'He wasn't caught. There were very few servants in the house as my mother had granted most of them two or three days free while she was away. Only the housekeeper and one maid were there, and the groom, who sleeps over the stables. No one heard anything, and the burglary was not discovered until the morning. It was difficult to discover what had been taken, because the contents of almost every drawer in the house had been turned out. Some money was gone – not a great deal, for mama never approved of keeping much in the house. She said it was an invitation to dishonesty. The burglar seems mainly to have taken small items of jewellery – nothing striking or especially valuable, but the kind of rings and bracelets and brooches that everyone has. Things that could be sold quite easily and unsuspiciously, I'm told, and very difficult to trace. If we thought about it at all, we thought he was unusually intelligent for a burglar.'

'What about papers?'

'Taken, you mean? Nothing, as far as I know, but it was almost impossible to tell. I've no idea what papers my mother had – other than the really important ones, I mean. And they were in such disorder there was no way of telling if anything had gone.'

Miss Malcolm suddenly returned to full awareness and sat up sharply, frowning at his lordship. 'Why are you so interested in the break-in? You don't think . . . Oh, no! Surely not the diamonds?'

His lordship had quite forgotten about the diamonds. Fortunately, his face was already set in lines of deep concentration, so he allowed a little time to elapse and then said: 'No, I think not.' What he did think was that Mrs Malcolm's papers had very probably included some that would have illuminated the problem of Caroline's paternity. Murder on Tuesday evening, break-in on Thursday. Just about the right lapse of time for someone busily engaged on covering his tracks.

Knowing what the answer would be, he said absently: 'I take it you went through your mother's papers and that they contained no clue to the mystery of your father?'

Miss Malcolm's delicate brows rose and her eyes widened. 'Gracious me!' she exclaimed. 'If only I had thought to look! Perhaps I need not, after all, have taken up so much of your valuable time!'

His lordship's intent expression dissolved into a smile as infectious as it was brilliant. It left Miss Malcolm, who had not hitherto been subjected to the full force of his charm, totally unnerved.

'My apologies,' he said. 'A digression from the main issue. Was anything else discovered in Wiltshire? What happened to the horse and gig?'

'The horse and gig?' she repeated weakly. 'Oh, the horse and gig. The horse was never found, but the gig turned up at an abandoned gipsy encampment near Wincanton, I believe. It was assumed that the gipsies had made off with them after my mother's accident.'

'Did anyone attempt to trace the gipsies?'

'I don't believe so.'

'Do you know the extent of the magistrate's investigations? Did he question many people?'

Miss Malcolm shrugged her slender shoulders. 'He talked to the tollkeepers round Atherton, and I think he had some enquiries made at houses in the area.'

'Hmmm,' said his lordship noncommittally. The magistrate had been looking for witnesses to an 'accident' near Atherton, whereas the real question was where had Mrs Malcolm been bound when she set off from Bishops Deverill in the landlord's horse and gig? Wherever it was, it was reasonable to assume that it was there that she had met her murderer or, at the very least, whoever was culpably involved in moving her body several miles from the scene of her death. And who had then ridden or driven up to town and broken into the house at Hill Street. Why, the earl wondered, *had* he broken in, when he could probably have stolen the keys from Mrs Malcolm's body and let himself in without trouble? The answer was obvious enough – a missing key would not only have linked the burglary with Mrs Malcolm's death, but would also have thrown suspicion on the circumstances of the death itself. The murderer, clearly, was not a fool.

Miss Malcolm, whose heartbeat had begun to return to normal, was looking puzzled. 'How does all this help you? I don't understand why you should be interested in such details. Surely if my mother's body was found near Atherton she must have been visiting someone close by? Assuming she *was* visiting someone, and not just proposing to ask for permission to see your gardens, which I understand are very fine.'

'Is that possible?' said his lordship, arrested. 'Or likely?'

'Quite likely, if she happened to be in the vicinity, though I don't think she would have made a special journey from London for the purpose. What I have never understood is why she should have been on foot when the accident took place. *Why* should she have descended from the gig?'

Hastily reminding himself that Miss Malcolm still believed her mother's death to have been an accident, the earl said: 'There could have been any number of reasons. The horse might have cast a shoe, or gone lame, for example. That was why I asked if it had ever been found.'

'Oh.' She did not sound convinced.

The earl, moderately certain that she had told him all she knew about the accident, decided to let the subject drop in case she should begin to ponder too deeply on it, which for her own peace of mind – and his – would be undesirable.

The fire had burned low and the grey afternoon was drawing in. There was no clock in the room, the earl noticed, nothing at all to break a silence that seemed to him not restful but oppressive. Four in the afternoon had always seemed to him to be the least congenial of all the twenty-four hours of the day, and he would have liked to throw an armful of logs on the fire and set a taper to every candle in the room. He sighed, soundlessly, but it was enough to bring Miss Malcolm back to the present.

She looked up and smiled, tentatively at first and then with more confidence, pleased with herself that she had succeeded in carrying out her resolve to remain composed, though it had been a close-run thing at times. So far, so good, she thought. But she also felt it necessary – for reasons she did not choose to analyse – that his lordship should be made to understand that this was the *real* Miss Malcolm. So she surprised him quite considerably by saying, in her liveliest manner: 'It's all right, you know. It really *is* all right now. There's no need for you to tiptoe round my feelings any more. My obsession, as you called it, made me most dreadfully miss-ish for a time, and quite unlike myself, but somehow, in the last two weeks – perhaps as a result of all those metaphorical douches of cold water you poured over me! – I have come to terms with it. I can, I assure you, look back on my mother's accident without making a melodrama of it, and wonder about my true father's identity as if it were not much more than an intriguing mystery in which I am only distantly involved.' She smiled again, and looked at him expectantly.

Like an enchanting kitten asking to be stroked, he thought. With very mixed feelings indeed he surveyed the vivid face opposite him, its planes, softly lit from below, showing the clear skin stretched over finely wrought bones that would preserve their beauty into old age. He swore quietly to himself, distrusting this vivacity though he sensed what was behind it and was not altogether indifferent. If the mood persisted, she might well decide she ought to play a more active role – just when he would much prefer her to remain in the wings, gracefully wringing her hands.

He conjured up a vision of how very difficult Miss Malcolm might be if she really set her mind to it. Why *should* she stay indoors? If she went out, why *should* she always be accompanied? Why *should* she keep those shapely lips closed if, by opening

125

them, she might induce someone to part with interesting information? Veiled hints would be useless, and he could not warn her openly that she might be in danger, for then he would have to reveal his suspicions about her mother's death – something he still hoped would never prove necessary. However sincerely she might believe she had recovered her equanimity, the first mention of murder would soon cure her of that misapprehension. The earl found himself at a standstill. What a problem she was, this pretty, piquant, wilful little client of his!

It had been a long silence, and Miss Malcolm broke it at last. 'You don't believe me!' she exclaimed. It was not quite Mrs Siddons, but not too far off, and she thought she detected a slight deepening at the corners of his long, firm mouth and a hairline engraving of amusement round his eyes. With a trace of relief, she rose to her feet and tugged the bell pull. 'If the inquisition is to continue, perhaps you would like some refreshment?'

Her servants were well trained, the earl noted. Almost at once, a footman entered to light the candles and replenish the fire, and he was soon followed by the butler and another footman, the first bearing a heavy salver with decanters and glasses, the second a silver tray laden with a teapot and hot-water jug, cream, sugar, wafer-thin slices of lemon, elegant porcelain cups and saucers, and a dish of almond-topped macaroon biscuits.

While the servants busied themselves about the room, Miss Malcolm remarked: 'I expect Richard to arrive from Oxford in the next hour or so – in time for you to meet him, I hope.'

'I look forward to it. Is his departure from university voluntary or – er – involuntary?'

'Both! Yes, pull out the quartetto tables, Winton, and one can go by his lordship's chair.' She turned back to the earl. 'Having decided that he wished to be sent down – only for a few weeks, you understand? – he took steps to arrange it. A very efficient young man, my brother!'

Sime having set the tea tray on a table by her side, she nodded dismissal. 'Indian habits,' she remarked, and was surprised and pleased when the earl said he, too, would prefer tea.

When the ritual of pouring had been completed, Miss Malcolm bit into a macaroon and said, her diction admirably unimpaired: 'What next?'

His lordship, having rather more to say, took care to swallow first. 'Let's leave the subject of your mother's accident for the moment. There's something else I want to ask you about, though it may seem quite irrelevant to you. I believe that if we could find out more about your mother at the time of her marriage to Colonel Malcolm, it might be helpful.'

'Yes?'

'It occurred to me that there might be someone among Colonel Malcolm's acquaintance who was present at the ceremony. What about the Duke, for example?'

Miss Malcolm considered. 'No, I am almost sure he and my father had not met before he arrived in India. Papa Malcolm, you see, was home on furlough in 1795 when he met and married my mother. His family lived somewhere on the Borders. He had been in the Indian Army since he was a boy and was to be transferred to the political service when he went back. It was much more interesting, he always said, because it meant that he wasn't restricted to waving a sword around but could dabble in diplomatic affairs *and* wave a sword around as well.' She smiled reminiscently. 'And that was just like him. He looked very serious and authoritative, and, I think, had quite considerable acumen – but underneath there was a tremendous sense of fun. Richard's very like him in some ways.'

'Not the Duke, then. Someone else, perhaps?'

She sipped her tea, her brow deeply grooved with thought. 'No one we knew in India – it was such a changing society, you see. People were always pulling up their roots and being sent somewhere else. If you were acquainted with someone for as much as five years, it was the equivalent of a lifetime. I'm trying to think of anyone who might have known my parents before they were married, but . . . The thing was that they were such a – I don't know – *complementary* couple! Quite unlike each other. My mother was calm and restful, whereas Papa Malcolm was full of life, boisterous sometimes, quiet and intense at others.' She gave a little chuckle. 'Even when he was quiet, he still seemed to vibrate! The point I am trying to make is that even people who may have known them before they were married always thought of them, not as Robert and Jane but as Robert-and-Jane – as if it were all one word, as if they were one, composite personality rather than two separate ones. Do you understand what I mean? Even people who may once have known them as individuals came to think of them as a joint entity!

'I remember only one thing that might help. My step-father did once mention his former commanding officer as having been a witness at the wedding. It was when he was talking about losing touch with people. This man – oh, dear! what *was* his name? – was also from the Borders and had been home on leave at the same time as my father. They both went back to India at much the same time, but Papa Malcolm was stationed in the Bengal Presidency, while the colonel and his regiment were sent to Bombay. It was early in the Maratha troubles. The colonel occasionally turned up in Calcutta, but it always seemed to be when papa was in Delhi, or one of the cis-Sutlej states. I think he did come and pay his respects to my mother once or twice, but I was too young at the time and I should hate to swear to it!'

'Have you any idea where the wedding took place?'

'None, I'm afraid.' She shook her head helplessly.

'Do you remember the regiment?'

'Oh, yes! It was the 28th N.I.' The earl's air was a little abstracted, so she added kindly: 'Native Infantry, you know?' His lordship had been contemplating the prospect of telling John that he was going to have to go back to the East India House to search the records again, but he had heard her and his thanks for this enlightenment were just a shade too smooth. Miss Malcolm giggled. 'Well, not everyone is as well informed as you appear to be!'

He ignored the provocation. 'What about friends in this country?'

'None. My step-father was in India for most of his adult life, and my mother, as I told you, never spoke of any family or friends here.'

'But I had the impression that the Homes, for example, were friends of long standing?'

'Gracious, no. We met them only last year, a few weeks after my mother died. In fact, when I say "we", I mean Rich. I don't recall the occasion, but I know Lord Caslon introduced him to Ludovic and Louis.'

'I see. I wonder . . .' he said, just as Miss Malcolm asked: 'More tea?'

He handed over his cup and just as she stretched out for the teapot she gave an exclamation. 'Of course! Teasdale – that was it! How silly of me to forget. Colonel Teasdale. Does that help?'

'Indeed it does. John will be most grateful to you.'

'John?'

'Didn't you know? Investigations at the East India House are strictly his department. Without the colonel's name he would have had to go to regimental records to discover who commanded the 28th N.I. in the middle of the 1790s. But now, a few questions to the clerks will probably be enough to elicit whether your colonel is alive or dead, here or in India. There can't be too many Teasdales in the India service.'

'But what do you propose to do when you find him?'

The earl's chivalrous instincts were temporarily in abeyance, his mind wholly occupied by the problem in hand. He replied in the long-suffering tone he might have used to his sister when she was being obtuse. 'Ask him,' he said, 'about the wedding!' Miss Malcolm was by no means accustomed to being spoken to in such a way. She was, in fact, quite prepared to be offended, but the door opened at that moment and instead she jumped to her feet with a pleased cry of, 'Rich, love! Don't tell me – you've been rusticated? You poor thing. You look quite crestfallen!'

He grinned down at her from his muscular six feet, and said cheerfully: 'Shocking, isn't it? I am completely unmanned with the shame of it.'

She laughed and drew him towards the fire to be introduced. What a contrast to his sister, the earl thought, amused. It was the bone structure that did it, of course. Caroline looked as if she had been finely moulded out of porcelain, while Richard had been hewn from marble. His physical development was remarkable for a boy not yet nineteen. The earl smiled into the frank hazel eyes, so nearly on a level with his own, and liked what he saw. The boy's face was serious, almost grave in repose, and this, in combination with his size, made him appear several years older than he was. If the earl had not observed the mischievous grin of a moment before, he would have taken Rich for a handsome, responsible, and possibly rather dull young man in his middle twenties.

When his favourite chair had been drawn forward and fresh tea brought, Caro beamed upon her brother once more and asked, in the tone of one who expected a routine reply: 'What kind of journey did you have?'

Richard's tranquil expression dislimned and reformed into one that would have done credit to a hanging judge. 'Really,' he said severely. 'I can't imagine what this country is coming to! In India, men set out on journeys measured in hundreds of miles, and many – it must be admitted – never reach their destination. They disappear by night, stealthily, in jungle clearings, in the ruins of mysterious temples, or in some dark defile among the secret hills. But I ask you, do they – *do* they? – find themselves held up by highwaymen in broad daylight on Ealing Common?' He took a punctuating gulp of tea and his eyes glazed slightly and began to turn pink around the edges.

Caroline stared at him. 'Highwaymen!' she exclaimed. '*Highwaymen?*' It was almost a shriek. 'I don't believe it! Richard, will you stop drinking tea in that provoking fashion and tell me what happened?'

Her brother was a picture of injured innocence. 'What are *you* provoked about? It's I who've scalded my throat. The tea's too dashed hot, that's what it is.'

'Richard Robert McGregor Malcolm! *Will you tell me what happened!*'

The earl was forcibly reminded of his own sister dealing with John, and found it difficult to repress a grin. All the same, highwaymen on the Common these days were rare enough. Interested, he waited to hear more.

'Oh, well, since you are so anxious to know! After all these weeks of being lectured in stuffy halls I wanted the freedom of horseback, so instead of travelling in the curricle I decided to ride. Benton was with me, and we set out late yesterday and passed the night at Maidenhead.'

'Really, Richard! Travelling on a Sunday!'

'Caro has scruples,' Richard explained to his lordship, 'and dashed inconvenient they can be!' He turned back to his sister. 'We had a perfectly good journey and I was feeling much refreshed. Even Benton had recovered from the gloom that always afflicts him when he's asked to do something he hadn't expected. Anyway, we reached the Common some time after noon. There's a place where the road passes close by a small clump of trees – I don't know if you know it, sir?'

'Just beyond where the Brentford Road crosses? Yes, I know the spot. People tend to avoid it because there was a spate of robberies there a few years ago.'

'Oh, was there? The road was certainly very empty. We were just coming level with the trees when I saw a horseman standing half hidden among them a little way ahead, and at almost the same moment he rode forward yelling "Stand and deliver" and let off a pistol in the air. I was quite taken aback, I can tell you! I'd no weapon, but I didn't have any intention of standing and delivering, either – not that I *had* much to deliver, for there were only a few guineas in my purse. So I shouted to Benton to ride for it, and as I did so the man raised his second pistol and pointed it straight at me. He was very close indeed, and I felt that to try throwing myself on him would be asking for disaster.' Richard paused, his face lit by that mischievous grin.

'There seemed to be only one alternative. You remember Chunder Row, Caro?'

A smile of reluctant comprehension dawned on his sister's face. 'Yes.'

'He would have been proud of me. As the man pulled the trigger, I simply slid out of the saddle and dropped right under the girth, hanging on like an upside-down crab. One thing I didn't know before – it's not a position for hilarity. I saw the fellow's face as I went down and dashed nearly fell off trying not to laugh!

'I was just emerging, right side up, and thinking that Benton and I could deal with him now he'd let off both pistols, when there was another shot from behind that nearly parted Benton's hair. Another man had appeared from the trees behind us and was riding up like the hammers. The first man shouted to him, "The other one, you fool!" – which made me stare, I can tell you! Fortunately, Benton was still riding level with me and we were still going at a great pace, so as the second man turned his pistol towards me and prepared to fire I kicked my stirrups free and, still holding on to my own reins, leapt sideways for Benton's horse. I landed on its rump and the ball zipped under my own horse's belly, just where I would have been if I'd tried the crab trick for a second time. Mind you,' he went on judiciously, 'I think it was luck, for you have to be pretty good to get in a shot like that from a galloping horse. However, I decided it wasn't a time for hanging about to discover whether there were any more villains concealed in the trees, so I told Benton to ride hell-for-leather – or as near as the beast could manage with two men on his back and another horse out of stride at his tail! We were all a little blown when we drew up after another couple of miles, but there was no sign of the highwaymen by then and we were beginning to get some very strange looks from other travellers. At any rate,' he wound up, unabashed, 'it was all very exciting, and no harm done.'

Caroline turned to the earl. 'Surely highwaymen don't make a practice of trying to *murder* their victims? Especially when they're unarmed?'

'It does seem curious. On the other hand, you can rob someone of a great deal more if he's wounded or dead than you can if he is conscious and vocal.' And 'curious', he thought, was a very mild word indeed for what had happened. But *why* Richard – who was not even distantly involved in the mystery of the diamonds? To Richard he said: 'You've certainly left a disconsolate pair of highwaymen behind. Where on earth did you learn your circus tricks?'

Richard was reproachful. 'Circus tricks?' he repeated. 'Cavalry skills at their finest, you mean!'

'Do I?'

'I was taught by a man who used to be a trooper in Skinner's Horse – the Yellow Boys. There's no one in India to equal them.'

The earl knew where he was now. 'Or anywhere else, if what I've heard of them is true. Colonel Skinner must be a remarkable man, mercenary or not. I'm told his irregulars have a skill in the saddle that's nothing short of breathtaking.'

'*And* you ought to see their marksmanship, even at full gallop,' Richard said eagerly. 'I was never as good at that as in the equitation exercises, though I pride myself on being a fair shot, but it's such a joy to be taught by someone who is a real master. At anything! Our head syce in India – head groom, you know? – was a Yellow Boy until he was wounded in the leg and came to us. He was tremendously enthusiastic, and there was nothing that made him happier than to pass on his skills – even to a five-year-old *chota sahib*. "Little sir", that means, though I admit I didn't stay little for very long. But it's surprising what weight a horse will carry. Proper rhythm seems to matter more than avoirdupois.'

'And I suppose,' his sister interrupted acidly, 'that Benton's horse found it perfectly rhythmical to have an extra two hundred pounds of humanity land unexpectedly on his back?'

'He sagged a little,' Richard conceded, 'but I think Benton was more surprised than the horse!'

His sister had found the whole story less than amusing. 'Well, *I* don't like it. It all sounds a great deal too deliberate to me!'

Richard looked at her in surprise. 'You can't think it was an ambush designed for me personally?'

'No? What about the first man shouting, "The other one, you fool" after his confederate had shot at Benton?'

Her brother pooh-poohed it. 'I've no doubt it was merely a reminder that I was the master and likely to have more valuables about me than my groom.'

The earl, deciding that it was time to intervene, smiled beneficently upon them both and said that he had an engagement which compelled him to leave almost immediately. 'But before I go, Miss Malcolm, may I see that portrait of your mother just once more? There's a detail in Susan's copy,' he explained, ruthlessly sacrificing his sister's artistic reputation, 'that isn't quite clear. Nothing important, but I should just like to make sure I have the image sharp in my mind.' Her thoughts were so much taken up with Richard's misadventures that she failed to recognize how unconvincing an excuse it was, and she rose without a murmur and left the room.

'Richard,' said his lordship swiftly, 'I have something to say and I want to say it while your sister is absent. It is this. She will, no doubt, tell you what I have found out – and not found out – about the diamonds and about her real father. She doesn't know everything, for the sake of her own peace of mind, but I can tell you that some of the things I have discovered have given me – let's say, cause for concern. There is a streak of violence in at least one of the people involved that quite frankly worries me. My brain tells me that your sister is in no danger, but my instincts are uneasy. Your arrival could scarcely have been better timed. Would you, as tactfully as possible, try to make sure that she is never alone, except in the safety of this house? And even here, make sure that everything is well locked up at night!'

Young Mr Malcolm was studying the earl in a serious, considering way – very much, the earl thought, as the late colonel might have done, if Caroline's description of him was accurate. 'Very well,' he said at last. 'If we were to meet soon, perhaps you might like to tell me more?'

'Agreed.' There was the faint whisper of approaching footsteps. 'But in the meantime, I repeat, don't allow your sister to go tempting fate. And don't, if you can avoid it, tempt it yourself, either.'

✖ *Chapter Twelve* ✖

One afternoon later in the week, Lady Susan strolled into the library at St James's Square still wearing her outdoor clothes, a cinnamon velvet pelisse jauntily frogged, an extremely dashing Cossack hat in rich brown fox fur, and a matching muff of luxuriant proportions. Casting the muff on a chair and beginning to draw off her gloves, she announced to her brother in tones of the greatest satisfaction: 'Well, I have found your Uncle Edmund for you!'

The earl, his mind on other things, did not immediately recall possessing an Uncle Edmund, and certainly not having mislaid him.

'I beg your pardon?' he said.

'For goodness' sake, Charles! Sir Augustus's long-lost brother. The mithing kith – missing kith, I mean! The vanished kin! The one who went to America.'

'Oh, him?'

'Yes, him! Do you or do you not want to know?'

'Of course I do. Sit down,' said his lordship invitingly, 'and tell me all about it.'

Slightly mollified, his sister sank into a chair. 'I thought it might be productive if I went to see Aunt Stapleton. You know what a memory she has for gossip, and I thought she might be able to tell us something about Wayne and his sons in the early '90s. But no luck there. She pointed out rather sharply that she had ceased going about much by then.' Lady Susan interrupted herself. 'Did you realize that she's ninety-three years old? I didn't. All she knew was that the elder of the two boys was in the army and was killed in about 1790, and that the other died in an accident two or three years later. There was something havey-cavey about it, she said, but it was all hushed up and she never did discover the truth. She said that in spite of Wayne's being so unlikeable, she pitied him. *There*'s Christian charity for you! Although he does appear to have suffered one shattering blow after another, all in a short space of time. First his sons were killed, then there was his own accident, and then his wife died. His heir, according to Aunt Stapleton, proved to be as dynamic as a limp rag, and then Uncle Edmund deserted the family without so much as a by-your-leave and ran away to America – which she still insists on referring to as "the Colonies"! She couldn't remember precisely when he went, though she was sure it was in the '90s some time, but surprisingly enough she did remember which of the States he settled in. It was Ohio, and she remembered because she had been reading Crèvecoeur's *Letters* not long before, and he had made Ohio sound like a gentleman farmer's paradise – "merely scratch the soil and Nature will do the rest while you pursue more genteel occupations – like hunting and fishing". You know the kind of thing!'

The earl smiled absently. 'Ohio. I wonder how long he stayed there. She didn't know anything else?'

'No, but with your American connections surely you ought to be able to find out.'

'It's possible. Anyway, thank you – you've been very helpful.'

'Don't mention it! How are your other little irons heating up?'

His gaze had been fixed on his hands, lying loosely clasped on the desk before him, but now he looked up. 'Slowly,' he said. 'Slowly. Adam should be here soon. He was going to the Admiralty today to try and confirm Wayne's version of his accident, and John is visiting Colonel Teasdale.'

'Colonel Malcolm's commanding officer? You traced him, then.'

'John did, through East India House records, and discovered he had retired from the Company's service and was now living in Kensington.'

'Oh, dear. How very provincial. A chicken nabob?'

'It certainly sounds as if he must have been behind the fair when it came to lining his pockets. However, we'll see. I was just trying to decide whether to send John up to Northumberland when he gets back, or off to Wiltshire to give Francis and Matthew a hand.'

'They should be there by now, of course. But I should have thought it would be a mistake to send John, too. I gather you don't want to raise a hubbub.'

'That's the problem. Three would make faster progress than two, but whereas Francis and Matthew can probably ask questions without arousing too much gossip, if the Honourable John were to become involved the entire county would soon be talking.'

Lady Susan chuckled. 'On the other hand, I'm sure John would much rather go to Wiltshire than to Northumberland, and I can't say I'd blame him. It's such a distance away that one wouldn't think it physically possible for anyone there to have had anything to do with what you are investigating.'

'No one resident there, certainly, but people have been known to leave home. Sister Emily, I have discovered, gave birth to no less than seven children. I am ignorant of the subsequent history of six of them, and John might be able to find out something if he were on the spot. The seventh, a son, moved south many years ago. Would you care to hazard a guess at where he settled?'

Susan looked at him.

'Not Wiltshire, no,' he said. 'But just over the border in Somerset. Interesting, isn't it?'

'Fascinating! But surely that makes it all the more desirable to send John down to join forces with Francis and Matthew. It might hurry things up, and I can't see that it greatly matters if people *do* talk.'

'Oh, but it does! For it might come to the ears of our villain, whereas I would much prefer that he remained in the dark about our enquiries for as long as possible.'

She regarded him speculatively for a moment and then asked: 'Why? What is so unusual about *this* particular villain? Why are you so uneasy about him – for you can't deny that you are!'

He unclasped his hands and laid them palm down on the desk, and then leaned back in his chair. 'I don't think you quite realize,' he said carefully, 'how far we've come from that innocuous little problem of the diamonds. We are as sure as it is possible to be that Mrs Malcolm's death was either murder or culpable homicide. Wayne attacked *me* with a venom that could easily have ended in murder. Richard Malcolm was held up on Ealing Common and would almost certainly have died if he had been less quick-witted or less agile.

'So – where does that take us? Mrs Malcolm's death looked like an accident. Wayne attacked me in the hottest of hot blood, when I had deliberately provoked him. Richard would have appeared to be the victim of a crime that isn't altogether unusual. All unrelated events, you might think. But I *don't* think so. Coincidence can be stretched too far, and it is my belief that there was one guiding brain behind all these "unrelated events", and one that is quite capable of instigating more lethal accidents if the need should arise.'

'But surely,' said Susan, who had been listening in growing consternation, 'even if there was a "guiding brain" behind Mrs Malcolm's and Richard's accidents, the attack on you cannot have been planned unless the guilty party was Wayne himself.'

'To begin with, I thought that too. But he was in a savage mood when I arrived and it's just possible he may have been worked up to it by someone who knew how to handle him. I certainly wouldn't be prepared to swear that either my visit or my questions came as a complete surprise to him. There's something else – all the signs indicate that our villain is a blood relation of Wayne who may have the same undoubted streak of violence. And when you have a man who is prone to violence, but clever enough and cool-headed enough to cover up its results in the way our villain does, then by my reckoning he is a very dangerous man. Which is why I'm uneasy about him. The violence makes him unpredictable. The cleverness protects him.'

A note of vexation came into the cool voice. 'What is so profoundly irritating, of course, is that if we knew more about the history of the Wayne family, the villain would probably be self-evident. But the fact of Wayne himself being so secretive, and of having outlived most of his contemporaries ... Well, it's tiresome, to say the least.'

'Never mind,' remarked his sister inadvisedly. 'Perhaps Adam or John will bring back something useful.' She was rewarded with a look that decided her it was time to go and remove her pelisse while her brother recovered his temper. As she rose to leave, however, the door opened to admit both Adam and John, who had met on the front steps.

Adam's eyes lit up at the sight of his betrothed. 'That's a very fetching rig!' he exclaimed appreciatively as he came forward and planted a kiss, with careful precision, in the space between her right eyebrow and the fur rampart of her rakishly tilted bonnet. But she shook her head at him satirically and said: 'This is no time for gallantry, Adam! Charles is sunk in gloom. Tell him something that will cheer him up, if you please!'

Adam surveyed the earl for a moment in silence and then shook his head. 'Not I. My research has been productive of nothing but the information that Wayne was telling the truth about what happened in Holland and on the *Barfleur* in 1793. He was completely incapacitated, just as he said. The Admiralty has a great deal of correspondence on the subject, for Wayne's injuries didn't affect his tongue or his ability to write the most astoundingly rude letters!'

'I knew it,' said his lordship balefully. 'So that rules Wayne out of the paternity business beyond a shadow of doubt. Not out of Mrs Malcolm's murder, though. I don't think I told you – Girvan discovered that Wayne wasn't in Norfolk in September of last year, although he couldn't find out any more than that. His servants were unable to remember where he was, and the groom who went with him was noticeably tight-lipped on the subject.'

'It must have been like a conversation between two clams,' John said with a grin.

Lady Susan cocked her elegant head. 'Perhaps I'm being obtuse, but if Wayne was involved in the murder he must have known Mrs Malcolm was dead. He must have known she was in England, too. So why trouble to send off the twenty-first diamond to India?'

Captain Gregory regarded her fondly, but her brother's gaze was reproving. 'Dates,' he said. 'As your affianced husband pointed out on another occasion! Mrs Malcolm died when?'

'September.'

'And the last diamond was despatched from London when?' Lady Susan's face fell. 'August,' she remembered.

'Precisely,' said her brother in his most irritating tone. He turned to John, who had been listening with a faintly sanctimonious smile, and asked with the utmost politeness: 'And how did you fare with Colonel Teasdale?'

John gulped. 'Er, oh!' he began, and then tried again. 'Yes. A nice old gentleman. He's been back in this country for four years but he still feels the cold dreadfully.' He caught his brother's eye and hurriedly gathered his wits together. 'I told him a yarn about there being a legacy and that we were trying to trace other members of Colonel Malcolm's family and thought they might have been at the wedding. Since he knew the Malcolms, I decided perhaps it would be better not to tell him the true story?' The earl nodded, and John resumed: 'He was at the wedding, but said neither the bride nor groom had any members of their family present. It was his impression that the bride had no surviving family. He described the bride . . .' John paused, hoping to tantalize '. . . as a beautiful young *widow* with a small child. It was in June 1795, by the way, and the happy couple sailed almost immediately for India. Colonel Teasdale had another two months' furlough before he followed, and after that he scarcely saw the Malcolms again. He was very sorry to hear they were both dead and asked to be remembered to the children.' John's voice tailed off. 'Well, at least it tells you that Miss Malcolm *was* born in wedlock,' he said defensively. He looked round at three discouraged faces and tried again. 'The wedding was in Glasgow . . . What *is* the matter with you all?'

'Have you finished?' his brother asked.

'Yes, I suppose so.'

'The colonel hadn't met Mrs Malcolm before the wedding, and scarcely saw her after it? There were no members of either family at the ceremony. Were there any outsiders other than the colonel himself?'

'An acquaintance of Mrs Malcolm's – the woman whose house she lived in. That was all.'

'In Glasgow?'

'Yes.'

'No name or address?'

'What – after one meeting and twenty years? No.'

The earl sighed. 'Not a great deal of help, I fear.'

'But at least we know Mrs Malcolm was a *widow*, so we can rule out all the problems of illegitimacy that were worrying you!'

Susan looked at him pityingly. 'John, dear,' she said. 'Hasn't it occurred to you that any young woman with a child but no husband would inevitably represent herself as a widow?'

It had not occurred to him.

The earl said: 'Nevertheless, it's suggestive. You remember I mentioned the possibility of a runaway marriage to Gretna? The fact that the wedding to Colonel Malcolm took place in Glasgow is interesting. Mrs Malcolm herself was English. Why should she have been alone with her child in Scotland?'

Adam joined in. 'You mean she fled across the Border to Scotland, where the laws are less stringent, to be married, and that she was widowed there and had a child – and then remained in Scotland instead of returning south as she would probably have done if her husband had lived?'

'Something like that. It's worth bearing in mind. But I hope Francis and Matthew,' concluded his lordship, scanning the faces of his indignant aides, 'will be able to come up with something more productive than you three!'

※

The weather in southern Wiltshire was clear and mild, and the sun shone palely in a vault of faded blue. The landscape was wide and open, patches of turned earth scarring the sallow gold and washed-out green of the fields, swathes of creamy white showing where sheep grazed far across the vale. The trees still held their leaves, amber and citrine, copper and dying brown that rustled, dry as tissue, and drifted down to earth in the wake of Francis Mervyn and Matthew Somerville as they rode at a leisurely pace out of the village of Bishops Deverill and along the toll road to the east.

'First of all,' the earl had said, 'I would like you to quarter the roads round Bishops Deverill in search of someone who may have seen Mrs Malcolm in the gig. The magistrate was concerned only with the accident, which he believed occurred at Atherton – so that was where he looked for witnesses. We, on the other hand, are fairly certain that whatever happened to her happened not at Atherton but within the general area of Bishops Deverill itself. I am assuming that her body was transported to Atherton so that it would be found some way away from where her death occurred, for the obvious reason that the murderer could not afford to have enquiries made in his own locality. Since Atherton lies to the north of Bishops Deverill, and since Mrs Malcolm set out on the road to the east, I would suggest you begin asking questions on that road and its side roads, and then work round to the south-east and the south. A ten-mile radius should be ample, and my feeling is that you will find traces within that east-to-south segment of the circle round Bishops Deverill.'

Francis and Matthew were armed with a copy of the Chinnery portrait, and had been primed on local topography by the ostler at the Ship Inn. 'But,' that worthy had added, 'tha won't find anyone to tell tha owt close by. Talk of t' neighbourhood, 'twere, when it happened, and 'tweren't no one came into t' town who diddun discuss it for weeks. We'd have 'urd if'n anyone had seen t' poor lady.'

'You saw *every*one within ten miles?' asked Francis, and the ostler hesitated. 'Most everyone,' he said.

'That's no good,' Matthew said with unaccustomed decisiveness when they left the inn, and Francis agreed. So they turned their horses' heads towards the east and clopped gently along the toll road. The task of questioning was initially left to Matthew, whose half-sentences seemed likely to be more productive than Francis's silences, and the answers he received at the first three houses he visited – built of fieldstone and quilted with thatch down to the eyebrows – were all positive. The womenfolk, wiping floury morning hands on their aprons, had all seen the pretty lady drive past in the Ship Inn's gig and had all wondered why the Quality should be travelling in such a vehicle, and unattended. But after that things became more difficult. Outside the village houses were fewer and side roads more frequent. It was Matthew's task to take the side tracks while Francis carried on along the main road, stopping at each house on the way and halting to wait for Matthew at the next junction. By this method they progressed quite unproductively for several miles, and each time Matthew seemed to take longer to catch up.

'Whew!' he exclaimed on one occasion. 'It was all of a mile up to the farm and nothing on the track except one gate after another. And nothing when I got there, either. I was pretty sure not, anyway. With all those gates, Mrs Malcolm would have taken a groom. Your turn next, Francis, my boy!'

Towards noon, having traversed an endless series of side roads, turn and turn about, they arrived at the first toll gate, bestriding the road in bleached and sagging authority, two of its crossbars sprung and its uprights worn away at the foot with years of dragging over the rutted surface. There was no one in sight.

'Gate!' shouted Matthew, but nothing stirred. He tried again. 'Gate, I say!' He exchanged glances with Francis. 'Deaf or asleep. Probably wouldn't pay any attention if the Prince Regent himself was standing here holloaing.' He let out another resounding bellow that caused Francis to grit his teeth, and at last the door in the centre of the gatehouse opened a fraction and an ancient face peered out. 'Well, come along!' said Matthew impatiently. 'We want a word with you!'

'Thruppence each,' said the ancient malevolently. 'An' it opens the next two gates.'

Matthew sighed and murmured to Francis: 'How often do you think the Trustees of the Wiltshire Toll Gates come round on inspection?' He jangled sixpence at the old man, who plodded out reluctantly and set the gate juddering on its hinges.

'Do you know the gig that belongs to the landlord at the Ship Inn?' Matthew asked.

'Where?' said the old man, allowing the gate to subside, half open.

'The Ship Inn at Bishops Deverill. Is there another?'

'"ow should I know? Ain't bin in t' village this last five year.'

'Would you recognize the gig?'

'Might,' admitted the old man grudgingly.

'See many pretty ladies driving alone round here?'

The gatekeeper looked at him, a gleam in his rheumy eye.

'Ever see this one?' Matthew pursued. 'Driving in the gig from the Ship Inn?' He held out the portrait, then hurriedly twitched it out of reach of the gatekeeper's dirt-ingrained fingers. The old man looked at it and then without a word turned and disappeared into the gatehouse, leaving Matthew staring after him in astonishment. Francis, more familiar with the habits of the taciturn, sat and waited patiently. Sure enough, the tollkeeper reappeared after a brief space, clumsily hooking a pair of battered spectacles around his ears. He curled a grubby finger at Matthew who, after a momentary failure of comprehension, once more held out the portrait of Mrs Malcolm.

'Arrrh!' said the old man. 'That wur 'ur.'

'When did you see her?'

'Must be going on a yurr, mebbe more. A'ernoon, it wurr. Diddun come back this way.'

'Did you see which way she went?'

'That way, o' course. Bain't no other,' he added morosely, as if he held it personally against the Trustees.

Francis spoke for the first time. 'Was she alone? No one else in the gig?'

The old man looked at him, arrested. 'Got a voice, 'ave yur?'

'Mind your tongue!' snapped Francis, as much to Matthew's surprise as that of the keeper. 'Just answer our questions sensibly and there will be something in it for you. There's no need to play the yokel with us – we know enough about the toll gate Trustees to know that you wouldn't hold your job for as much as a week if you were even half as slow-witted as you choose to appear!'

It had a salutary effect. In a matter of minutes the keeper had remembered it was last September when he had seen the lady because old man Wharton had been through that very morning with his lambs and he always took them to market in September. It must have been about two in the afternoon when she passed through the gate, for he always had a nap after his dinner and disremembered when he'd been woken from it, before or since, by a *lady's* voice. What had she been wearing? A cream-coloured coat – 'pelisse, d'ye call it?' – because he had thought it would get muddied in that old gig. And she hadn't known the charge and had to rummage in a pretty little purse she carried, smiling at him while she did so almost as if he were human. Not like most of the Quality, who treated you as if you were an unlettered clod instead of someone holding down a responsible job that required you to be wide awake, sober, and as good at your sums as that fellow Yuckuld. Incorruptible, too, he concluded, sliding the shilling Matthew gave him into the pocket of his greasy leather waistcoat.

'Yuckuld?' said Matthew, his eyes round, as the two young men passed through the gate and rode on.

'Euclid, I imagine,' and Francis relapsed into silence again.

Soon they reached a promising-looking side road leading north. Ahead, they could see two other side roads, one leading north and the other roughly south. 'What do you think?' asked Matthew.

'Now we know she was on this road,' Francis replied after consideration, 'I think we should go on to the next toll gate. If we find she passed through there, we needn't waste time on all these roads in between. If not, then we can work back here again.'

Matthew having agreed to this sensible suggestion, they rode straight on to the next gate, where the keeper was somewhat younger than the last but no less surly. Some more silver changed hands, but this time there was nothing forthcoming. The keeper knew all about the disappearance of the pretty lady last year and had discussed it with his cronies in the taproom of the Ship Inn. But the portrait elicited nothing other than appreciative admiration and confirmation of the fact that Mrs Malcolm had not passed through his gate. Matthew and Francis turned back the way they had come and spent what remained of the daylight hours vanishing in turn up side roads and farm tracks, bridle paths and sheepways – any trodden route that looked as if it might possibly give passage to a country horse and gig. They learned a great deal about the standards of farming in the district, the state of repair of barns and gates and hedges and ditches, heard an astonishing amount of gossip, and in the interest of courtesy downed considerable quantities of home-brewed ale.

At dusk, they gave up and rode back towards Bishops Deverill. 'I am awash,' Matthew groaned. 'Can you hear all that ale swilling about inside me? God help our livers if tomorrow is like today!'

The next day, however, was more profitable. They had already investigated all the farm access tracks off the main highway, leaving themselves with only two roads that ran ten miles across country to connect with another pike road to the south. By the time they had progressed a mile down the first of these, which cut across a wide expanse of rolling chalk land, it was clear that habitations were few enough for one man to deal with them alone. Matthew and Francis therefore agreed to separate, Matthew continuing along the first road, and Francis returning to the pike and taking the second. 'See you back at the inn, Matt,' said Francis as he departed.

Dusk was closing in when, within a few minutes of each other, two weary young men rode back into the yard of the Ship Inn. Francis, who had been travelling faster and was less accustomed to long hours in the saddle than his colleague, groaned as he dismounted. 'Not a word,' he said forbiddingly, 'until I have changed my clothes and quenched my thirst.'

'No home-brewed today?' Matthew asked, and was rewarded with a glare.

An hour later, slightly restored, Lord Moriston's hardworking assistants sat down to take stock. Matthew's day had been stale, flat, and unprofitable. His route had been roughly U-shaped – east from Bishops Deverill, south across country, then west along the pike road for seven or eight miles. He had found no witness who had seen Mrs Malcolm drive by in the gig. At the pike on the southern road he had thought to ask about other traffic on the day in question, and the keeper, somewhat to Matt's surprise, had remembered. This, it turned out, was because the original search for Mrs Malcolm had extended as far as there. It had been a quiet day, the man said, with nothing but local traffic. Mr Heath from the farm had been back and forward, and Joe Trigg from the inn. The carrier from Mere had passed, and a curricle from the big house, and the parson on his way to visit old Mrs Gaskin, and the sawbones to see Mrs Hodge whose rheumatics were turrible bad.

'And that was it,' Matthew concluded. 'There was no answer at one or two of the houses on the way out, but I saw them on the way back. So all I have to report is that Mrs Malcolm almost certainly didn't go that way.'

Francis Mervyn's saturnine face was thoughtful. His own route had been longer than Matt's. Reaching the southern end of the cross-country road, he had first turned west along the pike until he reached its junction with the road Matt had travelled, and had then, for reasons of his own, turned back to the first junction and continued along the pike road for several more miles to the east.

'I'm not sure your day *has* been wasted,' he said. 'On my road there were no side tracks for about six miles, but several houses close to the road itself. I found three people who had seen Mrs Malcolm.' Matthew brightened perceptibly. 'Yes, no doubt about it. They all recognized the portrait. Then suddenly,' Francis went on significantly, 'that was the end. I could find no other trace at all – on that road, *or* on the pike road though I rode five miles west of the junction and five miles east of it.'

Matt looked at him. 'Could she have gone off on a side track?'

'I checked all the tracks off the pike road. Nothing. And there was only one on the cross-country road, about half a mile south of the last house that had seen her pass. It was a crossroads of sorts, with a funny little signpost, so old that it was almost illegible. It must have rotted in the ground, I should think, because it was very short – as if someone had broken off the sound piece and hammered it back into the ground. I had to dismount and bend down before I could even attempt to read it. All the track did when I followed it was curve away for miles round the boundary wall of the big house further down the road.'

'Did you ask at the house?'

'No, only the lodge. I take it to be the big house your pike keeper mentioned – which was why I said I didn't think your day had necessarily been wasted. Do you know whose house it is?'

Matthew shrugged. He was a single-minded young man and not much given to speculation. 'Should I? I hadn't thought about it. I have been used to ride this way so seldom. I suppose it must be . . . Oh!' He stopped. 'You don't mean . . .' His voice trailed off again.

Francis picked up his glass and stared into it for a moment. Then he raised his slanting dark eyes to Matthew's face. 'I'll wager our employer knew, though! The name of the house is Priory Court, and its owner is Sir Augustus Home.'

There was an ominous silence. Then, with the extreme reverence of a conscientious churchgoer, 'My God!' said Matthew.

✹ *Chapter Thirteen* ✹

'I have to go to Atherton,' announced his lordship two days later in the brisk and businesslike tone that never failed to infuriate his family. 'As if he were presiding over a Cabinet meeting,' John had murmured on one occasion in a voice that, unluckily for him, had not been sufficiently *sotto voce*.

'And I should like it,' the earl continued benignly, 'if all of you were to accompany me.'

John, recognizing that his social arrangements were about to be disrupted yet again, was unwise enough to open his mouth, but before he could voice his objections, his brother went on: 'A small and select house party would be best, I feel. Adam, you will join us, won't you?' He did not wait for an answer. 'And we must have Miss Malcolm and her brother Richard. Who else?'

'The Marquis of Wayne?' her ladyship suggested dulcetly. 'Or don't you think the furniture could stand it?'

Captain Gregory, accustomed by now to the Dornays' style of conversation, joined in mildly. '*What* are you up to?'

The earl rose to his feet and made for the door, where he turned, his hand on the reeded gilt knob. 'Matthew and Francis have found something, I think – enough to make it necessary for me to be there. But I want to keep Miss Malcolm and

Richard under my eye, and since I can scarcely whisk them off to a house populated only by myself and the servants . . .

'I am going round to Hill Street now, where I hope to find Miss Malcolm and that foolish Nicholas woman out, and only Richard at home. I will leave for Wiltshire tomorrow, and I should like you, Adam, and you, John, to escort Susan and the two Malcolms on the journey as soon afterwards as may be contrived.'

'Don't forget you must invite Mrs Nicholas, too!' called his sister as the door began to close.

It opened again and his lordship's head reappeared. 'No!' he said with absolute finality, and vanished before his sister could say another word.

Lady Susan's gaze was thoughtful as it rested on the place where he had been, but John's was expressive of the blankest astonishment. 'What is the matter with him?' he exclaimed. 'He is behaving in the oddest way!'

'I think Miss Malcolm's problem is very much on his mind,' Adam intervened soothingly.

'Yes, but he's never been like this when he's investigated *other* people's problems, has he, Susan? He thrives on mystery. It usually puts him in the best of tempers.'

There was a faint gleam of amusement in her eyes as she turned to him. 'Very true,' she agreed. 'In fact, there's just no accounting for it, is there?'

Whatever arguments the earl used to Richard, or Richard to his sister, Miss Malcolm was perfectly docile when the Dornays' travelling carriage rolled up to Hill Street three days later, John on horseback beside it. Lady Susan had announced that she could not possibly leave London for at least another day, and Captain Gregory was to remain behind to accompany her. 'Charles will be furious!' John had said, the matter of his brother's uncharacteristic behaviour still teasing him, but his sister was scornful. 'Pooh!' she replied. 'As if Richard Malcolm and that dour maid of Caroline's were not chaperons enough for her for two nights!'

The journey passed pleasantly and without incident, but the day was cool and the sun low in the west when the carriage arrived at Atherton and rolled past the castellated lodge and up the sweeping drive to the Palladian east front of the house, flanked by a planting of ancient cedars and silhouetted against a sky that shaded from peach to palest saffron to aquamarine. The failing light gave Caroline no very clear idea of the exterior.

All that she was aware of was a long Classical façade with a graceful portico and a double flight of steps leading up to the stately front door under the pediment. Inside there was a blazing fire in the great hall, casting a warm glow on the veined marble floor and flickering on the family portraits that clothed the walls.

'Alarming, isn't it?' said John's voice in her ear. 'Two centuries of Dornays, and every last one of them as autocratic as Charles!'

Miss Malcolm gave a little choke of laughter and turned to smile at Mrs McColl, who led her to the fire and begged her to sit by it and warm her chilled hands. With an imperious finger, the housekeeper summoned a footman who had just appeared bearing a heavy tray. 'Hot beef tea,' she announced, distributing little two-handled silver cups to the new arrivals. 'Nothing like it on a cold day. No, Mr John, you may not have a glass of Madeira, not until you've drunk your beef tea.' John obeyed with a grimace, reminding himself to warn Richard that he was unlikely ever to meet a finer specimen of the velvet hand within the iron glove than Mrs McColl.

His lordship, Mr Somerville, and Mr Mervyn were all out, it appeared, riding up and down one road after another 'just like hens on a hot griddle' said the housekeeper disparagingly. The travellers, therefore, were firmly escorted upstairs to their bed-chambers to recover from the fatigue of the journey before it was time to change for dinner. Caroline, who was not in the least fatigued, was surprised to discover how swiftly the time passed. Her room was charming, decorated in white, gold and blue, and with a delightful painted ceiling that had been done many years ago, Mrs McColl told her, by a French gentleman called de Clermont. On the walls were a number of watercolour sketches of antique ruins, and there was a small library of folio volumes of travel and topography, including two on Wiltshire. Remembering Priory Court, whose few books were confined rigidly behind glass in what was known as 'the bookroom', Caroline warmed to Atherton. The watercolours were signed only with initials, but the flyleaves of some of the books were dated in the 1740s and '50s and bore the signature, in what she thought was the same hand, of one Peregrine Dornay.

'The third earl,' said his lordship some little time later as they entered the spacious chamber known as the small dining-room. 'My grandfather. That's him over there on the wall to the left of the fireplace – backed by the Parthenon, no less. He was a dedicated Philhellene. The house was built before his time, but he was responsible for commissioning the design of the gardens.

Fortunately, he had too much sense to try and reproduce the Greek landscape in the heart of Wiltshire, but he did allow himself one *jeu d'esprit*. You'll see it from the window of your bedchamber, a pretty little marble temple on the hill. Unfortunately, it's the only part of the main gardens that can be seen from the house – which I must say I regard as a serious failure of design.'

The talk at dinner was light and civilized and laced with wit. The earl controlled it, skilfully and unobtrusively, so that Caroline – one woman among five men – was scarcely aware of the disparity. The conversation moved easily from the house and its art treasures to the garden and the countryside, the eccentricities of other lands, and how the very fabric of a country could affect the people who lived there. The earl compared Europe with the Americas, and drew Caroline and Richard to talk of India, then smoothly brought the conversation back to the comforting gossip of London and the *haut ton*, balls and routs and drums and masquerades, so that dinner ended in a ripple of humour and scandal. Caroline, who had anticipated that the occasion might prove something of an ordeal, was interested to find, in retrospect, that she had seldom enjoyed an evening more.

No mention was made of the problem that now possessed the earl's mind to a far greater degree than Miss Malcolm's. His lordship, sharing the task with Francis and Matthew, had covered a great many miles in the past few days and had questioned, with infinite tact and delicacy, a great many people. There was just one section of the nearby countryside that remained to be dealt with, and he intended to ride over that tomorrow. But it would do no more than confirm something of which he was already convinced. He knew now, almost beyond doubt, who had killed Mrs Malcolm.

Who, but not why. And until he knew why, he could do nothing and say nothing for fear of setting the man on his guard.

After dinner, he carried Richard off to his study where he gave him the promised account of his discoveries. It was heavily edited but, he hoped, strongly enough stated to start the boy thinking both about his mother's death and the attack on himself. 'Will you sit down quietly somewhere,' he suggested at the end, 'and just concentrate? Everything suggests that it should have been Caroline who was in danger, but the attack was made on you. Perhaps if you devoted your mind seriously to it, you might be able to come up with a reason.' Richard promised, and went to

148

bed that night with every intention of remaining awake and thoughtful for as long as might be necessary. But he fell asleep within minutes.

Next morning, the earl and his two aides set out early, and when Richard and Caroline descended to the breakfast parlour they found John in sole possession – 'waiting to do the pretty,' he said, and show them all they wished to see of the house and grounds. In the morning, he escorted them round the house, through the State Apartments – 'shocking great draughty places; we never use them unless we have to' – the Picture Gallery, the Music Room, the Library, the various saloons, and the Gothic Hall. 'My mother had a fancy for the picturesque,' John said apologetically, 'so you'll find rather a lot of rib vaults and pointed arches around.' Caroline was impressed to find that he talked with perfect fluency about the architecture of the house, the paintings on the walls, the Chinese porcelain in the display cabinets, and the books in the library. And in the afternoon, he was as informed and informative about the gardens.

'Ride, or walk?' he asked. 'The path that runs round the lake is wide enough to take the gig, if you wish, but you'll have to get out to admire the grotto, which is our *pièce de résistance*.'

Caroline elected to walk, and they strolled in perfect amity round the lower reaches of the gardens for almost two hours, resting occasionally on one of the rustic benches, pausing to admire the turfed, urn-decked terrace where the family and their guests picnicked on sunny summer days, exclaiming over the subterranean silvers and greys of the grotto, with its presiding nymph, and coming at last to a halt at the late Lady Moriston's favourite conceit, a Gothic *cottage orné* where one could sit in perfect comfort even in the most inclement weather. It was a little rotunda, with flint walls and three slender lancet windows set in stone on either side of an arched doorway that would have done credit to a small cathedral. But the incongruity that gave it its main charm was the circular thatched roof, decoratively tied, and toothed around the eaves. 'For all the world like a Chinaman's Sunday-best hat!' exclaimed Caroline delightedly. Inside, it was surprisingly spacious, with a fancifully carved table at each side of the doorway, and a Gothic bench fixed all the way round the wall. 'We have cushions in the summer,' John said reassuringly, 'but they have to be taken indoors when the weather breaks. This place does tend to get damp . . .' For some time, he had been casting anxious glances at the sky, and had already vetoed a climb to the third earl's marble temple. Now he said: 'I think we should start back for the house. This kind of wind always brings rain and the clouds are building up. I should hate Miss Malcolm to catch an inflammation of the lungs on her first day here!'

Caroline agreed, readily enough, with visions of a roaring fire and a comforting tea tray. But Richard, who had found no opportunity for thought all day and was young enough to want not to have to report failure when he met the earl again that evening, was anxious to remain at the cottage for a little in the hope that solitude might bring inspiration. 'You go on,' he said, 'and I'll follow shortly. I don't mind getting wet.' As Caroline hesitated, he added mendaciously: 'I want to have a look at the roof of this place to see how different the thatching technique is from the one they use in India. Do you remember those village houses we looked at in Bengal?' Caro shrugged her shoulders despairingly. There was no accounting for brothers and the subjects they became excited about. John, too, was mildly surprised, but all he said was: 'There's a lamp there if you need one, but don't hold it too close to the thatch and set the place on fire, there's a good fellow!' Then, taking Miss Malcolm by the arm, he marched her firmly off in the direction of the house.

⚹

The man who lay concealed in the graceful marble folly on the hill watched the two figures as they walked away, the girl settling her shawl round her shoulders, and the tall, thin young man bending down to catch what she said against the rustle of the wind. Only when they had disappeared from view behind a sheltering bank of laurels did he move, quietly and cautiously, stretching muscles grown stiff from two hours of watching and waiting. Cat-like, he stretched again, flexing and relaxing – once, twice, three times – until he was satisfied that no knot of tension remained. Then, skirting the fragments of shaft and pediment that lay in artistic disarray around the little temple, he slipped silently into the trees and began a careful descent towards the lake, relying on the fluttering wind to cover the faint scuff of his feet among the fallen leaves. Once or twice he stopped, the breath arrested in his lungs, his skin grown chill as if invisible streamers of mist had wrapped themselves around him. But the sounds that halted him were only the natural whisperings of the countryside, and he moved on again, smooth, deliberate, absorbed.

Within five minutes, still breathing lightly and evenly, he

arrived at the *cottage orné*. The back of the cottage had only two narrow slits of windows, heavily leaded like those in front, and he flattened himself against the wall beside them and moved his head, with extreme slowness, until he was able to look inside. A smile of satisfaction flickered like a wintry shadow across his face, and he withdrew his head again, slowly and soundlessly as before. Though his glance into the cottage had shown him that there was no need for haste, he did not linger as he moved round to the front.

The door was closed. Beside it, on a hook let into the wall, there hung a key, massive, and black, and heavily chased. With the same circumspection as before, intensified, perhaps, because on this depended not only the success of his plan but his whole future life, he lifted the key from the hook and slid it into the lock. Slowly and gently he began to turn it, and smiled again to himself at the well-oiled ease with which the bar slid home. It must be pleasant to be the great Lord Moriston, with staff that attended to every minor detail of one's estate.

Then he stood back, flexing his shoulder muscles again and gazing at the door, a half-smile fixed on his lips. Three inches of timber in the door, and a lock of solid cast-iron, well sunk into the stone jamb. Impermeable walls. Windows no more than nine inches wide. And a thatched roof. He drew flint and tinder from his pocket and, coaxing a flame, set light to a spill of paper. Then, almost indolently, he strolled round the pretty little cottage, touching the blazing spill to the overhanging fringe of thatch, here and there as the fancy took him. At last, he stood away from the building, studying it carefully, until, with a nod, he withdrew into the shadow of the trees, prepared to wait again and watch, just as patiently as before.

※

Richard had been sitting lost in unproductive thought and quite unaware of his surroundings. But the first crackle of flame and the unmistakable whiff of burning brought him sharply out of his reverie and on to his feet. He could see the fire already, licking along the junction between wall and roof, growing and spreading hungrily even as he watched. With puzzlement and a first dawning of alarm he strode to the door. Men and buckets would be needed, but at least there was water close at hand. He turned the handle. And turned it again. It was stuck, God damn it. Gripping it with both hands he pulled, and pulled, and then paused and gave it a mighty heave instead. Nothing happened. He felt a long, icy ripple run down his spine and through his limbs, spending itself in a momentary paralysis of movement that he knew he could not afford. He turned and looked at the flames, a foot high now and beginning to gulp around the exposed roof beams. He tugged on the handle again, in vain.

The windows were impossible, far too narrow for his powerful frame. He peered out. It had been a grey day and dusk was coming early. There was no one in sight. He might break the windows and shout through the aperture. He already had the lamp in his hand, ready to hurl it through the glass, when he stopped. Anyone close enough to hear his cries for help would already have seen the flames, and to admit a rush of air into that enclosed space would do no more than feed the fire. With a hollow feeling in his stomach, he remembered that the gardens lay in a fold of the landscape and could not be seen from the house. Only the temple on the hill – and that only from the upper floors. To wait for help might be the same as to wait for death. If he were to survive, he must find his own way out. Gently, he put the lamp back on the table.

He was beginning to gasp from the heat and the smoke of the reed thatch, green and moist inside where the wind had not dried it. He had to think, and think quickly. Sinking to the floor, where the heat and smoke were less intense, he tried to concentrate. The door opened inwards, and the jambs were of stone. He would only be squandering his strength if he tried to kick the lock or hinges free, and the door itself was inches thick. Could he set light to it and burn it down before the thatch and timbers collapsed? He laughed, retching slightly. What the devil was the name his schoolmaster had given to the kind of question that carried its own built-in answer? Anyway, the answer in this case was no. Steadying himself, he looked at the Gothic bench. Could he climb on it and batter a hole through the roof – there, where it joined the wall and the thatch had already begun to burn itself away? More promising. He stepped up on to the bench, recoiling from the flame that flicked out at him like a lizard's tongue, and peered with eyes grilled by the heat at the base of the timbers. He soon saw that it was hopeless. The beams were braced with L-shaped supports and crossbars, and bedded in mortar. It looked as if the only part of the roof he could reach was the one part that would stand out forever against the flames.

His breath was coming fast and uneven now, and he knew that time was slipping away. Shreds of burning thatch were fluttering down around him. He took off his coat and, draping it over his head and shoulders for protection, looked round for some weapon, some tool he could use. The elegant little tables splintered like matchwood when he attacked the door with them, and the Gothic bench resisted all his efforts to tear it from the wall. There was nothing else, nothing at all. He collapsed once more on the stone-flagged floor, grimly holding back the panic that threatened him. That damnable door. He struggled to it on hands and knees and tried it again, and again. Maddeningly, the handle was still cool and soothing to the touch.

He peered at it. Why – *why* should it have jammed? And then he had the answer. In the hairline shrinkage gap between door and jamb, outlined against the flames reflected in the waters of the lake, he could just see the narrow, solid bar of the tongue bolt, shot home. Unbelievingly, he stared at it. *Locked in?* Locked in, and left to roast? He made a little sound that might have been stupefaction, recognition, or acceptance, or something of all three, and then shook his head to clear it. The roof above him crackled and roared with a mad, mind-wrecking dissonance.

Afterwards, he recognized that this had been the turning-point, the moment when despair was transmuted into a furious and reviving rage. With his lips clamped together and his jaw tensed, he put his entire mind to his predicament. The roof, the walls, the furniture had failed him. There only remained the floor. He looked at it through streaming eyes and saw, for the first time, that four of the flagstones in the centre, snugly though they fitted, were not, like the others, mortared into position. Was there – could there be – a cellar? Or even just a storage chamber for garden tools that might give him some purchase on the door? He ran shaking fingers round the joins, feeling for some handhold or grip, but found nothing. Then he discovered that the stones slid readily, as if they rested on runners. With growing excitement he pushed one slab until it butted against its neighbour. When he did the same with another, he found he had made a gap just large enough to give him purchase. With a breathless, silent prayer he gripped the edge of one of the slabs and lifted it clear.

He could not believe his eyes. There was no cellar, no storage chamber underneath, but a sheet of clear, tough glass – a window on a submarine world of pale, bleached fronds and dark water and scurrying fish surprised by the light. With burning thatch and fragments of flaming timber raining around him, he simply sat on his heels and stared. The glass was removable, too, he thought. Of course. It would have to be cleaned sometimes.

With a conscious effort of will he forced himself into activity again. He removed the three remaining flagstones, then, scrabbling with urgent fingers, found the bedding of the glass and prised it free. There was the faintest tinge of hysteria in his laugh as he thought of all the fashionable ladies who must have sat on the now smouldering Gothic bench – with cushions! – marvelling at the fish that swam lazily to and fro in the narrow ornamental pond at their feet. 'What a delightful idea, Lady Moriston!' he murmured giddily as he leaned down through the opening to trail his fingers in the cool, heavenly water. He tasted it, and it was fresh.

Gazing into the cavity he could see two opposing banks of the pond. But where the other two should have been there was only impenetrable darkness. Any sound of splash or flow was drowned by the deafening roar of the roof. The crackling was explosive now, and a burning shard dropped in the water beside him, sizzling. He looked up. Through the smoke and the glare and the wavering currents of heat he became aware that the whole roof was swelling, and moving, and shifting.

Taking a deep breath he threw off his protecting coat, freed himself of his waistcoat, and wrenched his cravat from his neck. Then, in the last searing moment before thatch, spars, sways, timbers and ties crashed in a seething inferno to the floor of the cottage, sending a towering volcano of fire and sparks high into the darkening sky, he plunged – blindly, fatalistically – into the cool, wet darkness under the floor.

⚄

When the roof caved in, the watching figure in the trees slipped forward silently and unlocked the door, shielding his face against the flames that now leapt from the window apertures. Then he hung the key on its hook, and as silently as he had come, stole off – up, over the hill, and away.

⚄   Chapter Fourteen   ⚄

Dismounting before the graceful portico of his home, it was the earl who saw the fountain of flame that shot into the air when the cottage roof collapsed. His exclamation cut through the mild pleasantries that John, who had come out to greet them, was addressing to the saddle-sore Francis and Matt.

154

Assessing the direction, 'It must be the cottage!' said his lordship, irritable but resigned. 'That damned thatch! Oh, well, it was bound to happen some day.' Then, turning, he caught sight of John's face, and his own changed. 'What is it?' he asked sharply. 'Is there someone down there?'

'Richard,' replied John, briefly and chillingly, as he made a dash for the stairs and the fire bell that hung in the corner of the portico. His voice, taut and apprehensive, floated back to them. 'We left him there less than an hour ago!'

The bell clanged out under John's vigorous hand until a footman ran up to take over. Loud and commanding, piercing yet mellow, the message rolled over the lawns and down into the valley, where the waters of the lake acted as a sounding-board to send it on, amplified and reverberating, to the estate village just inside the main gates, summoning all able-bodied men to the scene of the fire.

But even before the first villager had abandoned his supper and snatched up his bucket, the earl, flinging a hasty instruction to John to stay and look after Miss Malcolm, had spurred his horse back down the drive and along the path to the gardens. Pausing only to haul out the hand pumps from their concealed recess in the portico, Francis and Matthew followed close behind.

They hoped, all the way to the cottage, that they might meet Richard on the path, or even find him there trying to fight the fire, however uselessly. But there was no sign of him at all.

The earl and Matthew stood silent for a fraction of a second, and Francis said: 'He can't – he *cannot* – be inside!'

'We must find out,' the earl replied. He had already torn off his coat and waded into the lake with it, soaking his legs up to the thigh and steeping his coat in the water. Now, wrapping the wet coat round his right hand and arm, he strode up to the door and pushed. Smoothly, easily, it opened two or three inches and then hit an obstruction. He raised his soaking boot and kicked with all his force. Francis and Matthew, similarly protected now, came to his aid, and all three men pushed and thrust in turn, wet shoulders against the sizzling door, boots steaming at each kick against its timbers. It was a fallen beam that was holding the door, and gradually, inch by inch, they succeeded in shifting it until the gap was wide enough for them to see inside. Then they recoiled, their faces set. If Richard had been inside . . .

A faintly slurred voice behind them said: 'You should never leave a frying-pan unattended, you know. Look what happens.'

With extreme slowness, the earl turned, his aristocratic – if somewhat heated – countenance expressive of nothing but friendly interest. 'Richard, dear boy,' he said pleasantly. 'And where have you been hiding yourself while we have been indulging in all this healthy exercise?'

Richard grinned, a little weakly. 'I passed out,' he confessed.

In the glare from the fire, they could see that he was dripping from head to toe and liberally plastered with mud. Otherwise, though exhausted, he appeared to be whole, uninjured, and rather less scorched than they were themselves.

The earl opened his mouth to say something, but at that moment the first few village firefighters arrived. He gave them concise instructions, Matthew handed the pumps over, and they began on an exercise in which they had been thoroughly drilled but had never had the opportunity to practise. One youth, slightly over-excited, remarked brightly that it wurr handy to have the foyurr so near t' watter, but he was reduced to silence by an instant clout over the ear from one of his elders. The earl watched the action for some moments and then said: 'Back to the house, I think. Richard needs to be dried out, and I am feeling a little damp myself.'

They had just hoisted Richard up on to Francis's horse and were turning into the laurel walk when there was a thunder of hooves on the carriage drive ahead, and then the unmistakable sound of horses being pulled up sharply. In a moment, the hasty figure of Captain Gregory came striding into view.

'Well, if that's the way you treat your greys,' remarked his lordship cordially, 'I shall take very good care never to let you handle mine!'

The captain halted, a twinkle creeping into his eye. 'Well, there's gratitude!' he exclaimed. 'I arrive after a long journey, hear of the fire, tip your sister head over heels and protesting vociferously out of the curricle, and ride here *ventre à terre* to the rescue. And what do I get? Insults.' While he was speaking his eyes had been resting on the swaying form of Richard, held in the saddle by will-power alone. He transferred his gaze to the earl and raised his brows.

'Yes,' his lordship agreed. 'I think the curricle is just what we need.'

During the brief drive back to the house, the earl would not permit Richard to talk, but the young man was determined on saying one thing, because it had to be said and he did not wish to say it in his sister's hearing. 'The door,' he murmured.

'Someone locked it. I was locked in.'

'You're sure?' his lordship asked, and wished he could feel surprise or disbelief.

'Locked,' Richard insisted. 'Didn't hear him do it, but I could see the bolt spanning the gap. Definitely locked . . .' He fought to hold on to his consciousness.

A hand gripped his and a voice said commandingly: 'You must say it was jammed. Do you hear me, Richard? You must say it was jammed.'

Richard nodded once and then slipped into insensibility.

✄

By half-way through the evening, Atherton had returned to its usual calm. Richard, packed off to bed, was much restored by a couple of hours' sleep, and Caroline, who had been sitting with him, had progressed from anxious solicitude to a stringent commentary on people who were careless with oil lamps in thatched cottages.

'Be a good girl,' her brother begged at last. 'Go and have your dinner!'

His request was reinforced by the earl, who arrived at that moment and volunteered to keep the invalid company during Caroline's absence. 'A tray is being prepared for him,' he announced, 'laden with delights such as Epicurus never dreamed of. So you may go and partake of your own bread and gruel with an easy mind.'

Caroline was only too aware that her protests failed to carry conviction, and when his lordship held the door invitingly open for her she swept through it, head held high. For she was, she admitted to herself as she trod downstairs, quite ungenteelly ravenous.

Closing the door behind her, the earl turned towards the bed and surveyed its occupant gravely. 'Now, Richard,' he said. 'Tell me – if you feel able.'

It did not take long, and Richard finished just as a discreet tap on the door heralded the arrival of the tray.

As Richard removed the cover from the first dish, a heavenly aroma assailed his nostrils. He stopped for a moment, the cover poised in his hand, and then said, a slight break in his voice betraying what he had been through: 'I thought this afternoon I was never going to smell anything but burning, ever again!'

'I blame myself,' said the earl. 'I thought you would be safe here, but I should have known better.' He paused. 'But why *you*, Richard? Why you?'

The soup tasted like nectar. Swallowing it blissfully, Richard said: 'I don't know. I was trying to think this afternoon – but I was interrupted!'

The earl's set face relaxed. 'Well, thank God you found the stream, even if only in the nick of time. We cover it in at the end of September, as a rule, because despite the glass it seems to make the cottage damp and turns the furniture mouldy. John has been cursing himself back, forth, and sideways, for we always tell people about it – it's part of the charm of the cottage. Or was. He says he was just about to show it to you when he was distracted by the look of the sky and decided it could wait until tomorrow.'

'What is it? A tributary stream?'

'Yes. When my mother found what she thought was the ideal spot for the cottage she refused to be put off by a mere rivulet. I don't know whose was the happy idea of framing it to make it look like an indoor aquarium, but it was very successful. The stream rises from a spring in the hillside and of course flows beneath the foundations for a few feet until it emerges under that little bluff at the side of the promontory the cottage stands on.'

'Yes, I know the spot you mean,' said Richard, his carefree grin restored. 'But I can tell you it's a sight longer than a few feet under those foundations!'

'Fifteen yards, to be precise.'

Richard was addressing himself to the fish, white and flaky and delicate as falling snow, but he looked up at that. *'Fifteen yards?* Is that really all? It felt like a hundred miles. Mind you, I was doing a kind of dog-paddle. The channel wasn't wide enough to let me swim, and too deep for me to touch bottom, and I was bumping my head on the roof every two or three strokes! I suppose all that made it seem further. I couldn't see very well, either, for it was such a grey day that there was no light penetrating from the lake and my eyes were dazzled from the fire. To be honest, I wasn't even very sure whether I *was* going to come out in the lake or whether I was fated to dog-paddle on forever until my underground river finally debouched into the Styx. I think it was sheer relief that made me faint when I came out under the bluff.'

'It may have been as well that you fainted – and in such a concealed spot,' said his lordship. 'Our murderous friend probably waited until the roof collapsed, and then emerged to unlock the door. I don't imagine you would have been in much of a state to defend yourself if he'd seen you.'

'Is that what happened, do you think?'

'The door was certainly unlocked by the time *we* arrived.'

'Well, my God,' exclaimed Richard, his eyes kindling. 'I wish I hadn't passed out after all. Nothing would have given me greater satisfaction than to lay my hands on him!'

When Miss Malcolm returned to sit with her brother, the earl went back downstairs and found Susan, John, and Adam Gregory settled in one of the smaller saloons. He surveyed them thoughtfully for a moment and then, in response to their impatient enquiries, told them what Richard had said. 'But I don't think Miss Malcolm should be told,' he concluded. 'It is the kind of thing from which she ought to be shielded.'

His sister stared at him. 'Men!' she exclaimed. 'Doesn't it occur to you that she might not *wish* to be shielded from everything? Even if she doesn't already have her suspicions, she is certainly going to find out some time. And I can assure you that when she does she is going to be very cross indeed!'

'Oh!' said his lordship, disconcerted. 'Is she?'

Adam grinned. 'There's no accounting for women, is there?' he said. Then his eyes narrowed consideringly. 'But out with it, Charles. There's something else on your mind, isn't there? What is it? The name of the villain?'

There was a protracted silence, while the earl sat running two fingers lightly over a scorch on his temple. 'Something like that,' he said at last.

His sister gasped, and John stared at him, his mouth slightly open.

'I'm almost sure I know who, though I've no conclusive proof. And until the attacks on Richard, I thought I had an inkling of why. But now . . .' He shrugged his shoulders expressively.

'Perhaps Susan's researches might help you, then,' Adam said. He surveyed her with a faint smile. 'It's no use holding back with the dénouement, love. Richard has quite upstaged you!'

Lady Susan twinkled back at him. 'As if I didn't know that! I was merely waiting for a break in the conversation.' She turned to the earl. 'We have found out who Caroline's father was.'

The earl sat up. 'Have we, by God?'

'Verona returned from Paris three days ago. Really, Charles, you were unusually slow about that. Why did you think I was so anxious to see her? She and Mrs Malcolm were almost of an age, and if Mrs Malcolm came of the kind of family we thought she did, then it seemed to me excessively likely that they must have known each other at the time of their come-out. And I was right. As soon as I showed the portrait to Verona, she said, "Good heavens! It's Jane Stridon!"'

'Stridon,' the earl repeated, a frown in his eyes. 'Now, that means something to me. But what?'

'Patience! Verona was a little older than Jane, but they were at school together, and Jane, it seems, admired Verona – yes, real , ! – and fell into the habit of confiding in her. Verona was presented, but Jane was still too young, and before her come-out she ran away to Gretna Green – eloped, if you please! – with . . .' She paused mischievously.

'With Wayne's younger and quite legitimate son,' the earl said coolly. 'Yes. Go on.'

The captain drew an uneven breath, and placed one hand delicately before his eyes.

'As you say,' Lady Susan resumed, enunciating each word with extreme clarity. 'Are you quite *sure* that you wish me to go on? I have no doubt you know all there is to know, and I should very much dislike it if I bored you.'

'No, no. Pray proceed. There may be one or two details I'm not aware of.'

'Oh, hush, Charles!' John exclaimed. '*You* may be a polymath, but I'm not. Go on, Susan.'

'What's a polymath?' she asked, diverted.

'A know-all! Go *on.*'

'Oh, very well. Yes, she ran off with Lord Rivett, Wayne's son and heir.'

The earl snapped his fingers. 'Stridon. Of course! Berkshire family, yes? No title but impeccable lineage, and impossibly high in the instep. The last of them had only one child, a daughter, and her parents died while she was still a minor. She was brought up by trustees and then it was given out that she had died of a fever. So she didn't die after all? Well, well.'

'No, but young Rivett did. They reached the Border and were married, and then, only three or four weeks later, he was killed in an accident – putting his horse at a wall too high for it. He broke his neck.'

'But wait a minute.' It was John. 'Why did they have to run away at all? There could have been no objections on either side as far as money or birth was concerned.'

'There,' his sister admitted regretfully, 'Verona was a little hazy. Jane was under age, of course, but Verona thought it was Wayne who was the real stumbling block. Rivett, apparently, was an extremely wild young man and in his father's opinion no suitable match for a gently reared girl only eighteen years old. Rivett himself was approaching thirty. Jane's trustees might have given their consent to the match, but not when the young man's own father was so strongly opposed – and for such reasons! So they withheld permission, and Rivett persuaded Jane to elope.

'Verona said that, to do the girl justice, she had been very unhappy at home, for the trustees were not only elderly but very stiff and starched-up and had put her in the care of someone quite unsuited to handling a lively young girl. By eloping, however, she threw everything away, for her father's Will was positively gothic! If she married against her trustees' wishes while the trust was still in force – before she reached the age of twenty-five, in effect – she forfeited her inheritance. I'm glad *our* papa was less of a high stickler! Though I doubt,' she added, 'whether I myself would have thought Rivett worth giving up everything for.'

Her audience sat silent for a while and thought about this, and then the earl remarked in tones of mildly surprised appreciation: 'That was really very helpful, Susan. Thank you. I confess it had never even occurred to me to ask Verona.'

Lady Susan fluttered her eyelashes and smiled demurely. 'Feminine intuition, my dear.'

'Fiddle-de-dee!' said John.

'So that means Mrs Malcolm was Lady Rivett for a time,' Adam said. 'And Caroline must have been – must still be, I suppose – an Honourable?'

'Whereas, if she'd had the sense to be born a boy, she'd have been heir to the Most Noble the Marquis of Wayne!' John remarked.

'Yes,' said his lordship. 'However, she does at least have her very valuable twenty-one diamonds.'

The tea tray arrived, and Susan prepared to pour. 'Should I send to fetch Caroline?'

'No, leave it for the moment. In fact . . . Peter, have another tray prepared immediately and take it up to Mr Malcolm's room, will you? I imagine his sister is still there.'

The footman bowed and withdrew.

The earl stood in his favourite position before the fire, cup in hand. Looking down at his sister, he said: 'Exercise your feminine intuition a little more. Suppose you were a pretty, lively girl from a straitlaced background, who ran away for love, and then found herself widowed, pregnant, and completely alone. Bearing in mind what you've just told us, how would you react?'

Lady Susan expelled a small, surprised breath. 'Oof!' she said inelegantly. 'Well, I know it sounds sordid, but I'd start by counting my money. If I were almost penniless, I'd have no choice but to go back to my trustees on bended knee and hope they'd take pity on me, or else go to my disapproving father-in-law and beg on behalf of his future grandchild. If I did have money, on the other hand . . .'

'As you probably would,' her brother interrupted. 'I don't imagine Rivett would fly to the Border without adequate reserves of cash, and afterwards, of course, you would stand to inherit at least a proportion of his own, personal fortune. If any.'

'Yes. Well, if I did have money, nothing on earth would persuade me to go back to my trustees. And I think,' she went on, taking a thoughtful sip of tea, 'that I might feel almost as strongly about my father-in-law. After all, the whole thing seems to have been his fault, even if his motives *were* admirable.'

'On this occasion, if on few others,' the earl commented drily.

'Let me think,' she went on, slowly, as if she were testing each word before she used it. 'I have had an unhappy, repressed childhood, haven't I? And just when I think happiness has come at last, it is snatched brutally away from me. I suspect that, as well as being heartbroken, I might be very resentful indeed. You know – every man's hand is against me, so to hell with them all!' She broke off, blushing.

Captain Gregory surveyed her delightedly, but her brothers, assiduously drinking tea, appeared to have been afflicted by sudden deafness.

Lady Susan cleared her throat. 'Yes, well,' she said. 'I think I might persuade myself into hating the whole Wayne clan so much that I would refuse to have anything whatever to do with them. I would find somewhere to live and try to make a new life for myself, quite divorced from everything in my past. And when I met Colonel Malcolm, I would marry him. And if he were the kind of man I would be prepared to marry, after all I had been through, he would probably be the kind of man who would respect my desire to blot the past out of my life.'

She looked up at the earl, to find his blue gaze fixed on her but quite unfocussed. 'Will that do?' she asked.

He returned to the present. 'Admirably,' he said. 'Quite

admirably. There's only one thing you've left out – the diamonds.'

'Oh, bother! That's true.' She considered, while the earl watched her with a half-smile on his face.

'Very well. By the time the child is born, my resentment has died down a little – a very little. Just enough to make me realize that it would be quite improper to keep its existence secret from its father's family. So I write to the marquis, quite briefly, to inform him that he has a grand-daughter. I think I might add – indeed, I'm sure I *would* add – that neither I nor my child require anything from him or will ever make any claim upon him, and that he'll never hear from me again. Something like that, anyway.'

She made the mistake of pausing for a moment, and John, entranced by this new game, could not resist chiming in. 'And the marquis,' he said, 'with his strong sense of family responsibility, replies that while such an attitude may be all very fine for you, your daughter may feel differently when she grows up. He proposes, therefore, to send the child the family diamonds, and hopes you will not be so ungracious as to refuse. And being no fool, or perhaps something of a cynic, he sends the first one with the letter.'

'Not bad,' said the earl critically. 'But why send the stones one by one? Why not simply the whole necklace?'

John was silent, but Captain Gregory came to the rescue. 'As income, John! He was guaranteeing Mrs Malcolm an annual income amounting to several thousands of pounds. If he'd sent the whole necklace, she might have sold it and allowed the money to slip through her fingers. Or she might have felt unable to sell it, even if she was in dire straits. But a single diamond could be kept or sold as the need arose. It was the nearest he could contrive to ensuring that the child needn't ever go short.'

'I see!' said John, much struck. 'That was rather clever, wasn't it?'

'And I think probably the truth,' his brother said. 'Or near enough. But that problem having been solved to everyone's satisfaction – and I must say I think Wayne acted very responsibly, in the circumstances – we are still left with two questions. Why was Mrs Malcolm killed, and why has Richard been attacked? I think – I *think* I know the answer to the second question now. Something you said not so long ago gave me the clue, John . . .' John's mind, almost visibly, began to race back over everything he had said in the last hour, and his brother grinned at him as he went on, '. . . but I am still at a loss over the murder of Mrs Malcolm.'

He turned to the captain. 'Adam, I propose calling at Priory Court tomorrow to see Sir Augustus. I doubt if the interview will be pleasant, but I need a witness who will be prepared, if necessary, to swear to what has been said. Will you come?'

'Of course,' Adam said.

✖ *Chapter Fifteen* ✖

It rained heavily during the night, with the sheeting force of approaching winter, but the downpour had moderated by the time the earl walked down to the *cottage orné* soon after seven the next morning.

He found it a sodden, smoke-stained shell islanded in a sea of trampled mud. It was without any great optimism that he embarked on a minute study of the ground nearby, working systematically in ever-widening circles. He spent several minutes in a particular grove of trees where the earth had escaped the full force of the rain. There were footprints there, the heel marks heavily indented towards the back as if their owner had stood for a while leaning against a tree trunk. Apart from this, which merely confirmed what he had already suspected, the earl found nothing but a single scrap of paper, thrice folded, scorched along one edge, and so thoroughly soaked that he feared it would disintegrate when he unfolded it. But it was good, laid paper of sturdy quality, printed with the feint lines that denoted a business account. That it had been used as a spill to set light to the thatch he had no doubt, and whatever writing had been on it had burned away, but in the heart of the triple fold, partly scorched, were the lower parts of a series of figures. The earl groped for his quizzing glass and smiled as he found his labours had not been in vain. The clerk who had penned the bill had been blessed with a firm and forceful hand, and his quill had been running dry, so that despite exposure the figures were incised into the paper and only slightly blurred.

Close scrutiny, and some tilting of the paper so that it caught the light, rewarded the earl with the sum of £445.12s. An account due for settlement, undoubtedly, and unless he was much mistaken, a tailor's account. He felt in his pockets, profitlessly, for something he might use to protect his find, and then looked around him. In the end, with a mental apology first to the plant and then to his gardener, he tore two large leaves from one of the laurels and carefully sandwiched the paper between them.

For the next two hours he was exceedingly busy, and by the time his family and guests descended for breakfast, Francis and Matthew, as well as Girvan, Peter the second footman, Anderson the second groom, and Jamie, the youngest and one of the most promising of Girvan's underlings, had all been despatched from Atherton on a variety of errands. Pausing only to enquire after Richard's well-being and to recommend that he and his sister should remain indoors for the day – 'The weather is not at all pleasant, you know!' – the earl disappeared into his study and was not seen again until after midday.

Miss Malcolm might have thought this behaviour very odd if her attention had not been otherwise engaged. But as breakfast came to an end, Lady Susan said to her: 'Let's take our coffee into the Red Saloon, shall we? No, not you, Richard. I have something very particular to say to Caroline.'

What Lady Susan had to say to Caroline, that young lady was startled to discover, was that she had been deputed by the earl to tell Miss Malcolm the story of her parentage. As she had been vouchsafed no information at all since the day the earl had asked about her mother's accident – the day Richard had been attacked on the way home from Oxford – Caroline had assumed that the investigation was making little progress, although she suspected Rich of knowing more than he would admit. She had allowed herself to be coaxed to Atherton by means of a great many impenetrable hints, and had gone – she convinced herself – purely to please Richard. Certainly not from any other motive. And with no expectation of being told anything to the point. So Lady Susan's announcement found her quite unprepared – though that was nothing unusual, she reflected bitterly. Her dealings with the Dornays had nearly all been noteworthy for the ease with which they seemed able to throw her off balance.

She sat down with something of a thud and fixed her luminous grey-green eyes speechlessly on her hostess. But to Lady Susan's discomfiture she did not remain speechless for long. Indeed, her ladyship very soon realized that her brother had not been motivated solely by generosity when he left it to her to disclose a story which she had been partly instrumental in uncovering. Happy to be permitted to set Caroline's mind at rest on a subject that had troubled her for so long, she found almost at once that the path of good intentions was as liberally strewn with rocks as a mountain road after an avalanche. As she threaded her way with meticulous care through what Miss Malcolm *was* to be told and was *not* to be told, she discovered that Caroline had a genius for fastening on the most awkward questions. It was over the matter of relatives that her ladyship finally came to grief.

'I believe the marquis has no close family,' she said, trying to achieve a tone of finality. She did not succeed.

Miss Malcolm took her up. 'No close family – perhaps,' she said. 'But he must have *some* connections. Who, for example, is the heir?'

Lady Susan bent down gracefully to pluck an imaginary thread from the hem of her morning dress. Really, she thought, John was right. Charles *was* behaving badly. Why could he not have given her some hint of why she was not to mention the Homes? As it was, she was being forced to choose between the truth and a feigned ignorance that was bound to be exposed, sooner or later. She was beginning, however, to understand more clearly what had attracted the earl to Miss Malcolm. It was not just her undeniable beauty, but a certain quality of mind, a quick incisiveness that was scarcely apparent in everyday conversation but was given full scope in a situation such as this. Unfortunately.

'The heir?' said her ladyship abstractedly. 'A nephew. Middle-aged.' Then, abandoning the unequal struggle: 'In fact, I think you know him – Sir Augustus Home. He lives at Priory Court about ten miles from here.'

Miss Malcolm was very much surprised and, it seemed, not at all pleased. 'Good heavens!' she exclaimed. 'I asked his lordship to find my father – I can't *think* why! I must have been all about in my head at the time! – and now he appears to have found me a family as well.' A rueful gleam crept into her eye. 'And one I could very happily do without!'

This rider quite disarmed her ladyship, who had at first been inclined to feel offended at Miss Malcolm's cavalier attitude towards the earl's labours on her behalf. In a ripple of laughter, she exclaimed: 'Your restraint does you credit! I shudder to think what my own reaction would have been if I had found myself saddled with the entire Home clan!'

Caroline was considerably heartened by this very human response from someone of whom she stood a little in awe. She began to relax, and her delightful smile illumined her face as she admitted candidly: 'And what makes it worse than anything is that I cannot complain that your brother failed to warn me! I remember his words quite clearly. He said it would be necessary to ferret out a great many secrets from the past that I might find would have been better left to lie. How right he was!'

'And how very vexatious of him to be so!' agreed Lady Susan, a laugh in her voice.

Some little time later, wholly unaware that he had been the means of putting his sister and Miss Malcolm in perfect charity with each other, the earl, accompanied by Adam, set out to visit Priory Court.

Rain was rattling down sporadically on the roof of the chaise, and Wiltshire, Adam thought gloomily, looked almost as dispiriting as Norfolk. The earl, after mentioning that Sir Augustus expected them at two o'clock – Peter the footman having been sent over with a message earlier in the day – had relapsed into silence for the first part of the journey. Adam, too, was preoccupied with his thoughts. But as they crossed the toll road that led west to Bishops Deverill, he stirred and said: 'I think perhaps you ought to enlighten me as to the purpose of this visit.'

The earl turned his head, and sighed faintly. 'If you're to be an honest witness, Adam, you should have no preconceptions, so I can't tell you what I suspect. But I will tell you what I propose laying before Sir Augustus.

'Once we were sure that Mrs Malcolm had been murdered . . . Now, there's a preconception if you like! What I should say is that once we were sure Mrs Malcolm had been murdered *or* accidentally killed, tracing her movements on the day of her death clearly became of some importance. The magistrate, with an accident in mind and not having seen the position of the body when it was first found, centred his questioning on the area round Atherton. I, on the other hand, sent Francis and Matthew to investigate near Bishops Deverill. It was a gamble, as it was more than a year since she died, but they had the portrait and I hoped they might find something. In country districts they have long memories for strangers. It worked. Francis and Matthew found several witnesses who had seen Mrs Malcolm go by in the gig belonging to the Ship Inn. They tried all roads within a reasonable compass, and they traced her to within a mile of the gates of Priory Court – but not beyond.'

He could not have complained that his audience was inattentive, and he acknowledged it with a fleeting smile, as he went on: 'Well, I remembered Matt speaking of a curricle as one of the vehicles mentioned by a tollkeeper near Atherton during the

167

magistrate's investigations. And another keeper on the pike road south of Priory Court referred to a curricle from "the big house" going through on the day Mrs Malcolm disappeared. Don't laugh – I know the roads are thick with curricles! But for the last three days Francis, Matt and I have been pursuing *that* one.

'Now, as you know, Priory Court lies to the south of Bishops Deverill and Atherton to the north. We've confirmed that, late in the afternoon of the day Mrs Malcolm died, a curricle – occupant unknown, but certainly from "the big house" – passed westward through the pike on the south road. And we have traced "a curricle" at roughly the right time and, as far as it's possible to say, on the right day, all the way from that southern pike, up and round by the west, then back north passing Atherton and going eastward, then curving round south again in the general direction of Priory Court. A circular tour, never drawing attention by passing through the same gate twice, but finishing up where it began. I don't know what all that suggests to you . . .'

Adam whistled. 'Quite a lot!'

'Yes. Enough, at any rate, to risk asking questions of Sir Augustus.'

The captain sat deep in concentration. 'It's obvious enough who you have in mind,' he said. 'Has there been anything else to confirm it?'

'Pointers, no more. Passing remarks. Things overheard. As I said last night, Richard's so-called accidents are less of a mystery than the business about his mother. That still has me in a fog. But it's just possible that we may discover the answer this afternoon.'

There was a long silence as the flat, wet road unrolled over the chalk downs. Then Adam said suddenly: 'I've been meaning to ask you since we found out about Rivett – why on earth did Wayne attack you when you mentioned his sons? I thought at the time it was because he believed you were going to try and blacken their names!'

'Yes. I suppose a hundred explanations must have gone through my mind for that one! At first, I imagined he might be using a rather extreme method of steering me away from dangerous ground, but the very vehemence of his reaction made me think again. He was in a vitriolic temper, remember, and he regarded me as interfering in *his* affairs. When I mentioned his sons I suspect he thought I had known the answer all along – and it was simply too much for him.'

The captain grinned suddenly. 'You do have a talent for

infuriating people. Susan would cheerfully have clouted you with the nearest blunt instrument last night, when you stole her thunder about the identity of Miss Malcolm's father!'

His lordship grinned uninhibitedly back. 'But you must admit it was irresistible! As a matter of fact, I'd only just worked it out, though I'd no idea who the bride was or why she and Rivett should have run away. But once one put Wayne's son, Glasgow, and the diamonds together, and added a few normal human reactions to the equation, everything seemed to fit together. None of it, of course, explained Mrs Malcolm's death, and it was only when I forced myself to consider that as being something – not entirely separate but at least *detached* from the diamond business, that I began to get anywhere. Something other than the diamonds precipitated her death, and it must have been something related to the birth of the child.'

He leaned forward, brushing condensation from the window, and said: 'Here we are! Look your fill on the former residence of the priors of Merton. Depressing, isn't it?'

Adam had never been much taken by the Gothic style, whether genuine or Strawberry Hill, and as he descended from the chaise he saw no reason to revise his opinion. Nor was the prevailing grey angularity relieved by the visage of the Home butler, creased north to south and clearly indicating the need for two shaves a day.

As he and the earl followed the butler through the hall and along a cloister-like passage to Sir Augustus's study, Adam noted the shabbiness of the surroundings – not the comfortable shabbiness of a house that was lived in, but that of one where economy ruled. The fabrics were pretentious in design but poor in quality, and the dressing had worn out of them, leaving them limp and drab. The furniture, dyed and polished, revealed where the dye had worn away that it was made of cheap wood treated to simulate walnut. The vases had lost their lustre, and the oil paintings on the walls would have been the better for a good cleaning.

Adam shivered slightly and hoped they would not stay for long. He had not had the doubtful privilege of meeting Sir Augustus, but had heard enough about him to know what to expect. He was tall and well fleshed – not fat, not muscular, but vaguely soft and flabby. His countenance was that of a precocious child, small features closely set in the centre of an adult-sized face, the wide domed brow stretching baldly back to the crown of his head. A fringe of fluffy brown hair began above his ears and curved round, over-long, to the nape of his neck. His tailoring left much to be desired, and his manner could only be described as ingratiating. All in all, he was a mildly ridiculous and not very attractive figure. Trying to convince himself of an adage that experience had long disproved – that every human being had at least one virtue worth praising – Adam dutifully seated himself on a chair of remarkable obduracy, and awaited developments.

The earl, acquainted with the upholstery at Priory Court, remained standing. It gave him an advantage over Sir Augustus who, waving his hand toward the chairs, had seated himself behind his desk a little too quickly.

Hands clasped behind his back, the earl looked down on Sir Augustus with the expressionless detachment Adam was coming to know so well. 'You are aware from my note this morning,' he said, 'that I would be grateful for your help in a matter that concerns a young friend of mine. There is – a small inheritance involved. Through the mother.' Sir Augustus's face showed only artificial interest. 'As you will understand, I should prefer not to name names at the moment. But perhaps you would tell me if you have ever seen this lady before.'

This was shock tactics with a vengeance, and Adam felt a slight constriction in his chest as he watched the earl produce a rolled sheet of watercolour paper, smooth it flat, and then present it to Sir Augustus.

Sir Augustus, accepting it, felt for his quizzing glass, a somewhat tarnished artefact, and raised it to his eyes. Then it was as if some invisible hand had been smoothed over his face, wiping away all the lines of expression and melting both muscle and bone into a flat, caricature mask. Not a comedy mask or a tragedy mask, Adam thought, but something in between with blank eyes and a gash of a mouth bracketed at the corners by deep, circumflex lines.

It was a long time before Sir Augustus looked up and met the earl's knowledgeable blue gaze. His eyelids fluttered, and he made a faint, rustling sound in his throat. 'Jane Stridon,' he said.

'Jane Stridon,' the earl agreed placidly.

There was another long silence. 'She ran away with my cousin,' Home said. 'Years ago. More than twenty years ago.' A hint of feeling crept back into his voice. 'A dreadful, *wicked* woman.'

Adam was startled, but the earl said, passionlessly, as if it were a matter of documented fact: 'You quarrelled with your uncle over her.'

'My fault! He said it was *my* fault! I should have prevented it, he said! As if I could have done, when I was lying at death's door. Inflammation of the lungs,' he added in bleak parenthesis. 'It was *his* place to keep an eye on his son. He knew there was bound to be trouble. But, oh no! Off he went gallivanting to the Low Countries and got himself wounded. I wish he'd died of it.' His voice was vicious, and his lip curled rabbit-like over his front teeth. Suddenly becoming aware of the impression he must be creating, he took a deep, controlling breath and went on in more moderate tones: 'Rivett never paid any attention to me, you know. I could have argued myself blue in the face and he would still have run off with her. Headstrong, that's what he was. And my uncle was mad, trying to protect the girl. Oh, yes! She looked sweet enough – took my uncle in beautifully. But she and Rivett were well matched. My God they were!'

The precocious face was filled with loathing and contempt, and its colour was unnaturally high. Adam, his eyes contracted in puzzlement, watched it, and then saw the colour drain slowly and completely away at the earl's next remark.

'She came back, you know – to Priory Court. Last year.'

Surprise, concern, fear? Adam could not decide.

'From India,' his lordship went on. 'After eighteen years.'

The look was readable now. It was sheer, naked disbelief.

'No,' Sir Augustus said flatly. 'That's not true.' What wasn't true? Adam wondered. That she had come back, or that she had been in India for eighteen years?

The tall, flabby man behind the desk rose restlessly to his feet and turned to face the window. His hands clamped behind his back, he repeated: 'That's not true. I know it for a fact.'

'But it is true,' the earl said gently. 'Though she came back not as Jane Stridon, or as Lady Rivett, but as Mrs Malcolm.' The knuckles of Sir Augustus's twined fists whitened and the bones stood out, sharp and angular. 'You remember – the mother of Caroline Malcolm, who was your guest here not so long ago. The woman who was killed in an – accident.'

The atmosphere in the room was intolerable, and Adam felt as if his head would burst. An uncontrolled shudder shook Sir Augustus's frame, and he swayed as if he were about to faint. Adam half rose to his feet but the earl's hand stopped him. His lordship's face was pensive. 'We believe,' he went on mildly, 'that she was not just killed, but murdered.'

Adam wondered how many more shocks their host's constitution could take and flashed a frown at his lordship, but the earl's

171

eyes were fixed on Sir Augustus as he turned, his mouth opening and shutting, to face his tormentor.

'Murdered?' It was almost a croak.

'Yes.'

The man sank into his chair. It *could* not be acting, Adam thought.

Then he dropped his forehead on his spread fingers and muttered: 'She was a wicked woman. She deserved to die.'

The earl waited in silence. Another quiver ran through Sir Augustus, and he raised his head again and looked at the earl with a curious fixity in his gaze. 'Then that girl, that pretty little Miss Malcolm . . . Just like her mother. *Just* as wicked!'

The earl's eyes narrowed. 'This time,' he said slowly, 'you *have* surprised me.' His own quizzing glass swung idly in the long, beautiful fingers. At length he said: 'Blackmail?'

Drained, Sir Augustus sat back and looked at him. 'Blackmail,' he echoed. 'You must know about it, I suppose.' There was no question in his voice, only weariness.

'In March 1794, the Stridon girl wrote to me to say that a child had been born of her marriage to Rivett. Courtesy, she said, required that I inform me of it, but I could be assured that this was the last time I would ever hear from her. Her husband's family, she felt, had betrayed him, and she would never be beholden. She proposed making an entirely new life for herself and the child.

'I heard no more from her for eight whole years, then, out of the blue, there was a letter. It was from her – no, there was no doubt about it. I had kept the first one, here, in a corner of my desk, and the handwriting was the same. This time,' and he paused bitterly, 'she said she found herself in financial difficulties, but was sure I would wish to assist her. If I were prepared to pay her the sum of two thousand pounds, twice a year, in perpetuity, it would not be necessary for her to bring her son out of obscurity – or some such phrase! – to take up his heritage.'

A gasp was surprised out of Adam, but the earl's face, after a momentary stillness, suddenly relaxed.

'In other words,' Sir Augustus went on, 'if I paid her four thousand pounds a year, she would allow me to remain heir to my uncle.'

'Not a bad bargain,' the earl commented drily. 'I imagine the estate could stand it.'

The man behind the desk looked at him with dislike. 'Just, though I had to make some economies. But two or three years later, after a bad season, I sent a note with the money saying I couldn't afford such a large sum in future. She replied that I had made a commitment, and if I infringed it in any way . . . What would people say of me, she asked, if they knew I had been paying a beggarly four thousand pounds a year to defraud an innocent child of an inheritance worth more than ten times as much?'

'You never doubted that it *was* Jane Stridon you were paying? Or wondered about the child, whether it was really a boy or whether you were being bled for an heir who did not exist? The first letter, if I understand you, spoke only of a child, not a son.'

Sir Augustus raised a ravaged face. 'No,' he said simply.

'How did you pay the money?'

'Banknotes. A few days before each payment was due, I was sent a letter containing merely a name and address – always different, sometimes in London, sometimes outside it. The last one was St Albans. That was just last week. So if Jane Stridon is really dead, then either Miss Malcolm or the boy must have taken over from her.'

For the first time, there was a trace of pity in the earl's voice as he said: 'You're not thinking clearly. It was *either* Miss Malcolm *or* "the boy" who was born to Jane Stridon and Lord Rivett. Not both.'

Adam watched the painful comprehension dawn on Sir Augustus's face. 'You mean . . . You mean I've been paying that woman all these years for a *daughter*?'

The earl gave him a breathing space while he, in turn, strolled over to the window and looked out over the dripping garden. 'Was the writing on the last two – no – three name-and-address notes the same as it has always been?'

'Yes,' he replied without thinking. 'The girl must have forged them, I suppose.'

His lordship turned. 'No. They were forged by the same person who forged all the earlier notes, someone who, knowing that you were unaware of Jane Stridon's death and did not connect her with Mrs Malcolm, saw no reason to change the handwriting. If he had changed it, you might have begun to suspect the provenance of the notes, might you not?' Sir Augustus nodded blankly.

'It's not Jane Stridon – Lady Rivett – you have been paying out to all these years, I'm afraid. She married again in 1795 and went to India, and only returned early last year. Your

173

blackmailer is someone entirely different.'

He stopped, and Adam could see him wondering how much more to say. 'Your blackmailer is someone who knows you, and knows you very well indeed. And I fear you have to prepare yourself for something else.' He looked down at the drawn white face of the man whose manner was no longer ingratiating and whose fluffy brown tonsure and childlike features appeared no longer even mildly ridiculous. 'For he was also, at the very least, culpably involved in the death of Jane Stridon, and has since made two attempts on the life of Miss Malcolm's half-brother Richard.'

The reply was no more than a whisper. 'Who?'

'No,' said his lordship matter-of-factly. 'You must work that out for yourself.' Then he added, in a gentler tone: 'And I would advise – in privacy.'

Chapter Sixteen ✕

Miss Malcolm had retired to the Music Room, which was in a long wing of the house that curved forward at an angle to the main block. Along most of one wall was a series of casement doors opening on to a wide terrace, which had a balustrade of stone and a long, wide flight of steps at the end leading down to lawns sunk below the level of the house. It must be a delightful room on a sunny day, Caroline thought as she sat down at the piano and absently picked out a few notes on the keyboard. Lady Susan was conferring with the housekeeper, and John and Richard were playing billiards, so Caro had taken the opportunity to escape into solitude. There was so much to think about, and she supposed she also had some decisions to make.

Casting her mind back to what Lady Susan had told her, she was more than ever convinced that her ladyship had read mama's mind correctly. She could perfectly understand her mother refusing to have anything to do with her husband's family.

For a moment, she wondered wistfully what her father had really been like. Not as wild as he had been painted, surely. She had heard it said that a man who had been wild in his own youth was always intolerant of excesses in his c' 'ldren, and perhaps that had been the case with Wayne and his son. Or possibly her father *had* been wild, and her mother, with all the romantic ardour of a young girl in love for the first time, had believed she could reform him. He had died before she could find out. Caroline smiled and ran her fingers up the scale to end on a high C. At least she now knew which side of the family her own temper came from!

It was a relief, too, to know at last that there was nothing reprehensible about her parenthood – apart from that long-ago elopement – and that her mother's wounding secrecy had not been secrecy at all, but merely a sign that she had succeeded in wiping one short, tragic episode out of her life.

Though Lady Susan had been oddly reticent, mama must have been proposing to visit Priory Court when she came to Wiltshire. It seemed strange until Caroline thought that perhaps she had merely meant to look at the place from the outside – as a kind of final exorcism. But why had she gone as far afield as Atherton on that last, fatal afternoon? To pass the time by looking at the gardens, after all? Saving Priory Court for the morrow, when she would have the whole day available? Caroline shrugged her shoulders. It seemed to be one of those questions that would never be satisfactorily answered.

She wondered what would happen now. Nothing, she supposed. There were no problems of inheritance. She could simply stay Miss Malcolm. The Marquis of Wayne sounded like the kind of person she would prefer *not* to acknowledge as a grandfather, and since she and Richard were already acquainted with the Homes, their relationship could continue much as before – friendly, but not too close. She could almost hear Lady Home addressing her as 'Coozeen Caroleen' and shuddered. If anything it would be worse than 'Mees Mallycollum'!

Suddenly, with a peculiarly empty feeling, she recognized that it was all over and that the mystery she had lived with for more than a year had gone, vanished into the air as if it had never been. But to feel deprived – purposeless, even – was too ridiculous. Almost involuntarily, her fingers had been straying over the keyboard, and now, in irritated amusement at her own sense of let-down, she launched into one of the liveliest, most testing works in her repertoire. As the fast, percussive notes of the Turkish *rondo* from Mozart's eleventh piano sonata clamoured through the long room – whose acoustics, she noted, were superb – she began to feel much more like herself, and at the end, after the last bravura flourishes had died away, she sat, slightly breathless, and savoured the silence.

'Bravo!' said a voice behind her, and she jumped like a hare startled from its form. It was, of all people, Ludovic Home, hat and gloves in his hand, cane under his arm, leaning his stalwart shoulders negligently against one of the open doors to the terrace as if he had been there for some time, and smiling at her with an approval that held just the merest trace of – what?

'Good gracious, what a fright you gave me!' she exclaimed crossly. 'Do you always walk into other people's houses unannounced?'

'Not usually,' he admitted, slightly mortified by her tone, 'but I was coming across the lawn and I couldn't resist finding out who the talented musician was. Lady Susan hasn't quite your panache, and Moriston and John are sadly short of practice, I would imagine. I believe they're too busy with other things, most of the time,' he added, and went on at random, as Caroline showed no signs of contributing to the conversation: 'I didn't expect to find such congenial company in this majestic pile. When did you arrive?'

Caroline looked at him. She distinctly remembered telling him of the proposed visit three or four days previously. What *was* the matter with him? Surely he could not have forgotten? She collected the rags of her courtesy and, her eyebrows slightly raised, replied civilly enough: 'Two days ago.'

'And how do you like the house? Large, isn't it? Very stately.' He smiled deprecatingly. 'Not at all like Priory Court.'

Caroline felt a lead weight settle somewhere in the region of her breastbone. This, she thought, was really too much. Ever since she emerged from the schoolroom she had been sought after and admired, and on more than one occasion had found herself faced with having to cool the ardour, kindly but firmly, of some impassioned suitor who had contrived to detach her from her chaperon. Ludovic appeared for the moment to have his emotions under control, but his hesitancy, his embarrassment, the slightly feverish sparkle in his eye were all symptoms that, in Caroline's experience, could mean only one thing.

With a trace of desperation she said: 'But then it doesn't have quite the interesting antiquity of the Court, I believe?'

If only someone else would come in! If only the roof would fall! Anything – *anything!* – to save her from finding Ludovic on his knees before her, clasping her hand in his, and protesting his undying love!

'Did you come to visit anyone in particular?' she ventured

into the uneasy silence.

'I hoped to have a word with Moriston about a project I have in mind.'

'I am afraid he has ridden out. Could John help you?'

'No, no. It's of no importance. Is Richard with you? And well, I trust?'

Her smile of acknowledgement seemed, even to herself, a little perfunctory.

Silence fell once more. Nervously, Caroline eyed her visitor, who was looking thoughtful. Perhaps he was not on the verge of declaring himself, after all? But she still wished he would go away. It was quite improper for a young, unattached woman to be entertaining a young man unchaperoned. Especially in someone else's house.

He straightened up from the doorway and walked forward, laying his hat and gloves on a chair but keeping his cane in his hand and waving it gently back and forth, like a conductor's baton in time with some remembered melody. She stiffened, and then relaxed again as he strolled past her and over to the wall, where he bent to study a picture, a charming little oil sketch of one of the friezes discovered at Herculaneum.

Really, she thought illogically, it was too bad of him!

'The work of the third earl, I imagine,' he remarked, and went on pontifically: 'There is really no doubt in my mind that our grandfathers had a great deal more talent and sensitivity than we have.'

A gurgle of laughter was surprised out of her. From all she had heard of her own newly-discovered grandfather, sensitivity was one of his less striking virtues. Ludovic turned, frowning, as if he suspected her of mocking him, and she suddenly felt a surge of compassion. He might be tediously self-righteous, and sometimes pompous, but he was kind and reliable and in love with her, and she ought to be gentle with him. She was concerned lest she had hurt him. How nonsensical it was, she thought, that they should be sparring in this foolish fashion.

Deciding that she might as well settle the matter once and for all, she rose to her feet and began: 'I believe I must learn to call you cousin. I hope you don't object to the relationship? At least,' she added mischievously, 'you must be relieved that I was born a girl and not a boy, otherwise it would be a case of the missing heir returning to deprive you of your inheritance!'

She had intended to go on, but the words remained frozen on her lips. For Ludovic's face had become quite stark and his

177

lips were parted slightly, as if he needed to draw more breath into his lungs. He stood perfectly still.

And Caroline, looking at him, was engulfed by a wave of appalled enlightenment.

For a fraction of a second, she thought it was merely that Ludovic had been taken aback by the revelation of their relationship. Then she perceived that it was not this that had stunned him, but her frivolous, ill-chosen words about the missing heir. Stunned him, and brought a look of naked savagery to the wide grey eyes.

In the instant of recognition – long as eternity, brief as the moment of death – everything became clear to her. 'Richard,' she whispered.

He had thought Richard was older than she, the son of her mother and Lord Rivett, and heir to the Wayne title and estates. He had tried to have him killed, once on Ealing Common by a pair of hired bullies, and again, yesterday, when Rich – covering up his own carelessness, she had thought – had been trying to spare her worry. She remembered it was Ludovic who had first made Richard's acquaintance, Ludovic who, at the Seftons' ball, must have overheard her say to the earl, 'It's a wise child who knows its own father.' He had been at her party, too, when she had mentioned the day – almost the time! – when Richard would be on the road from Oxford to London. And she herself had told him at that boring breakfast party of Miss Parker's that Richard would be here at Atherton this week.

She could not disguise the understanding on her face, and Ludovic recognized it for what it was. She had not moved. She was still standing by the piano, isolated, infinitely removed from the bell pull that would summon aid. Smoothly, Ludovic moved to stand between her and the wall, and his smile, as he drew the short, slim, deadly sword from his innocuous-looking cane, was the smile on the face of the tiger.

'When will the footman come in to light the candles?' he asked softly. 'Five? Half-past? And there will have been an accident – so sad. You will have gone out on the terrace as the light was failing, and slipped on a fallen leaf, and tumbled head over heels down that long, hard, sharp-edged flight of steps. Alas for Miss Malcolm! She was a pretty girl, and witty, but she knew too much.'

Although Caroline heard and understood what he had said, it was not his words that held her mesmerized, grey-green eyes wide in a face that had turned pale as death, but the transformation

178

of his whole personality. She was scarcely able to recognize in this taut, predatory creature the respectable, responsible, moderate young man who had looked at her, not so long ago, with a warmth that had both embarrassed and a little moved her. The familiar gravity had been replaced by a light, theatrical extravagance. The studied calm had been wiped away from his features to reveal them in a new, sharp, sculptural light. Even the way he moved had changed, so that he was sleek, springy, and menacing as a jungle cat.

He flipped the sword, still smiling. 'Come, turn around. It will soon be dark enough.' She heard his footsteps stride swiftly, too swiftly, towards the door, and a click as he locked it. Then he was back, and she could hear his soft, excited breathing as he took up his position behind her again. But his voice was perfectly even when he said: 'We don't want to be interrupted, do we? How fortunate that I left my horse tethered to a tree. Sometimes my instincts are so nicely tuned that it surprises even me! No one saw me come, and when we have finished our business I will simply fold my tent and softly steal away. As the saying has it. Though I mustn't forget my hat and gloves, must I?' He bent to pick them up, and tipped the hat awry on his head while he stuffed the gloves in the tail pocket of his coat. 'So bad for the cut,' he mourned.

Caroline had half turned towards him so that her back was towards the open keyboard of the piano, but he paused in his flow of inconsequent chatter, and his mouth curled up at the corners. He gestured with the sword. 'Back, my dear! Into the centre of the room.' He closed the cover of the keyboard, saying: 'No clashing chords, if you please. *So* painful to the ear.'

It had been a forlorn enough hope, but he had recognized the intention and she began to be seriously frightened. Could she keep him talking until help came? He might recognize the intention there, too, but it was just possible that vanity might overcome caution.

'What I don't understand,' she said, her voice trembling, 'is how you knew who we were. For it was you who asked Lord Caslon to introduce you to Richard.'

Ludovic's eyes widened. 'You mean our busy friend hasn't found out? How convenient. Perhaps we should exchange notes, for I will confess that my future activities are somewhat dependent on Moriston's progress in this foolish investigation of yours.' The smile slid across his face again, like oil on water. 'All right, why not? Turn and turn about?

'I knew because your mama told me. When I met her almost at the gates of Priory Court in – September, was it? – last year.' Caroline turned perfectly white. 'You didn't know I had met her? Oh, dear! Moriston *has* been wasting his time, hasn't he? She was standing by a little signpost we have, quite illegible, and she asked me – me! – the way. I'd seen her once before, when I was a child, and I had never forgotten that astonishing hair. So like yours.

'I said I lived at Priory Court and would show her the way, and she said, "Then you must be Ludovic, surely!" And she looked at me and nodded – approvingly!' His shoulders shook with gentle laughter. 'She said, "I remember your uncle talking about you, saying what a handsome little boy you were. He hoped our son would be like you." We had the most delightful conversation and she very obligingly told me that she had kept her visit secret so that she might surprise you with its results. *So* trusting!'

Throughout this slightly febrile recital, he had been watching her, reading in her eyes that all of it was entirely new.

His own eyes gleamed. 'I don't know how it happened. Horses are so sensitive to one's mood, don't you think? Anyway, Prince reared up suddenly, and . . .' his lashes fluttered affectedly '. . . *poor* Mrs Malcolm.

'So I tucked her up in my curricle and took her away. I didn't want to be involved in the matter, you understand? But I'm sure you do. I confess it was sheer naughtiness that led me to Atherton with her. I've never liked Moriston, you know.'

Caroline wondered whether she was going to be sick, or faint. 'I didn't know,' she whispered.

'I had a very exhausting two or three days,' Ludovic resumed brightly. 'For after that I had to go up to your house in London and search it for papers – just in case.' Caroline felt as if her shudder jarred every bone in her body. This was dreadful, hideous. 'Your mama had left you a note. Did you know?' Unable to speak, Caro shook her head. This was worse than anything she had ever dreamed of. 'Oh, yes! It was addressed to you and Rich, and it said that in case you returned while she was still away she was going on a visit to Wiltshire, and you were to prepare yourself for a great surprise. She would tell you all about everything when she returned. I took the letter, of course. There was nothing else of interest – in fact, as dull a collection of personal papers as I have had the misfortune to see. How very respectable you all are, to be sure. Or were.'

He cast a glance out of the window. It was growing dark.

She contrived to say: 'And it was afterwards that you arranged the introduction to Richard?'

'I was moderately sure you knew nothing – the note, you know? – but I thought I should keep an eye on you. And everything was going perfectly calmly and peacefully until . . .' he shook his head reprovingly at her '. . . until you dragged Moriston in to discover Richard's real father. Oh, no. Of course – *your* real father. And then I had to take steps to ensure that the missing heir never turned up, or not alive, and preferably without it being known that he *was* the missing heir. I've had a very trying few weeks.' He sighed. 'There, now! You've let me do all the talking, and we haven't time for you to tell me how much Moriston's found out. Just tell me one thing, though. What was the verdict on yesterday's little episode?'

'Rich was careless with the oil lamp, and the door had jammed.'

'Oh, well. That's not too bad,' Ludovic responded gaily. 'I'll just have to try again.'

Caroline swayed.

'Now, now, Cousin Caroline! This is no time to faint!' He backed towards the open window second from the end and motioned her to make her way round to the first. 'Open it when you reach it,' he said softly, 'and then step outside.'

She wondered whether she dared run for it. If she were to make for the front of the house, where there might be people, she would have to pass Ludovic. In the other direction there lay the threatened flight of steps and the wide expanse of lawns hidden from the house. Either way she would be hampered by her skirts, but the way to the front of the house would bring her within certain reach of that murderous glinting blade.

She opened the window and stepped through, and at the same moment Ludovic slipped through the second window on to the terrace.

As he did so, there was an unbelievable, heart-stopping scurry of feet and the whole terrace seemed to fill with belligerent male figures, shouting, tussling, swearing. Richard was there, and Matthew Somerville, and the earl, and a funny little man she had seen somewhere before. Caroline, clinging to the open door as if it were the only stable thing in a collapsing world, at last saw Girvan strike Ludovic's sword down with a long cudgel, and then Ludovic himself was locked, struggling like a fiend, in the iron grip of John Dornay and Adam Gregory.

The earl, his left arm bloody from Ludovic's sword, reached her just in time to catch her as she fainted clean away.

※ *Chapter Seventeen* ※

For two tantalizing days, Lord Moriston was either absent from Atherton or else closeted in his study and not to be disturbed. The rest of the household, each of its members possessed of only part of the story, fretted and fumed and attempted, without success, to piece the whole together. Caroline, kept firmly in bed by Mrs McColl and visited occasionally by Lady Susan and Richard with news of all the comings and goings that were setting everyone about the ears, rested quietly for most of the time and went over and over the events of the past few weeks until her mind and her emotions were exhausted. Her maid, Dutton, who disapproved strongly of Atherton and felt that it was not at all what a gentleman's residence should be, merely folded her lips and confined herself to oracular pronouncements about making beds and lying on them.

On the third day, however, when Miss Malcolm descended the stairs, a little rubbery about the knees and strained about the eyes but almost restored to her usual self, she was informed by an elated John that Charles had decreed a family conference after dinner – 'when all will be revealed, thank God!'

It was an expectant company that assembled after dinner in the comfortable Red Saloon, the gentlemen with their brandy, Lady Susan with coffee, and Caro with the tea she preferred. The curtains were drawn against the night, the candles lit, and a splendid log fire crackled and glowed in the marble fireplace. John was there, and Captain Gregory. Richard shared a vast, padded sofa with Matthew Somerville. Francis Mervyn, with the fatigue of almost four days' hard travelling shadowing his brow, sat half hidden in a wing chair, and Louis Home, drawn-looking and unusually subdued, was perched uneasily on a chaise longue.

The earl began: 'I know you're all anxious to hear the story, but I had better tell you its end first.' He looked enquiringly at Louis, and then turned back to the others. 'It was, I sincerely believe, the best thing that could have happened. Earlier today, Ludovic was being moved from Bishops Deverill to Salisbury and made an attempt to escape. He succeeded in opening the door of the coach while it was travelling at speed, and jumped for it. In the noise and excitement as he broke away from his guards, he can't have heard the coach that was approaching from the other direction. In any case, he landed on the road right in front of it. There was nothing the driver could do.'

Louis gulped as every eye in the room was turned towards him. Lady Susan said: 'Oh, Louis!' in distressful tones, but Caroline could not bring herself to speak. Since she had last seen Louis, only a week ago, he had taken the single stride from lively, volatile youth to responsible adulthood. She thought what Priory Court must be like at the moment, and shuddered. Louis caught the movement and misinterpreted it. 'Thank you, Susan,' he said, 'but Charles is right. At home, we've been in ignorance all along, so for us the misery was just beginning. Mercifully, it's been cut short. Charles thought I should be here tonight so that I might begin to understand why Ludovic did what he did, and I'm grateful. But the real reason I came was to say to Miss Malcolm and Richard, on behalf of my parents, my sister, and myself, that we are more grieved than we can possibly say at the pain and suffering Ludovic's actions have caused them.'

The stilted words fell huskily into silence. Richard, with the resilience of eighteen, thought that there was no possible way of replying to them. One could scarcely say, 'We accept your apology and regret the necessity for it,' any more than one could brush it aside with a jovial 'That's all right, old fellow! Don't let it bother you!' He looked hopefully at his sister, and she settled the problem.

'We understand, Louis,' she said with a little difficulty. 'But it's all over now. There's a doctrine in India known as *karma* which I've sometimes thought was invented for the sole purpose of consoling people in trouble. A Hindu would say that it was in your brother's *karma* to do what he did, and in my mother's *karma* to die as she did, that their fates were ordained and that nothing they could do could alter them.' She smiled suddenly. 'And, of course, it was in Lord Moriston's *karma* to solve the mystery, and in mine to be absolutely furious at not being kept informed about what he was up to!'

Everyone laughed in relief, and there was a general relaxation of tension. The earl raised an appreciative eyebrow, and Captain Gregory thought, surprised, 'Clever girl!' Louis sent her a speaking look and then sat back more comfortably on the chaise longue and gazed expectantly at his host.

With a faint feeling of deliverance, the earl said: 'Now to the story. You all know, more or less, about Mrs Malcolm's first marriage to Lord Rivett and how Wayne came to despatch the diamonds to her on Miss Malcolm's behalf. Everything seems to have happened much as we guessed, and I hope that now we've solved the mystery Wayne will be prepared to confirm it. I've written to him.

'The other matter was more complex. I hope Miss Malcolm, Richard, and Louis are sufficiently reconciled by now not to be unduly upset by what I'm going to say?' He looked round, and all three nodded agreement.

'Very well, then. When Caroline was born, Lady Rivett, as she then was, wrote to the Marquis of Wayne and told him about it. Since he was the child's grandfather and closest living relative apart from herself, the letter was probably lucid if by no means friendly. In other words, she took a degree of care in writing it. She also felt it incumbent on her to notify the man who was now Wayne's heir, but since this was very much a formality her letter was brief to the point of curtness. She probably didn't even realize that her one reference to her daughter described her merely as "my child", or if she did, assumed that Wayne would enlighten him. She didn't, of course, know of the quarrel that had resulted from Wayne blaming Sir Augustus for permitting the elopement.

'At this time, Ludovic was nine years old, just old enough to be aware of what was going on. He was a lonely child, and until the previous year, when Louis was born, had been an *only* child. His mother seems to have reared him almost exclusively on bedtime stories about the horrors and brutalities of the Revolution in France, and I would imagine that, as a result, he may have become inured at an early age to the inhumanities of man, so that he grew up seeing nothing reprehensible or even particularly unusual in them. I suspect, too, that the general atmosphere at Priory Court was hardly calculated to foster warmth of heart in an impressionable child.'

Louis, as the earl's gaze came to rest on him, smiled ruefully and shook his head. 'If you mean that love and gentleness were conspicuous by their absence, you are perfectly right. Marie and I were sufficiently of an age to keep each other company, so we suffered less than Ludo, and we were lucky in having a nurse and then a governess who tried to make up for our parents' deficiencies. But I gather that Ludo's governess was a dreadful woman, and sheer self-preservation may have forced him to take on the role of paragon in the beginning. Later, he seems to have derived some strange sense of power and excitement from the deception, especially in his dealings with our parents, whom he despised. Marie and I have always known that he was by no means as prosy as he appeared but neither of us realized that he was an actor, through and through.'

'Anyway,' the earl resumed, 'eight years passed and Ludovic was a young man only too aware of how cribb'd, cabin'd and confin'd his life was in comparison with that of his contemporaries. Sir Augustus's natural instincts were miserly, and perhaps he even felt he was holding his estates on sufferance. Priory Court and its lands are part of the Wayne inheritance. He felt justified in spending money to keep the land and the fabric of the house in order, but nothing much beyond.

'It is to be supposed that Ludovic, one day, found in his father's desk the note from Mrs Malcolm written eight years earlier. He wanted money, and the note suggested a way of getting it. So he began to blackmail his father. He knew, no more than his father did, whether "the child" was a son or a daughter, but he offered Sir Augustus the continued possession of his estates and his future inheritance in exchange for the sum of four thousand pounds a year. The sum was carefully calculated. Much less, and Sir Augustus – naïve though he was – might have been suspicious. After all, a genuine heir would be unlikely to forgo anything as substantial as the Wayne inheritance for a mere pittance. Much more, and Sir Augustus might have been unable to pay.

'Every six months, Ludovic sent his father a note in the same carefully copied handwriting, giving him an address in some town or other in the south of England. Ludovic had a growing acquaintance and could usually arrange to visit someone in the country whose estates were in reach of a substantial town. It was ingeniously simple. When he was invited to visit friends with an estate in Buckinghamshire, his father would be instructed to send the money to Aylesbury or perhaps somewhere over the county border, like Northampton. In Leicestershire, it might be Melton Mowbray, or over the border in Nottingham. Ludovic would ride over from where he was staying, and simply pay some respectable-looking person to collect the package from the receiving office for him. So even if his father had had enough sense – sorry, Louis! – to try and find out who was collecting the packages, he would probably have been unsuccessful. And Sir Augustus was so little interested in his family that he rarely even knew of Ludovic's country visits. Ludovic, in fact, took care to be away from Priory Court as much as possible, not only from choice, but for fear his father might begin to wonder how he contrived to stretch his allowance so successfully.

'Everything went beautifully for eleven years, and then, one day, Ludovic, on a duty visit to the Court, rode out of the gates and a short way up the road, and found standing there – trying to decipher the directions on a signpost – the woman Wayne's son had run away with twenty years before. Without a qualm, she told him who she was and why she was there. Richard suggests that she had decided to let bygones be bygones, and hoped that the Homes would help to provide Caroline and Rich with an entrée into London society.'

'Of course!' Caroline exclaimed. 'Now, why didn't I think of that? It's just what she would have done, for she was concerned that we knew no one here of our own age!'

'She also mentioned a son, saying that Lord Rivett had "hoped our son would be like you". Ludovic, understandably enough, failed to realize that she meant Rivett had hoped that "if or when we had a son, he would be like you." But his first reaction was that if Mrs Malcolm and his father were allowed to meet, the whole profitable blackmail scheme would be blown sky high. He kept his grip on reality just long enough to ascertain that no one knew of all this, and then in fear – and, I suspect, sheer vicious rage – he forced his horse back on its haunches, and forward again to deal the blow that killed her.

'What happens next is conjecture. He must have hidden her body temporarily in the undergrowth while he drove the horse and gig off somewhere and turned them loose. It was probably found by gipsies, who abandoned the recognizable gig but kept the horse. Ludovic then returned to the Court, took out his curricle, and hid Mrs Malcolm's body under the seat.'

'Charles, for heaven's sake!' his sister exclaimed, rising and going across to Caroline who was looking exceedingly pale. 'Pass me some brandy, Adam.' There was a few moments' pause while Caroline recovered her composure. At last, she gave her head a little shake and attempted a smile. She was angry with herself for being upset, and with the earl for a great variety of reasons.

'Please go on,' she said.

'The worst is almost over.' His lordship smiled back at her, quite unfeelingly, she thought. 'Ludovic drove the curricle by a circular route to Atherton and back, leaving Mrs Malcolm's body – from sheer maliciousness, as he said – at my back door. He then bade a swift farewell to Priory Court and departed for London. Fortune favoured him, and the house at Hill Street was almost unoccupied . . .'

'How did he know the address?' It was John, whose long, self-imposed silence had finally become too much for him.

Before the earl could reply, Lady Susan said: 'From something in Mrs Malcolm's reticule, of course!' Almost simultaneously, Adam pointed out that it might easily have been mentioned during the conversation at the signpost, while Matthew embarked on a half-sentence which had to do with making enquiries at receiving offices in the better parts of town.

His lordship regarded them benignly. 'I am relieved. The beargarden is back in business. I was wondering how long this unnatural restraint would last.' Not surprisingly, this reduced the disputants to silence. 'May I go on? He burgled the house at Hill Street, pocketing a few easily disposable articles for the sake of verisimilitude, as well as from a natural inclination to take advantage of circumstances whenever possible. The papers he discovered, which included a note from Mrs Malcolm to her children, suggested to him that they knew nothing of the association with Priory Court, but he decided it would be wise to scrape up an acquaintance with them so that he might keep an eye on the progress of events. This was easily enough arranged.

'His mind was already adjusted to the idea that Richard was the child of Rivett and Mrs Malcolm, and when he met Richard he saw no reason to change his opinion. Richard . . .' and the earl smiled at the young man, '. . . had all the appearance of being older than his sister.'

'Now, that's very true!' John intervened again. 'And it's not only a matter of size.' He turned to Richard. 'For your company manners are really remarkably – er – majestic!'

Fortunately, Richard was the first of the company to give way to laughter. Caroline, with a faint gasp, said, 'Yes, indeed! What a splendid word!'

'It was only,' the earl resumed, 'when I was brought into the picture that Ludovic became seriously worried. He didn't quite know what I was up to, but he overheard something Miss Malcolm said to me at Lady Sefton's ball. Then he called casually at St James's Square just an hour or two after Adam and I had left for Norfolk, and was told – there was no reason why he shouldn't have been – that we were proposing to stay at Fakenham. No doubt he drew his own deductions from that. In fact, it wouldn't surprise me if he sent off a hasty, probably anonymous note to Wayne warning him that I was coming to pry into his affairs. From the point of view of timing, it could have reached Wayne an hour or two before I went to see him – and it would certainly explain some of the oddities of *that* interview. Next, of course, John arrived in Wiltshire, and with highly suspicious innocence began asking about the events of the year 1793.

'Ludovic was no fool, and it was clear we were interested in Rivett's marriage and in the child. His fear that his source of blackmail income would dry up now became subsidiary to the fear that the missing heir, so to speak, would be discovered and oust his father, and then himself, from the Wayne inheritance. It seemed to him just possible that if Richard died, by accident, the whole matter would be dropped. Even if it wasn't, as long as the death appeared to be an accident he himself would still, in due course, inherit the title and estates.

'There followed the two attempts on Richard's life, which you know about. In the first case, Ludovic employed hired assassins, though I imagine he himself was present to identify Richard and remained in the trees while they made the attempt. On the second occasion, he acted by himself, lying in wait in the gardens ready for any suitable opportunity that presented itself – as one did.

'What he didn't realize was that I suspected him almost immediately, not only because he always seemed to be within earshot on the appropriate occasions, but because I was sure Priory Court was the key to the mystery and there was no one else there who *could* be responsible.'

'There you are, Louis!' said the irrepressible John. 'An unsolicited testimonial for yourself and your papa!'

His brother ignored him.

'Francis and Matt had traced Mrs Malcolm's route in the gig, and when I arrived here a few days ago we were able to chart the progress of the curricle. Then, on the morning after the fire, I found near the cottage a fragment of scorched paper that looked as if it might have been used to set the thatch alight. All that was legible on the paper was a sum of money. It was a substantial amount, which made me think of a tailor's bill. As you know, there are only a handful of really fashionable tailors, and a great many of their clients make no haste to pay their bills. It seemed to me perfectly possible that Ludovic might have used one that happened to be in his pocket to light a bonfire! In any case, I compared the quality of the paper with one of my own bills and was fairly sure that I knew the tailor who had sent it out.'

'Gracious me!' exclaimed Lady Susan. 'That was very clever of you!'

'I have my moments,' her brother replied modestly. 'I sent Francis straight up to town with it, and it turns out I was right. The sum shown on the paper was enough to identify it as an account that had been sent to Ludovic just before he left London.

'While Francis was on his way to town I sent Matthew in search of the magistrate.' He smiled at Caroline. 'Your friend, Mr Hopkinson. It seemed to me that the fire ought to be reported, and even if the visit Adam and I proposed making to Priory Court that afternoon turned out to be less productive than I hoped, I still felt Richard's testimony about the locked door should be placed before the magistrate. The tailor's bill, I thought, might also turn out to be valid evidence, and I thought it worth while to send young Jamie, from the stables, over to the Court as if he were in search of employment – on the chance that he might pick up some useful gossip. By sheer luck, he was able to confirm something that, at the time, I didn't even know about. Sir Augustus mentioned that he sent one of the blackmail payments to St Albans in the last couple of weeks, and Ludovic's groom, trying to impress the eager young Jamie, said, "Very interesting working for Mr Ludovic. We fairly get about. One day London, next day somewhere else. We were up near St Albans last week, then back to London, and now down here. Never a dull moment, and the master's very free with his money if he wants you to do something special for him."

'And that's very nearly all. I was concerned about Ludovic. I thought there was a faint possibility he might ride over to Atherton on a reconnaissance on the day after the fire, so I sent Girvan and Anderson to the Court first thing in the morning to keep an eye on him as best they might. It's very tricky following someone in the open countryside, but they managed admirably, and Girvan left Anderson at the gate to warn me, when I returned, that Ludovic was up at the house.

'By pure coincidence, Adam and I arrived back at the same time as Matt and the magistrate, and we met John and Richard on the way up the drive.' He was talking only to Caroline now. 'Girvan was standing at the corner of the house signalling us to be quiet, so we all crept with enormous care on to the terrace, and during the moments when Ludovic's back was turned we contrived to plaster ourselves to the stonework between the windows.' His lips twitched. 'In other circumstances, I should have been strongly tempted to laugh, especially when the magistrate stubbed his toe on an urn and was unable to give vent to his feelings.'

He surveyed Miss Malcolm's slightly pink countenance tentatively. 'We *do* owe you an apology for leaving you to suffer what must have been a very trying interview. But it enabled the magistrate to hear the evidence at first hand, and clinched the case perfectly. And, you know, it would have been impossible to lay hands on Ludovic while he held you at sword point without putting you in serious danger. He was more than a little mad by then, as I'm sure you realize. So we waited, and it all turned out – er – very well.'

'Yes,' said Miss Malcolm, her colour still high. 'I am extremely grateful to you for what you have done.'

She was aware that her voice was taut, and that everyone else in the room was regarding her in mild surprise. Except the expressionless Francis Mervyn, of course – which quite irrationally increased her annoyance. If she were sensible, she would leave it at that. But she couldn't. There was something she had to say, and if she said it here she would be considered both ungracious and ungrateful. So she went on: 'If I might have a word with you in private?'

The earl's expression did not change as he stood up courteously and ushered her into the hall and then to his study.

She remained just inside the door while he lit more candles and stirred up the fire.

'I repeat,' she said in a brittle voice, 'that I am extremely grateful to you. But you knew – *you knew* – that my mother's death had been no accident, and yet you allowed me to find out for myself, and in such a way!'

He rose from the hearth and turned to face her. 'I hoped you would never find out, and no one regrets the manner of your enlightenment more than I do.'

'And Richard's accident, that – that burning *ghat*, that funeral pyre down there!' She gestured wildly with her hand. 'Why couldn't I have been told? Instead, I was left trying to convince myself that it *was* an accident, when all the time I knew it wasn't. The highwaymen and then that! It was too improbable.'

'I was trying to spare you,' he said with restraint.

'But you must have known I should find out one day?'

He sighed. 'Perhaps, but I hoped that when you found out everything would be so long past that it wouldn't matter any more.'

'And even *that* was not all! A little warning, just one word of warning about Ludovic, and I should have been prepared – instead of being cast, wholly unsuspecting, into a situation the like of which I hope never, *ever*, to have to experience again.'

The earl's patience snapped. He had had several thoroughly exhausting days, and several more during which he had been a prey to a great deal of worry and concern. He had ridden three horses almost into the ground, and sustained a number of extremely wearing interviews. He had been attacked by a madman, scorched by a fire, and his left arm, bandaged from shoulder to elbow, was throbbing with unabated fervour from the wound Ludovic had inflicted on him in that last frantic struggle on the terrace three days previously. No matter that – if the truth were told – he had found it all extraordinarily stimulating. Enjoyable, even. What *did* matter was that here was this chit of a girl, on whose behalf all his labours had been expended, actually daring to take him to task.

'Madam!' he said furiously. 'How dare you! When I think how much time and energy I and my entire household have devoted to discovering the identity of your father and bringing to justice the man who killed your mother, *I will not tolerate it*!'

'Will you not?' she flashed. 'Then give me leave to tell you that what you will tolerate, and what you will not tolerate, is a matter of supreme indifference to me.'

'Oh, is it, indeed? This is a new come-out! The first time we met you almost fainted at the sight of me. The second time, you would have shown me the door in two minutes flat, if you'd had your way. The third time, in full sight of a ballroom crammed with people, you made it clear to all that I terrified you out of your wits. You must forgive me if I over-estimated your sensibility, for I have been to a great deal of trouble to keep you in ignorance of what I believed would hurt you and to shield you from every unpleasantness that I could. And now you dare to upbraid me for it!'

'Oh!' she spluttered. 'You are arrogant, and over-bearing, and autocratic. Don't *speak* to me like that. You cannot ride roughshod over *me* as if I were a member of your unfortunate family!'

The earl had opened his mouth to reply, but he closed it again rather suddenly. He drew a gasping breath, and then another, and then, under Caroline's astonished gaze, dissolved into a peal of laughter. Sinking into a chair by the fire, he sat there for several seconds, head lowered and hands hanging loose between his knees, trying to control himself.

'And what, pray, is so funny?' Caroline asked tartly, if a little uncertainly.

His lordship gasped again and said with a catch in his voice: 'I do apologize. But if you had ever seen me trying to ride roughshod over my family, you would know!'

Caroline, very much disconcerted to discover that the earl was human after all and quite as capable of losing his temper as anyone else, said rather weakly: 'Oh.' Her own temper had spent itself, and she felt both foolish and singularly forlorn. Tears very near, she turned without another word to leave the room.

But as she held out her hand to the doorknob there was a light step behind her and his lordship, grasping her by the shoulders, swung her round to face him. He looked down into the swimming grey-green eyes, and his own blue ones were lit by a mixture of amusement, sympathy, warmth, and – what?

Reminded of something, she said with watery indignation: 'And another thing! You allowed me to think Ludovic was truly in love with me!'

'I – I? – allowed you to think . . .?'

She realized that she was being foolish beyond permission, and her eyes fell. 'Well, if you had told me what he *was*!'

'You little vixen!' he said, the laugh still in his voice. 'You are the most beautiful, provoking, infuriating, delightful, detestable client I have ever had for my detective services, and for weeks now I have been wanting to take you in my arms and comfort you. But it's bad policy to hug clients during the course of an investigation and, besides, I thought you might have heard the phrase *caveat emptor*.'

He smiled down at her. 'But now you are a client no longer,' he said, and before she could reply he swept her into his arms, not in the least gently, and kissed her for a long time.

Emerging at last, flushed and breathless, from his embrace, Miss Malcolm – who did not give in easily – looked up into the arrogant, over-bearing, autocratic face that gazed down into hers with such affectionate mockery, and said: 'What does it mean? *Caveat emptor?*'

He threw back his head and laughed. 'It means, my ungrateful little love, "Let the client beware!"' And he gathered her back into his arms again.